My Perfect Ex-Boyfriend

a novel by
Annabelle Costa

My Perfect Ex-Boyfriend

ISBN: 9781790527403

Prologue
14 YEARS EARLIER

My mother has spent the last ten years trying not to die.

It all started when I was barely eight years old. My parents brought me into the living room and solemnly sat me down on the couch. I thought for sure they'd found out I'd been sneaking candy at my friend Brianna's house. I had my face all screwed up, ready to start crying when they confronted me about those Jolly Ranchers. But they didn't know about the candy. It was much, much worse.

"Bailey," my father said to me as my mother sat beside me and held my hand. "Mommy is sick."

He always called my mother "Mommy," even though I'd stopped calling her that over a year ago. She was "Mom" to me, but always "Mommy" when my father said it. He still says "Mommy," even though I'm now officially an adult, of the age when I can legally smoke cigarettes and vote and play the lottery.

The details came spilling out. Breast cancer. Chemotherapy, whatever that was. Radiation, whatever *that* was. And a surgery. I understood the surgery part, and that's when I started crying.

"Don't worry, Bailey," Mom said as she squeezed me close to her. "I'm going to be fine. I'm going to beat this."

I still remember the warning look my father gave her, telling her not to promise anything she couldn't deliver. I knew it even then, at age eight.

But she was right. She did beat it. And when the cancer came back five years later, she beat it again. When it came to breast cancer, my mom was winning, two and oh.

And now, just three weeks before I start my first semester of college, I find out that she's going in for Round Three.

I'm lying on my bed in my small room, my CD player beside me, headphones on my ears, when my mother enters my room. I'm listening to an album by the Strokes, and the current song blaring into my eardrums is called "Last Nite." I know I'm going to remember forever that I was listening to "Last Nite" at this moment, the same way I still remember I was reading *Freckle Juice* by Judy Blume the first time my mother told me she had cancer.

"Can we talk for a minute?" Mom asks me.

I pull the headphones off my ears, my stomach sinking. The tears are already welling up in my eyes. I know. I *know*.

She perches on the edge of my bed, on my Hello Kitty bedspread I've had since I was nine. When I was very young, my mother had dark brown hair like mine that everyone used to call "chestnut." She confided in me that she had some gray strands she would dye. After the second bout of cancer, her hair grew back entirely gray and she left it like that. At first, I hated it. I wanted her to color her hair and be who she used to be. But now… I don't know. I like the gray. Her hair is thick and healthy and beautiful.

Although not for long.

"It's back," I say, before she can get out the words.

She nods. "I know the timing couldn't be worse."

Is the timing ever *good*? Has anyone ever said, "Gee, this was such a great time to get cancer!"

"I'm going to postpone the chemo until after we bring you to college," she says.

I frown. "When do they want you to start?"

"Next week." She shakes her head. "But an extra two weeks won't matter. I want to help you get to college."

"No." I sit up straight in bed. I will not be responsible for my mother failing to win Round Three—I want to stack the odds in her favor as much as I can. "If they want you to have the treatment next week, you should start next week. I can drive to college on my own."

"Bailey..."

"I won't let you come with me."

My mother can be stubborn, but it's a trait I've inherited. And I'm much worse.

"Daddy will come with you," Mom finally says.

"No," I say again. "Dad should stay with you."

My father will be on my side with this one. A bunch of my friends have divorced parents, but I know this is something that could never happen to my parents in a million years. My parents met during their second week of college and fell instantly and desperately in love. Mom got a care package from her parents and she was having trouble carrying it up the stairs—and then Dad appeared, skinny and not muscular by any means, but he still hoisted that big box up three flights of stairs to her room. She offered him a cool glass of water in her room. And as they say, the rest is history.

They're still absolutely infatuated with each other. It's really sweet and only sometimes a little bit sickening. I'm embarrassed to admit my personal romantic ideal is to end up with a guy who I love the way my parents love each other. So far, I'm batting zero. I've never even had a serious boyfriend.

"I'm going to be worried sick about you," Mom says, a crease between her eyebrows.

"Well," I say, "I could take off the first semester. I mean, you could probably use my help..."

She doesn't even hesitate. "No. You are not giving up college for me, young lady."

"It's just one semester…"

"Out of the question," she says sharply. Her eyes soften. "What if your future husband is right down the hall from you and you miss out on it because of me?"

I laugh. "How likely is that?"

Mom winks at me. "You never know…"

"Oh, come on…" I say, although I don't want to admit there's a small part of me hoping she's right. Maybe the love of my life *will* be living down the hall from me at college. You never know.

"We don't need your help," she says. "To be honest, you're probably the worst person to have around while I'm going through this."

I open my mouth, but it's hard to protest something I know is true. You'd think with a mother who spent the last decade of our lives going in and out of hospitals, I would get immune to illness and needles and blood, but I somehow went in the opposite direction. My mother's illness did a number on me. Whenever I get near a hospital, I break out in a cold sweat. When I see blood or an IV, my head starts to spin. Even when I have a bad papercut, I get a little woozy.

I probably need therapy.

"Okay, fine," I agree. "But I promise you, I can make it to college on my own. I'll be fine."

Mom reaches out and grabs my hand. Usually I pull away quickly when she tries to touch me these days. Not that I don't love my mom, but what teenager wants to hold her mother's hand for an extended period of time? But now I don't pull away. I squeeze her hand back, wondering if this could be one of the last times I'll feel her touch.

No. It can't be. She'll win again.

"We'll see," Mom says. "I think I can spare Daddy for a couple of days."

I don't argue with her, knowing that once she's vomiting from the chemo, she won't have it in her anymore to insist. I will drive out to college on my own. I'll be fine.

Chapter 1
PRESENT DAY

If I were to murder my ex-husband, I don't think I'd go to jail.

They would certainly arrest me—that part is unavoidable. There would have to be a trial and all that. I'd probably be convicted because I've never killed anyone before and I'd certainly be terrible at covering my tracks.

That said, when the sentencing came and the judge heard about the kind of person Theodore Duncan really is, I'd probably get a slap on the wrist. Maybe I'd be sentenced to community service—and that community service would have already been served by ridding the world of that man.

I'm joking, of course. I wouldn't really kill Theo. I'm not the murdering type. But at this moment, watching our six-year-old daughter sitting on the steps of our apartment building in Fresh Meadows, her pink backpack tucked between her knees, her head perking up every time a car turns the corner before her face falls when she realizes it's not her dad, I definitely want to commit an act of violence against him. If he's going to make Lily suffer, he should suffer.

"Is it two o'clock yet, Mommy?" Lily asks me.

Theo was supposed to get here at two. It was two o'clock twenty minutes ago. But fortunately, Lily has the worst sense of time of anyone in the universe. If I tell her we're going to the museum tomorrow, she will ask me every half hour if it's tomorrow yet until I want to gouge out my eyes. So for the last half hour, I've been telling her it's "almost two" and she's somehow buying it. But considering she's six years old, her patience will very likely wear thin in the immediate future.

"Not yet, sweetie," I say.

Lily gives an exasperated sigh. A blue Kia rounds the corner and her eyes perk up, despite the fact that she knows her father drives a red Ford. When I see the disappointment in her blue eyes, I whip out my cell phone and angrily pull up Theo's number.

I'm ready to leave an enraged cell phone message, but to my surprise, Theo picks up. His voice is breathless, which isn't a surprise. Theo always sounds like he had to stop something really important so he could answer the phone. Possibly sex.

"Where are you?" I hiss into the phone. I glance over at Lily, who looks forlorn. I never even knew what the word "forlorn" really meant, but at this moment, Lily personifies "forlorn." If you looked the word up in the dictionary, you'd find a photo of my daughter waiting for her ever-absent father.

"Where am I?" Theo repeats, parsing each word of my question as if he's only first learning the English language.

"You said you'd be here at two!" I'm so angry, I'm practically spitting. "You're supposed to take Lily to the movies."

"No, I'm not," he says. "That's tomorrow."

I am seething with anger. Once you finished looking up "forlorn" in the dictionary, you could look up "seething" and find a photo of me gripping my cell phone, my face bright red, the veins standing out in my neck.

"No, it was *today*," I say through my teeth.

"I'm certain it was tomorrow," Theo says with all the confidence of a man who hasn't stood up his daughter on multiple occasions.

"Why on earth would we arrange for you to pick Lily up tomorrow at two?" I snap into the phone. "Tomorrow is *Monday*. She'll be at school tomorrow at two."

Theo is quiet for a minute before he finally says, "Tomorrow is Monday?"

Oh, for God's sake.

"Look," I say, "how soon can you get here? I'll tell Lily you got hung up and you can catch the next showing of the movie."

"Bailey, I can't just drop everything I'm doing," Theo says. "I've got a gig in a few hours."

I groan. Theo is thirty-seven years old, and the starving musician bit is getting old. It's amazing how the things that attract you to a man when you first meet him are the very things that make you hate him years later, when he skips multiple child support payments because he's dead broke. It's tempting to remind him I could have him thrown in jail for the fact that he hasn't given Lily and me one red cent in over a year, but I'm trying not to morph into the stereotype of a bitter ex-wife. It's not easy though.

"Can't you cancel the gig?" I press him. Lily has just leaped off the stairs at the sight of a red BMW, which is about as far from Theo's beat up old Ford as a red car could possibly be. She splashes into a puddle on the sidewalk, drenching her formerly pink sneakers that are now gray.

"No way," Theo says. "I heard that record producers show up at this joint. This could be my big break."

I guarantee this will not be Theo's big break. I would take every cent I have in the bank and bet it on this not being Theo's big break. Granted, we're not talking about much money here. I'm a social worker—we don't make the big bucks.

"You take her to the movies," Theo tells me. "I'll pay you back for the tickets."

12

Ha.

"She's going to be crushed, Theo," I murmur into the phone.

"I'm sorry, Bailey." I hear someone talking in the background. Someone female. Theo laughs loudly. "Listen, I gotta run. Tell Lily I'm sorry."

Before I can even say goodbye, the phone is dead.

I shove my phone back into my purse, resisting the urge to hurl it to the ground. I can't afford a new phone—I can barely afford the one I have, which already has a cracked screen. I force a smile and sit down next to Lily on the steps of our building. I put my arm around my daughter's skinny shoulders.

"Lily," I begin.

She looks up at me with those big blue eyes. They're Theo's eyes. She looks just like him, with her heart-shaped face and straight reddish-brown hair—even that tiny bump in her nose is his. It's conflicting to feel so much love for someone who looks so much like someone I hate. I squeeze her tighter.

"Daddy had an emergency come up," I say.

"Ugh!" Lily yelps. It's a sound she makes whenever she's disappointed, a habit I only recently realized she got from me. Lily makes me aware of all my bad habits by copying each and every one of them. "He's supposed to take me to see *Dogcat*!"

Dogcat is the newest hot children's movie, about a cat that becomes a dog, or a dog that becomes a cat, or something inane like that. I have been hearing about *Dogcat* for the last two weeks, but movies aren't in my current budget. The amount it costs to go to the movies in Queens is nothing short of ridiculous. I'd rather spend the money on shelter and food. It would be lovely if I could save up enough money so that Lily and I didn't have to share a one-bedroom apartment. It puts a crimp in my social life.

Actually, that's not true. It doesn't put a crimp in my social life. Sadly.

"I'll take you to see *Dogcat*," I tell her just as the first tear falls from her eyes. "We'll go right now."

"But it's in 3-D," Lily says. "That's too 'spensive."

Ugh! If the movie is in 3-D, that means a three-dollar surcharge will be tacked onto each of our tickets in addition to the already exorbitant cost of the movie. "It's okay."

"And can we get popcorn?"

"Sure!" I say. "Why not?" This week can be an exercise to see how far I can stretch a box of spaghetti because that's all I'm going to be able to afford to eat for dinner.

Lily snuggles happily against my chest. "Thanks, Mommy!"

I allow myself to smile. When Theo and I got divorced, I vowed Lily wouldn't become one of those miserable kids I see as a social worker whose single mothers make them pay for the sins of their fathers. I will not be that. I'm going to make sure Lily has a good childhood, no matter what. Even if it means that I'm wearing the same jacket I've owned since college.

Chapter 2
PRESENT DAY

"I'm getting married."

I nearly spit out noodles, tomato sauce, and ricotta cheese dramatically when my father says the very last thing I ever expected him to say in a million years. You don't expect your sixty-three-year-old father to announce he's getting married. You might expect him to say his gout is acting up, or he's going to move down to Florida, or he'd like to turn in early after dinner. Getting *married*? Is he kidding me?

"Married?" I manage, as I choke down a sip of water from one of my father's chipped ceramic cups.

Dad nods. "That's right."

It's not that my father and I aren't close. I come to his apartment every Sunday night for dinner, and he helps me out a lot with childcare because he's retired and I'm destitute. We talk in a friendly way, usually about Lily or how my job is going. But let's be honest—most women don't feel comfortable confiding in their father about their dating life. And vice versa.

So I don't tell him about my personal life and he doesn't tell me about his. Of course, my personal life has been so nonexistent since Theo that I just assumed the same was true of his. As far as I knew, my father hadn't been on a single date since my mother died. It comforted me to think that way.

Apparently, I've been completely wrong. My father is a player. How could he do this to my mother—the love of his life?

"Grandpa's getting married!" Lily looks thrilled. "Can I be the flower girl?"

"Of course you can, my angel," Dad says to her.

I push away my fleeting concerns of how much a flower girl dress is going to set me back. There are much more pressing things to worry about.

"Are you okay, Bee?" Dad asks.

My father has always called me "Bee." He is absolutely the only one in the world who is allowed to do that—Theo tried it once and I let him know in no uncertain terms it was *not* okay (I wish I'd been as persuasive about his cheating). "Bee" is the first letter of my name, but also, when I was little, I had a round face and yellow hair, and Dad always said I looked like a bumblebee. My hair has since darkened to more of a chestnut shade like my mother's used to be, and thanks to my poverty diet, my round face is a lot narrower than it used to be. But to Dad, I'm still "Bee."

"How can you be getting married?" I feel like I'm about to burst into tears. "What about Mom?"

Dad frowns and the wrinkles on his face deepen. "Bee, Mom's been gone for nine years."

17

Technically, he's right. But here we are, eating dinner in the two-bedroom apartment that he and my mother purchased together, eating at the creaky wooden table she picked out, drinking from cups she bought at Pottery Barn. How could she not constantly be on his mind? How could he move on? I repeat: *she was the love of his life*.

You can't move on from something like that. You *can't*. I should know. A horrible accident took the love of my life away from me, and look what happened. *Theo* happened.

"Her name is Gwen," Dad tells me.

Gwen? What kind of name is Gwen? I've only known one Gwen and have nothing but bad associations with the name. I dislike her already.

"You'd really like her," he says. "She made this lasagna."

I look down at my plate of flat noodles in disgust. I can't believe I've been eating *Gwen's* lasagna. How could my father not have told me? I'd never have touched it.

"How did you meet her?" I ask.

"Through mutual friends."

My father has *friends*? God, so many revelations tonight.

"I like lasagna!" Lily says happily. "When can we meet Gwen?"

Never. Please let the answer be never. She can marry my father as long as I never have to see her or look at her.

"Actually," Dad says, "her son lives in Manhattan but he owns a cabin down in Maryland and she invited the three of us to spend a week out there."

I slam my fork down on my plate. "And you expect me to drop everything and go down to Maryland? I have a job, you know. I can't just… jet off to Maryland."

Dad smiles crookedly. "Yeah, but Lily's spring break is in a week, and you told me you were taking the week off with her. So I thought that would be a perfect time to go."

Damn it. He actually listens to things I say to him.

"I'm sorry this is coming as a shock, honey," he says softly. "I was afraid to tell you about Gwen or any other women because I thought you might… get sad. I know how close you were with Mom and… you know I miss her so much too…" He takes off his glasses and rubs his eyes. "I love Gwen though. And I'm certain you'll like her too."

It's hard to look at my father's face and not agree to go along with this. It's not like losing his wife has been easy on him. And he took care of her the whole time I was off in college. I'll always regret that I wasn't there for her those four years. I kept offering to come back, but they kept telling me no. Stay. Enjoy college, Bee.

"Fine," I mumble. "I guess a week in a cabin wouldn't be horrible."

Dad beams at me. "I think you and Lily will have a great time. Gwen's son also owns a boat, so that will be fun. Wanna go on a boat, Lil?"

This guy owns a cabin and a boat? Wow, he must be loaded. Maybe he's single. Probably not. Guys with spare cabins and boats don't tend to stay single long, in my experience.

As Lily and my father discuss the upcoming week, I have to admit, I'm not dreading it. Maybe a week away is just what we need right now.

Chapter 3
PRESENT DAY

Lily is in rare form on the Amtrak train down to Maryland.

It's like she read a magazine article before the trip on how best to annoy your parents during a long train ride. First she's hungry. That's an easy one—we feed her. Then she's sick to her stomach from the food she just ate and wants me to fix it somehow. Then she's bored. So bored. Soooo boooooored. I brought a stack of activity books for the train, but none of them hold the slightest interest for her. She starts kicking the seat in front of her, oblivious to the glares from the passenger unfortunate enough to be sitting there.

Now, with twenty minutes left until we arrive at the Baltimore station, Lily has gotten stuck in an endless loop. For the last hour, every five minutes, she has asked, "Are we there yet?"

I thought kids saying "are we there yet" was one of those stereotypes about kids that doesn't really happen. But I assure you, it does really happen. Over and over and over. And there's no way to stop it. No way for me to say "not yet" or give her a sense of the arrival time that will keep her from asking.

"Are we there yet?" Lily whines.

"Not yet, Lily!" snaps my father. Even *he's* lost his patience with her.

Lily's never been yelled at before by Grandpa, and immediately, her little heart-shaped face crumples. And now she's wailing hysterically. She's six years old and she's louder than the newborn infant two rows down. I'm scared someone's going to throw us off this moving train.

Dad is profusely apologizing for his outburst when my cell phone rings. I see Theo's number on the screen and consider not answering. I'm not in the mood for Theo right now. Well, I'm never in the mood for Theo, but especially not now. But then again, it will be a break from the monotony of this ride and Lily's screaming.

"Hello?" I answer.

"Hey, Bailey," he says. "I was just thinking about taking Lily out for dinner tonight. Maybe we could go see *Catdog*."

"*Dogcat*," I correct him, although I'm not sure why.

"Sure—that," Theo says.

"Too late," I say. "I already took her last weekend after you bailed."

"Fine," Theo says. "I'll take her to some other movie."

"Sorry," I say, even though I don't feel at all sorry. "We're taking a trip to Maryland for the week. We're actually almost there."

"*What*?" Theo has a temper. It's one of the many, many things I've come to dislike about him. And it's flaring up right now. "You never told me you were taking Lily to Maryland!"

"It didn't even occur to me that you'd care," I reply honestly.

"You're supposed to tell me when you take Lily on a trip!"

"Yeah, well, you're supposed to pay me child support."

Theo snorts. "Are you trying to shame me, Bailey? You know I pay what I can."

Yeah, and that's apparently nothing.

"Look," I say, "I don't know what to tell you, Theo. We're nearly in Baltimore."

"Are you going with some guy?" he growls. "Is that what this is about?"

Ha. That's so far from the truth, it's depressing. But I'm not going to tell him about my father and offer any window into my life.

"It's none of your business," I say.

"The hell it's not!" Theo yells. "Lily is my daughter! You can't just jet her off wherever you want with your... your man-whore!"

Back when Theo and I were married, I had to listen to him scream his head off at me when his temper was flaring. Fortunately, we're not married anymore. So I can click the "end" button and our conversation is over. He calls me back immediately, but I put my phone on "silent" and shove it back in my purse. If only I could temporarily put Lily on "silent," this would be a great trip.

I hear the conductor announcing overhead that the next stop is Baltimore. I breathe a sigh of relief. "How are we getting to the cabin?" I ask my father. "Do we need to call a taxi?"

Dad shakes his head as the train whistle sounds overhead. "Gwen's son is picking us up at the station."

"The son's *here*?" I imagined that Gwen's son was lending us an empty cabin to stay in. I didn't know we were going to have to share it with the son and likely his family. Fabulous.

Dad nods. "I haven't met him either, so Gwen thought this would be a nice introduction for everyone. He sounds like a nice kid."

Kid? How old is this guy? Old enough to drive and old enough to own a place in Manhattan *and* a cabin in Maryland. Of course, my father probably still refers to *me* as a kid, so for all I know, this guy could be fifty.

"How are we supposed to know it's him?" I ask. "Is he going to be holding up one of those big signs that says, 'CHAPIN'?"

He laughs. "Maybe. I don't know—I didn't ask her. Apparently, he thinks he'll be able to find us."

The train skids to a halt at the Baltimore station. I stand up, stretching out the crick in my neck from the long ride. Lily leaps out of her seat and smooths out the dress she's chosen to meet her new step-grandmother-to-be. The dress has a lot of cats on it. And when I say that, you might be imagining a dress that has three or four cats on it, so let me rescue you from that delusion. Every inch of this dress is covered in multicolored pictures of cats. It's almost dizzying how many cats are on her dress. There's got to be, like, fifty of them. It's her favorite dress.

"Come on, Lily," I say as I grab my duffel bags down from the compartment above the seats. My father was bright enough to purchase luggage on wheels, but I was apparently not. All our clothes and supplies for the week are stuffed into these two giant bags. Well, aside from the few things I fit into Lily's miniscule backpack. I hope Gwen's son is strong and likes carrying luggage.

We dismount the train, my father holding Lily's hand as I struggle with my two pieces of luggage. I really hope this guy is waiting for us and we don't have to look everywhere for him. Dad is looking around, shading his eyes from the sun with his hand. That's when I notice that there's a man walking in the opposite direction of the passengers coming off the train. He's clearly coming toward us.

It's very sunny and I squint to see him better. The first thing I notice is the tousled dark blond hair and strong, solid build—this is a guy who should have no trouble throwing a couple of duffel bags over his broad shoulders. As he gets closer, I can see the muscles filling out his blue T-shirt. Damn, this guy is a hottie.

And then his features come into better focus. The stubble on his chin. The blue eyes. The solid jaw.

Oh my God.

It's Noah.

Oh no.

Chapter 4
PRESENT DAY

Not Noah. Anyone but Noah. Please, God, let him be here for some other coincidental reason completely unrelated to me and my father.

But no, I'm not that lucky. The man I haven't seen in a decade strides in our direction and comes abruptly to a stop in front of us. I don't see any trace of surprise on his face, which makes me think he knew I was Leonard Chapin's daughter. He hasn't been blindsided like I was.

I also notice he isn't smiling. No big shock there.

"Mr. Chapin?" Noah nods at my father. "I'm Gwen's son, Noah."

"Nice to meet you!" Dad's face lights up and he thrusts his hand in Noah's direction. "Please, call me Lenny."

My father has no idea who he is. Not a clue. He has no idea he's already shaken Noah's hand before and commanded him to call him Lenny. I, on the other hand, get a sickening sense of déjà vu.

"And this is my daughter, Bailey," Dad tells him.

Noah faces me and one corner of his mouth lifts in something that is a poor excuse for a smile. "Actually," he says. "Bailey and I have already met."

"Have you?" Dad squints at Noah, clearly trying to place him. Mom would have known Noah in an instant. She loved Noah. But my father is struggling. It takes him several seconds, but finally, I see the color leave his face and I know he's made the connection. "Oh. You're…"

He doesn't complete the sentence. I think we're all grateful for that.

"What about me?" Lily yelps.

I laugh shakily. "Oh, um… Noah, this is my daughter, Lily."

Noah looks down at her and offers his first genuine smile since we arrived. "Well, hello, Lily."

Lily blushes and hides her face in my jeans. I think she's smitten. I can't entirely blame her. That bastard has only gotten handsomer in the time since I've last seen him. Back in college, he was good-looking, but now he's gotten *sexy*. So sexy. His face has filled out and the muscles in his arms and chest seem more pronounced under the light blue T-shirt that makes his eyes look oh so blue. His blond hair always used to be shaggy back then, but now it's clipped short and professional, making it look darker than it used to be.

I glance down at the fourth digit of his left hand. Bare, like mine.

"Let's go to my car," Noah says. He eyes my two bulging duffel bags. "I'll carry those for you."

"No, that's okay," I say quickly as I tighten my grip on the straps. "I can manage."

28

He raises his eyebrows. "They look heavy."

"No, don't worry about it!" I say quickly. "They're not as heavy as they look."

Noah narrows his eyes at me, but then shakes his head. "Fine. Suit yourself."

I regret my decision as the straps of the duffel bags dig into my shoulders. I hurry after Noah, who is walking just a little too quickly. As he pulls ahead of me, I examine the way he walks. He limps. It's definitely noticeable if you're looking for it. I glance over at my father, wondering if he's noticing too.

Noah's car is parked so far away, I'm beginning to feel like we probably could have walked to the cabin faster. I'm covered in sweat and there are painful grooves in my shoulders where the straps of the duffel bags have been digging in. When I see the gray Toyota 4Runner light up, I nearly collapse with relief—I drop my bags to the ground and rub my aching shoulders. Noah pops the trunk so I can throw the bags inside. I can't help but notice he's got handicapped plates on the car, although he obviously decided to park in the next town over rather than use them.

Noah lifts one eyebrow. "Where's your booster seat for Lily?"

"Oh." Somehow it didn't occur to me we'd be riding around in a car much. Considering I live in the city and don't have a car of my own, car seats aren't

29

something on my radar. After all, you don't need one on the bus or the subway. Theo had a car seat up until Lily was three, when he said she was "too big" and that it was a "pain in the ass." Oh, and also "Lily agrees," as if we're taking the opinion of a six-year-old into consideration on major safety issues. It's something Theo and I have argued about multiple times, although it's hard to refute his argument that neither of us were in booster seats when we were six.

"I don't have one."

"Aren't kids supposed to be in a booster seat?" Noah presses me.

I glare at him. "I said don't have one. So what am I supposed to do?"

He mumbles under his breath, something that sounds like, "Way to be a responsible parent." But who is he to judge me? I'm a freaking single mother. He doesn't even *have* kids.

Dad is too quick for me and jumps into the back seat next to Lily before I can claim it. So now I'm stuck sitting next Noah. Who smells nice. It must be his aftershave. Theo was all about being a grungy musician, so I've forgotten what it's like to be near a man who smells so…

Good. He smells good. Let's leave it with that adjective.

I watch Noah start up the car. It seems like a completely normal Toyota—it's got what appears to be automatic transmission, and when I lean over, I think I can see pedals for the gas and brake.

"Excuse me?" Noah says as I'm practically leaning over him to check out the pedals.

"I just…" I swallow and attempt a smile. "I noticed it's a normal car."

He rolls his eyes. "Yeah. How about that? I can drive a *normal car.*"

I need to shut up. Permanently.

Noah pulls out onto the road and it looks like he's right—he can drive a normal car. That's not to say I'm not worried about the whole thing though. I'm really beginning to wish Lily had that booster seat.

"You don't have to cling to the dashboard," Noah says to me. "I'm a safe driver."

"I'm not clinging to the dashboard," I lie. Truthfully, he's driving very carefully, staying around the speed limit and not tailgating the way Theo always does. Still, I'm hoping this isn't a long drive.

Noah's blue eyes stay pinned on the road, and he doesn't even attempt to make conversation with me. He turns on the radio and generic pop music fills the silence of the car. Usually I can count on Lily to chatter through any break in conversation, but she must be worn out from the train ride, because she's completely silent.

The car glides past a hospital. I watch an ambulance pulling into the entrance, its lights flashing. My head floats back to a conversation fourteen years ago.

"So, Noah, you're pre-med, huh?"

"Yeah. I'm planning to become a surgeon."

"Seriously? That sounds hard."

"I know, but it's my dream. I've wanted to be a surgeon as long as I can remember."

"Are you a surgeon?" I blurt out.

Noah slows to a stop at a red light before answering: "I'm an ER physician."

"An ER physician," I murmur. "That sounds… really fulfilling."

"You don't have to patronize me, Bailey," he says. "I'm a *doctor*."

My cheeks grow warm just as Lily blurts out, "Mommy is a social worker!"

Noah bursts out laughing. I'd forgotten what the sound of his laughter sounded like, and even though I know he's laughing *at* me, it still fills me with an almost painful sense of nostalgia. I missed Noah's laugh.

"You're a social worker?" he says incredulously.

I sniff. "What's so wrong with that?"

"Nothing. I mean, it's *admirable*." He smiles crookedly. "I just never saw you as someone who was interested in *helping* people."

Well, that's insulting.

"Bailey did an amazing thing for this woman who was a hoarder," Dad speaks up. "She got the whole neighborhood and all the woman's friends together and they all pitched in to clean out her two-story house. The house was going to be condemned, but they got it spick and span by the end."

I smile at the memory. That was one of my successes. I've had plenty of failures, but the success stories make it worth it.

"Is that so?" Noah pulls onto a road that leads out of the city. "Didn't you always want to be an artist or something like that?"

"Mommy's a really good artist!" Lily pitches in. "She draws all the time."

I look away from Noah, out the window. I did hope to have a career in art at one time. The reason I'm a social worker is because of Noah. It's part of my penance.

"I need the bathroom!" Lily abruptly calls out. She used the bathroom no less than one-thousand times on the train. It was tiny and smelled like urine. I don't know what's wrong with this child—it's like her bladder is the size of a pea.

"Sweetie, you just went on the train," I remind her. "You've been going every five minutes."

"I have to go again!" she whines.

"Maybe she has a urinary tract infection?" Noah suggests.

"She does *not* have a urinary tract infection," I snap at him. "This is a behavior issue, thank you very much."

Noah shrugs. "Well, if she can't wait, I'll find a gas station."

"How long till we get there?"

"Fifteen minutes maybe."

Lily agrees to hold it in for another fifteen minutes. If she soils Noah's car, I'll have to quit social work and become a nun.

"My mom is really excited to meet you, Lily," Noah calls to her.

I vaguely remember Gwen Walsh. She was a sweet woman with a chubby but beautiful face and blue eyes that reminded me of Noah's. The last time I saw her, she greeted me with a warm hug that felt like it would never end. The thought of seeing her now makes me physically ill.

"Does your mother… remember me?" I ask him.

"You sound like you hope she doesn't," he observes.

I squeeze my palms together. "Well…"

"Why?" He raises his eyebrows. "Do you think you did something extremely despicable to her son that you'd hope she wouldn't remember?"

Okay, Noah's being a jerk right now. I think my best bet is to avoid speaking for the rest of the weekend.

Starting now.

Chapter 5

PRESENT DAY

Noah's cabin isn't as small as I feared it would be. I expected some tiny little hut wedged between two trees where we'd all be forced to share one giant bed, but this cabin is more like a single-story house, with a large patio containing a porch swing and a rocking chair. I catch a glimpse of the back porch, which seems to have a barbeque grill, as well as a table and chairs set up. There's a chimney, as well as a paved path leading to the front door. It looks large enough that we'll probably all be sleeping in at least two giant beds.

True to form, the urge to use the bathroom has completely left Lily by the time Noah pulls up in front of the cabin. I'm not sure of the mechanism behind how all the pee vanishes from her bladder the second we actually find a toilet. Maybe Noah the Doctor could explain it to me.

Noah doesn't even offer to take my bags this time. I heave them out of his trunk and he waves a hand to lead us inside. There are two small steps to get up to the patio, and I watch him hold onto the railing as he carefully climbs the steps.

Thank God, it looks like this cabin has all the comforts of home—there's a fully stocked kitchen, a sofa, a loveseat, and at least one indoor bathroom. I had been seriously worried I might be squatting in an outhouse. I think I can deal with being here for a week.

"Gwen!" Dad calls as the woman I recognize as Noah's mother comes out from a room in the back. She looks mostly as I remember her, although slightly older. The lines on her face are deeper, but she still has the same strawberry blond hair pulled into a messy bun.

"Hi, Lenny." Gwen's face breaks into a smile. "How was the trip in?"

"Long," Dad admits.

Gwen bends down next to Lily. "And you must be Lily!"

Lily nods shyly.

"I'm so glad to meet you," Gwen says. "I got you a little present, if that's okay."

Lily nods more eagerly this time. Is it *okay*? When has being given a present not been okay with a six-year-old? What planet does she think this is?

Gwen straightens up and comes eye to eye with me. She has blue eyes—Noah's eyes. None of the warmth that was in her voice when she spoke to my daughter is in her expression anymore.

"Hello, Bailey," she says stiffly. "It's good to see you again."

"Yes," I murmur. "Good to see you too."

Gwen glances at Noah's grim expression, then back at me. "It was quite a surprise to realize who you were, but…" She shrugs helplessly. "It will have to be water under the bridge, I suppose."

"Yes," I say again. "Water under the bridge."

Ha.

"Come on, Bailey," Noah says to me. "I'll show you your room."

I follow him down a short hallway to a set of closed doors. He indicates the first door, "That's the bathroom. We've got one and a half bathrooms, so we're all going to be sharing a shower for the week."

That's fine. Lily can go a shower-free week without blinking an eye—actually, it would be her preference.

He opens the second door to reveal a room with a small queen-sized bed and a cot on the floor next to it. There's a small dresser and a window that gives us a great view of the woods.

"This is great," I say as I drop the duffel bags on the floor. "Perfect."

Noah doesn't say anything for a minute. He leans over and shuts the door to the bedroom, closing the two of us inside. I suck in a breath, staring at those blue eyes, terrified of what he's about to say to me. Preemptively, I say, "I'm sorry."

He raises his eyebrows. "Oh, are you?"

I take a deep breath. "If… if it helps, I've spent every moment since then regretting it."

"It doesn't help." His blue eyes flash and I cringe. "You think I give a shit that you feel a little *bad* about the whole thing? Are you aware what you *did* to me? You have no fucking clue, do you?"

I squeeze my fists together. "Why did you invite us here? To berate me for a week?"

Noah snorts. "Please, Bailey. Don't flatter yourself. I invited you here for my mother's sake."

"Why? Does *she* want to berate me for a week?"

"No, but she wants to marry your father." He shakes his head. "Despite the fact that I told her it would be a *huge* mistake to get involved with anyone from the Chapin family. But she doesn't want to listen to me. She's *in love*. So you and I need to get along."

"Right," I mumble.

He frowns at me. "I'll be cordial, okay? For her sake, I'll pretend that…"

He doesn't complete his sentence, and for that, I'm glad.

"But let's get one thing straight," he says in a low growl. "I don't forgive you. I will *never* forgive you. We will never be friends."

I bite my lip. "You really hate me, don't you?"

Noah is quiet again, as if really thinking about his answer. "'Hate' doesn't even begin to describe how I feel about you," he finally says.

I wince. Somehow in the time since I'd last seen Noah, I'd thought he... well, maybe not *forgave* me, but at least didn't think back on me with feelings of loathing. I figured he'd moved on—got married, had a couple of kids, etc. But that's obviously not the case.

"I'm sorry," I say again.

He shrugs, like he couldn't care less about my apology. Which I guess is true.

If Noah Walsh murdered me, I don't think he'd go to jail. There would be a trial, of course, because there would have to be. But if the judge and jury heard the entire story, I think they'd let him off scot-free. They'd decide he did the world a favor by getting rid of me.

Chapter 6
14 YEARS EARLIER

I have just driven two-hundred miles to get to college, and now here I am, stopped five feet from the entrance to my new dorm, unable to go any further.

All around me, I see parents helping their children unpack their cars and carry their belongings to their new dorm rooms. They all seem so happy, so excited. I hear peals of laughter in the distance.

And then there's me. All alone. Surrounded by heavy boxes.

As I predicted, Mom got sick as soon as she started chemo. So sick that she couldn't keep down the Zofran tablets and they admitted her to the hospital for fluids last night. I went to the hospital to see her, pushing away the dizzy feeling I get anytime I enter any medical facility. I tried to focus on my mother's face, not on the IV line and not on the chemo port on her chest.

I begged her to let me stay. She told me she was just dehydrated—there was no reason to put my life on hold. She reminded me I needed to leave now to get to college before registration started.

The compromise was that Dad would stay with her. Mom wasn't happy about it, but neither of us could imagine him leaving her to skip off to college with me. I assured them both that I could handle moving by myself. Dad loaded my boxes into the trunk and back seat of my car, and I assured him I'd just get everything into the elevator once I got to the dorm.

But now that I'm here, there's a problem: My new dorm does not have an elevator.

I checked. I circled, I asked around, and ultimately concluded that this five-story dorm has only stairs. Which means I will need to carry each and every one of my many, many boxes up to my room on the fourth floor. Despite the fact that I could barely lift some of them out of my car. It never even occurred to me such a thing could happen.

It's so depressing that I want to sit on the pavement and cry.

But instead, I buck up and grab one of the boxes out of the trunk. It's not one of the heaviest boxes, but not one of the tiny ones either. It's a medium-sized box. I figure if I get some of the medium-sized boxes upstairs, I'll build my muscles up to bring the big ones up. And after I'm done with that, the smaller ones will seem like a piece of cake.

Unfortunately, the medium-sized box is still very, very big. So big that when I've got it in my arms, I'm having a hard time seeing over it. I start up the steps to the front entrance, but forget exactly how many steps there are and it's too hard to see what's ahead of me. I swear, if I go sprawling with this box, I will definitely start crying.

"One more stair," a male voice says from behind me.

I obligingly lift my legs up the next step.

"Okay, now go straight," the voice instructs me.

I have no choice but to listen, since I can't see a thing. I walk straight ahead, but slowly, so I don't crash.

"Now go left," he says. I go left. A pause. "No, your *other* left."

Jesus. I can't believe I have like ten more boxes after this.

"Listen, just give me that," the voice says.

I don't know who has been talking to me. At this point, I don't care if it's a burglar, because anyone who wants this stupid box can have it. I gratefully hand over my gigantic medium-sized box, and look up to thank the student (or burglar?) who took it from me. And…

Oh, he's very nice-looking.

He's about half a foot taller than me, which would put him at around six feet. He's wearing a worn T-shirt and baggy blue jeans, but I can see the muscles bulging in his arms as he holds my box. He's got shaggy blond hair and blue eyes that crinkle when he squints at me in the sunlight. At that moment, I fall just the tiniest bit in love with him.

Well, maybe not in *love*. In *lust* is more like it.

"Thanks," I manage.

The boy raises his eyebrows at me. "You're a freshman, huh?"

I nod. He's too hot. It's made me into a mute.

"All alone?"

I nod again.

"All right," he says. "Let's do this then."

I grab a duffel bag from my car so I don't feel like a helpless little girl who needs a big strong guy to help her lift stuff, even if that appears to be the situation. Also, I hold doors for him. I'm good at that part.

It takes him five trips with me helping. Five times up the stairs to the fourth floor, carrying the heaviest of my boxes while I follow behind with something embarrassingly light. He barely grunts when he lifts the box with my computer in it. He dumps the last of my boxes on the floor of my new dorm room, a light sheen of sweat dotting his handsome features. His shirt is sticking to his body, which, sadly, makes him all the more attractive. Unfortunately, I'm just as sweaty as he is and I've even got pit stains, which isn't making *me* more attractive.

"Thank you so much," I say to him, having rediscovered my voice. "I really, really appreciate it."

"No problem." He grins crookedly. Oh my God, he's good-looking. It's almost criminal how cute he is when he smiles like that. "I'm Noah, by the way. I live right down the hall in one of the sophomore rooms."

"Oh," I say.

His smile widens. "In normal society, this is when you usually tell me your name."

My cheeks grow warm. "I'm Bailey."

Noah nods, smiling politely. It's obvious he did this because he's a nice guy who felt like he needed to help a poor freshman in distress. He didn't do it because he's wildly attracted to me or anything like that.

"You okay now?" he asks me. "Anything else you need?"

I shake my head. "No, that's fine. Thanks."

"In that case," he says with a wink, "I'll see you around, Miss Bailey."

I can't help but think of how my parents met. My father helped my mother carry her heavy box up to her room, just like Noah has done for me, except times ten. And he lives right down the hall, just like my father lived down the hall from my mother.

Except instead of inviting me to coffee like my father did with my mother, Noah walks away.

Chapter 7
PRESENT DAY

I catch my father unpacking alone in the bedroom he'll be sharing with Gwen. He's pulling out a pair of boxer shorts and whistling to himself.

When is the last time I've heard him whistle like that? When is the last time I've seen him smile that wide? Especially while unpacking underwear. Some of his hair even seems to be growing back.

He looks up at the sound of my footsteps and his smile falters. I don't take it personally. He knows why I'm here. His smile shrinks further when I shut the door behind me.

"What the hell, Dad?" I snap at him, forgetting my age-old rule about never cussing in front of my parents. If there's ever a time to cuss, it's now, damn it.

"I didn't know," he murmurs.

"No kidding." I take a deep breath, trying to control my anger. I don't want to yell at my elderly father, especially when he looks the happiest he's been since Mom died. "How could you not know?"

"Well, she told me she had a son named Noah," he says. "But… I didn't realize he was *that* Noah. Noah Walsh isn't an uncommon name. It's not like he's called… Benedict Cumberbatch."

I wring my hands together. "Did Gwen know?"

Dad shakes his head. "No, she didn't. When I talked about you, I always called you Bee or just said 'my daughter.' She never put it together until… well, apparently Noah told her while we were on our way here."

I bow my head and rub my temples. "This is really awkward."

He shrugs helplessly. "I know, Bee. I'm sorry. I would never have brought you here if I realized…" He sinks down on the bed. "But we're here now, and I think you should make the best of it. Gwen promised me Noah is fine with the whole thing."

Fine with the whole thing. Right. Aside from despising me with every fiber of his being, he's totally fine with it.

"Obviously, he's doing really well for himself," my father points out. "He's very successful. He's got an apartment up in the city, and this cabin down here, and he's a doctor like he wanted to be, so…"

"Yeah," I mumble, looking away. I wanted Noah to be successful. I wanted him to have everything he ever dreamed of. But for some reason, now that I'm faced with it, it stings.

His brows knit together. "Bee, if you feel like you need to go back, I'll make something up to Gwen. Do what you need to do."

I look at my father's face. It's been less than ten years since Mom died, but Dad looks at least two decades older. I forget how hard it's been on him. He deserves happiness. I don't want to mess anything up for him by throwing a tantrum over something that happened a long time ago.

Noah says he's willing to try to put this behind him. I guess I'll stay.

———

Lily spends some time in the living room playing with her new Barbie doll while I hide in my room. I get my sketch pad out from my bag and attempt to draw a picture of the cabin from memory. I want to go out and take a look to see what details I'm missing, but I don't dare leave the room. I don't want to risk another confrontation with Noah.

A couple of hours later, Lily bounces into our bedroom, clutching her new Barbie doll. It has blond hair and an impossibly skinny waist. I've shied away from buying Lily too many Barbie dolls because they're expensive and also because I feel like it would be nice for her to have a doll that looked more like a real woman. Of course, now there are all these dolls from other television shows like *Monster High* that look just look Barbies. I mean, it's not like I'm overweight or anything—being destitute is a great diet. But it would be anatomically impossible for me to have a figure like this doll that Lily is fawning over.

At least, I think she's fawning over the Barbie. Then I discover it's not Barbie she's fallen in love with.

"Noah is going to cook us dinner tonight," Lily informs me.

"Oh, is he?"

"Uh huh." Lily nods excitedly. "He said he's going to make stuff on a grill. Like with a big fire."

"Ooh," I say. I wonder how old Lily will be before she can recognize my phony enthusiasm. I hope it doesn't happen until her artwork gets a *lot* better.

"He went out this morning and bought lots of hot dogs because Grandpa said I like hot dogs."

"That's nice of him."

"And he said he's going to take us to a movie this week! Maybe *Dogcat*!"

I grit my teeth. "We already saw *Dogcat*." We saw it, it's *done*, and we never have to see it again. Never.

"Oh." Lily's excitement seems dampened.

"Maybe he can take us to another movie?"

"Okay!" Lily agrees, and before I can stop her, she runs out to find Noah, who is apparently her new hero. Lord knows, she doesn't have a father to be her hero.

A minute later, Lily bursts back into the room breathlessly. "He says he'll take us to see anything we want."

Despite everything, I feel a rush of affection toward Noah for being so kind to my daughter.

"Also," Lily adds, "he's going to take us out on his boat and we're going to catch fish!"

I imagine being stuck out in the middle of the lake with Noah on a tiny boat while we wait hours for fish to nibble on our bait. Lovely.

"I like Noah," Lily says, her little face beaming.

"I can tell," I say. I grin at her. "Do you think he's handsome, Lil?"

She giggles and hides her face in her hands. "Mayyyyybe. A little."

I can't exactly blame her. I was certain if I ran into Noah by now, he'd have been long since snatched up.

"Is he married, Mommy?" she asks me.

"I don't think so."

"How come?"

I shrug. "I guess he hasn't met the right woman yet."

Lily nods solemnly. "Do you think he's looking for a woman to marry?"

"I…" I really don't want to have this conversation with my child. And I really hope Noah isn't able to hear us. "I don't know. Maybe he doesn't want to get married."

She thinks about this a minute. "I think he should get married," she decides. "He'd be a good husband."

I swallow. "You might be right."

I look down at my sketch pad, at the likeness of the cabin. I'll focus on my art this week. Try not to think too much about the past. I can't change it, after all.

"Mommy?" Lily says.

God, I can't talk about Noah anymore. "Uh huh?"

"Why is there a chair in the bathtub?"

I look up at Lily's wide blue eyes. "A chair?"

She nods. "When I went to the bathroom, there was a white chair! In the bathtub! And a bar sticking out of the wall!"

I bite my lip. "I don't know, sweetie. You'll have to ask Noah."

I don't dare tell Lily that I know the answer to her question.

Chapter 8
PRESENT DAY

By the time I emerge from the bedroom, Noah has already fired up the grill, and the tantalizing scent of grilling meat wafts from the back patio into the cabin. They've got a table out on the patio, and Gwen is instructing Lily on how to set the table. It's such a homey scene. I imagine an alternate universe in which the man grilling the meat is my husband, and the woman teaching Lily to set the table is my mother. Instead, the cook hates me and my mother is dead.

"Smells good," I comment as I emerge onto the patio. I hope the food is close enough to done that I don't have to make awkward conversation for too long.

Noah lifts his blue eyes briefly to glare at me as I take a seat. He doesn't seem quite ready to be cordial. It's a good thing we've got a whole week out here.

"I want a hot dog!" Lily calls out.

"Right, I got it," Noah says. "You want a hamburger."

Lily giggles. "No, I said a hot dog!"

"Two hamburgers for Lily, coming right up!"

"No!" Lily is laughing so hard now that her face is turning pink. "I want! One! Hot! Dog!"

Noah nods. "Got it. Ten hamburgers for Lily."

"Be careful," I say to Noah. "You're going to end up playing this game with her for the next hour."

He winks at my daughter. "At this rate, I'm going to be grilling hamburgers for Lily for the next hour. So you want *twenty* hamburgers?"

It's sweet. He's good with her—I have to give him that.

The hot dogs are done first. Noah grabs a paper plate, opens up a hot dog bun, and drops her hot dog inside. He asks her if she likes ketchup and she says yes. And before I can warn him, he gives the hot dog a spritz of ketchup.

He wouldn't know. He doesn't have kids of his own, so he probably has no idea that you never add a condiment to a child's food without asking exactly how it should be added first, because *omg, you could ruin it*. Lily likes ketchup, but is very clear about the fact that you never, *ever* put the ketchup directly on the hot dog. It's the eighth deadly sin, in Lily's eyes. Hot dogs can only be *dipped* in ketchup, never slathered. Now it's ruined. If we were at a restaurant, I'd be sending back the hot dog as we speak.

Lily looks down at the offending hot dog on her plate, then back up at Noah. I would have bet my life's savings that she wouldn't have touched that hot dog, but to my utter shock, she sits down and starts eating it. I can't believe my eyes. She must really love him.

53

"What do you want, Bailey?" Noah asks me without looking up from the grill.

"A cheeseburger, thanks," I say.

Noah finishes grilling burgers and hot dogs for everyone else. When he grabs the bag of hamburger buns off the table next to him, and they slip from his fingers and fall to the floor. He looks down at the buns on the ground and lets out a barely audible sigh. I open my mouth, ready to offer to grab them for him. But I suspect doing so will only make Noah hate me more.

I pretend to look away, but I can't help but watch him out of the corner of my eye as he holds onto the table for support as he slowly, carefully gets down on one knee. He picks up the buns, then hauls himself back up, still gripping the table for dear life. Once he's back on his feet again, he looks in my direction, but I've busied myself by staring out at the lake in the distance.

"These hamburgers are amazing," Dad says to Noah once we all have our plates of food.

"Thanks," he says.

"Noah loves the grill," Gwen says. "He buys charcoal by the truckload."

The cheeseburger in front of me smells so amazing that my stomach rumbles, reminding me that my lunch consisted of a bag of Doritos on the train. I pick up the burger and take a bite and…

Ugh, this is terrible!

The burger Noah served me is charred to a crisp. I feel like I just ate a mouthful of somebody's cremated uncle.

I look at my father and Gwen, who are happily munching on their burgers. There's no way their burgers taste like mine. This is practically inedible.

"What's wrong, Mommy?" Lily asks. "Don't you like your burger?"

I notice that Noah is watching me, a tiny smile playing on his lips. "Yeah, Bailey, is something wrong with the burger I made you?"

I swallow hard. "It's just…" I notice that everyone is staring at me. "It's a little bit burned. That's all."

Dad seems aghast at my comment. Gwen glares at me. "It's from a *grill*. They have a char to them. It's not going to taste like the burgers at *McDonald's*."

"Right." My cheeks grow hot. "Actually, it's fine. Just… you know, a tiny bit burned. Not even. I shouldn't have mentioned it."

I take another bite of my burger. It takes superhuman effort not to spit the damn thing out. I glance over at Noah, who is chuckling to himself. Asshole.

"If you don't like it, Mommy," Lily says to me, "Noah says we're having more for dessert."

I frown. "More? You mean, more burgers? For dessert?"

Lily nods eagerly. "Yeah, Noah says it's the best dessert. More!"

Noah grins at her. "No, that's *s'mores*. We're having s'mores for dessert. We can make 'em right on the grill."

"I don't think she knows what s'mores are," I tell Noah.

His eyes widen. "Lily, you've never had s'mores before?"

Lily shakes her head solemnly as she always does when she knows she's going to experience something really meaningful or delicious.

"Really?" Noah is incredulous. "But your mom and I used to…"

He cuts his own thought off mid-sentence. I wonder if he's remembering the same thing I am. The two of us, cuddled together by a campfire, roasting marshmallows on sticks we found in the woods. The woods used to scare me, but with my head resting on Noah's broad shoulder and his arm around me, I felt completely safe and warm and happy.

I used to love s'mores.

"Hasn't your dad ever taken you camping?" Noah asks Lily.

Lily crinkles her nose. "He doesn't like that."

"Theo isn't what you'd call the outdoors type," Dad volunteers. "He's more the lazy, deadbeat musician type."

And then everyone laughs. Ha ha, my ex-husband is a big loser and I'm a loser for having married him. Real hilarious.

"Well, I'll have to show you some cool outdoorsy stuff this week then," Noah tells Lily. "Starting with s'mores, okay?"

Lily nods eagerly. "What *are* s'mores?"

"Basically," he says, "you melt some marshmallow on a piece of graham cracker, then you cover that with chocolate."

I think he had her at "some marshmallow."

———

An hour later, everyone goes back into the cabin, bellies full of meat, marshmallows, chocolate, and graham crackers. Lily officially loves s'mores. And Noah. She definitely loves Noah.

Noah stays behind to scrape and clean the grill. I do my part by wiping down the patio table, but I'm watching him out of the corner of my eye. I see his impressive biceps flexing as he scrapes the char from the lines of the grill. He's still so built—it's hard to tear my eyes away.

"Thank you for being so nice to Lily," I say.

Noah glances at me briefly, then goes back to the grill. "I know what it's like to have a dad who isn't around much."

Noah's father left his mother when he was about ten years old, but was usually absent prior to that. There were issues with alcohol, but in general, he just seemed like he wasn't a great guy. *A loser*, Noah always called him. I remember Noah telling me about a heart-wrenching Boy Scout trip where every dad showed up but his. It was one of his goals in life to be completely different from his own father.

"Anyway," he says, "she's a sweet kid."

I smile at the compliment. "Thanks. She likes you too. Actually, I think she has quite the crush."

Noah snorts. "Yeah, I get that a lot from the little girls who show up at the emergency room."

"The moms too, I'll bet."

He doesn't look at me as he mumbles, "Yeah."

The female patients must go wild for Noah. A handsome, young doctor with no ring on his finger? He must have to bat them away.

"So," Noah says quietly, "does Lily know about me? Did you tell her?"

I bite my lip. "Tell her what?"

He turns to glare at me. "What do you *think*?"

I wince at his anger, which is probably deserved. "No. I haven't told her anything. Do… do you want me to?"

He doesn't look terribly surprised that I haven't told her. He shakes his head. "No, let me. I'm used to telling people." He shrugs. "Can't be any worse than telling a woman I'm out on a first date with."

"Oh," I mumble. "Is that... I mean, do they react... badly?"

Noah slams down the spatula and glares at me. "Well, gee, Bailey, how the fuck do you *think* they react? You think they rip their clothes off with desire?"

"No," I say quickly, then when I see the look on his face, I backpeddle. "I mean, I'm sure there are *some* women who... there *have to* be women who... I mean, you've had girlfriends, haven't you?"

I see the look on Noah's face and recognize at this point that I'm not making the situation any better. "Jesus Christ," he says. "Of *course* I've had girlfriends. What the hell do you think? This is really insulting."

"I'm sorry." I run a shaking hand through my hair. "I didn't mean to... I mean, *you're* the one who brought it up." I chew on my thumbnail—an old bad habit of mine. "I feel like I can't say anything without you yelling at me."

"Sorry to make things *uncomfortable* for you," Noah shoots back.

I scoop up a package of unused paper plates from the table. I want to throw them at him. "If you want me to leave," I say, "just say so. I'll have Lily and me on a train to New York first thing tomorrow."

He studies my face as if he's really thinking about it. I know he said he invited me so that we could learn to be cordial with each other, but I think it's a lost cause. It's clear Noah doesn't have it in him to be nice to me, even if he thought he did.

"No," he says finally. "I want this to work out. For my mother's sake. She deserves to be happy."

"Fine," I say, "but you have to stop being such an asshole to me."

He opens his mouth as if to protest, but then thinks better of it. "I'll try."

Our eyes meet across the patio. It surreal that we're standing here, struggling to be civil to each other. This wasn't where I thought we'd be ten years ago. Everything went horribly wrong, and I know there's nothing I can do at this point to fix it.

Chapter 9

PRESENT DAY

Sketching is better than psychotherapy for me. When I'm feeling awful, all I need to do is get out my sketchpad and let my mind go blank as I watch the image take shape before me. I don't think about anything else when I'm sketching other than the drawing in front of me. There was a year when I couldn't draw because of… well, everything that happened. That was one of the worst years of my life. I've probably saved thousands of dollars in therapy bills thanks to my hobby. (Good thing too, because I don't have thousands of dollars to spend on therapy.)

So instead of getting worked up about the fact that Noah is in his bedroom, thinking about how much he hates me, I sit out on the sofa and sketch while Lily plays with her new Barbie. Gwen and my father have gone out for their "nightly walk" so it's very quiet in here. I'm sketching Noah's small kitchen, with its small wooden dining table, creaky chairs, and humming refrigerator. (The challenge is to sketch "humming.") As the image takes shape, the tension gradually melts from my shoulders and the sharp pain in my temples subsides to a dull ache.

Until Noah comes out into the kitchen to pour himself a glass of water.

He walks into the room with that noticeable limp. His T-shirt is far from tight, but it still can't hide all the muscles in his chest and arms. I hate that he still looks every bit as good as he did a decade ago.

He grabs a glass from the kitchen cabinet and fills it with filtered water from his refrigerator. Before I can stop myself, I blurt out, "I thought you always said water filters were bourgeoisie."

Noah puts his water glass down on the kitchen table with an aggressively loud thump. Great—why did I say something to antagonize him? I should have stuck with a neutral topic, like the weather. Why oh why didn't I talk about the weather?

"This isn't the *suburbs*." He shakes his head at me like I've said something too stupid to believe. "You can't drink the water unfiltered out here. You'd get really sick."

"Okay," I mumble.

Given how much he hates me, I'm hopeful he'll bring the water back into his room, but he doesn't. He sits down with it at that wooden table in one of the rickety chairs with an ungraceful plop. And he sips his water painfully slowly, watching me over the rim of the glass. It makes it hard to do… well, anything.

"I wonder when your mother and my father will be getting back from their walk," I say, because sometimes it's hard for me to shut up when I'm nervous. And Noah is making me very nervous. "I hope they're okay."

Noah looks down at his watch. "They're adults. They'll come back eventually."

"Yes, but…" I look at the door. "Your mother took her purse, didn't she? Could they have gotten… mugged?"

"Mugged?" Noah snorts. "Here? You've got to be kidding me." He takes another sip of water. "No, around here, the bigger worry is coyotes."

My heart speeds up. "Coyotes?"

He nods solemnly. "And snakes."

He's messing with me. That's his *mother* out there—he wouldn't send her out to be eaten by coyotes and snakes. But my calm from a moment ago has been completely shattered, and I feel a rush of relief when I hear footsteps right outside our door. *Human* footsteps. Nothing four-legged or slithery.

Gwen and my father burst through the door, and I see right away that Gwen is limping. Despite the fact that I'm certain Noah was teasing me about the coyotes and snakes, he looks alarmed when he sees his mother.

"Mom!" His light brown eyebrows scrunch together. "What happened? Are you okay?"

I know how close Noah always was with his mother, especially since his dad walked out on them. As a teenager, he chased out a guy his mother was dating when the guy got too fresh. He liked being able to protect her. It must gut him to see her hurt.

"I'm fine!" Gwen hobbles into the living room and collapses onto the sofa. "I just got scraped up by some evil branches."

But Noah insists on taking a look. He is, he points out, a doctor. My father holds her hand while she straightens out her left leg—sure enough, there are angry red marks all over her calf, which are oozing dark red blood. I close my eyes, not willing to let them see how much the sight of Gwen's injury is bothering me. I'm trying not to think about that dark red blood.

"That's a lot of blood," Lily comments.

Thanks for the observation, honey.

"Let me get this cleaned up," Noah says. "Bailey, could you grab the first aid kit in the closet over there?"

He's pointing to the closet about six feet from where I'm sitting. It's an entirely reasonable request, except if I try to stand up, I will definitely pass out. Even without standing up, it's a coin flip whether I'm going to stay conscious.

"Um…," I murmur.

Noah raises his blue eyes to look at me. I see a flicker of amusement on his features—almost affection. "It still bothers you so much, Bailey?"

I turn my head away, unable to even mumble a response.

"I'll get it!" Lily yelps, abandoning her Barbie on the floor. She's too eager to impress Noah.

Unfortunately, Lily doesn't have the slightest idea what a first aid kit looks like. After a moment of contemplation, she pulls an umbrella out of the closet and holds it up triumphantly. I don't get that. Yes, she might not know what a first aid kit should look like. But she does know what an *umbrella* looks like. My father has to go over to help her, but he can't find it either. Noah finally has to fetch it himself.

While Noah is rifling around the closet, looking for the kit, my father holds Gwen's hand. He smiles at her in a way that makes me wish I had a boyfriend of my own around for all the various cuts and scrapes I've had over the years. Not only am I single, but there's nothing even remotely on the horizon. I am uber-single.

"Must be nice having a son who's a doctor," Dad comments.

Gwen smiles and nods. "Yes, it is." She flashes me a pointed look. "He always looks out for the people he cares about. That's just the sort of person he is."

Nice. Way to rub it in.

Noah fishes out his first aid kit from the closet after a minute of searching. The sight of it is painfully

65

familiar. I don't know if it's the same one he had in college, but it may as well be. I've been watching Noah break out his first aid kit for a long time, at even the slightest excuse. It was sort of his *thing*. I used to tease him about how a papercut doesn't warrant a first aid kit.

I still remember the first time I saw that first aid kit during my freshman year of college. My party animal roommate Carla had left a bottle of Corona on the floor of our dorm room, and I knocked it over accidentally, shattering glass all over the wooden floorboards of our room. During my angry attempt to clean it up, I slashed my hand on a large piece of glass.

I ran out of the room in the direction of the communal bathroom to get myself cleaned up. But it turned out I wasn't alone in there. The first thing I noticed when I got inside was a cloud of steam coming out of one of the shower stalls. And that's when I saw Noah, standing at the sink in nothing but his boxers, his usually light hair darkened from the water.

The sight of those tight muscles in his chest and arms made me forget all about my bleeding hand. It's not like I hadn't seen men with their shirts off at the beach or at the swimming pool, but none of them looked like Noah.

Wow.

He blinked water droplets out of his eyelashes. "Bailey, right?"

I just stared at him, somehow rendered speechless.

His light brown eyebrows bunched together. "Are you okay?"

"Yes?" I managed.

"Um… you're dripping blood all over the floor…"

Noah later claimed he saw my eyes roll up in their sockets. I'm not so sure. My knees were definitely very wobbly, but I don't think I was about to hit the floor. I do remember him yelling, "Oh, shit!" And then I felt his arms grabbing me, supporting me.

A second later, he was scooping me up in his arms like I was a princess and he was the gallant handsome prince carrying me off into the sunset. And also, he was shirtless. I wish I could have appreciated the sexiness of it, but I was mostly mortified that my hot neighbor had to rescue the dorky freshman from fainting.

"I'm okay," I murmured. "You don't have to…"

"You almost *fainted*," he pointed out.

My body was pressed against his own bare chest. I'd never felt such a troubling combination of turned on and queasy. I finally gave in, resting my head against his shoulder, and let him carry me back to his room, where he lay me down on the futon.

"Are you going to faint, Bailey?" he asked me.

I shook my head no.

"Throw up?"

My cheeks burned. "No."

"Let me see your hand."

I squeezed my fist shut and held it protectively to my chest. "I'm okay."

He rolled his eyes. "I'm going to go get my first aid kit."

Noah disappeared into one of the bedrooms. When he emerged again, he was fully dressed in a T-shirt and jeans, but he wasn't any less sexy fully clothed. He was also holding a plastic box containing bottles of antiseptic, band-aids, alcohol swabs, and gauze that he laid out in front of me.

Noah held out his hand to me. "Give it here."

I looked away as I held out my injured palm. I buried my face in the futon, trying to pretend this wasn't happening.

I heard Noah laugh. "Wow, you're really squeamish, aren't you, Bailey?"

"Pathetic, right?"

"No, it's cute, actually."

Cute. The hot guy next door who had to save me from face-planting onto the bathroom floor just called me cute.

I felt Noah wiping away the blood on my hand. It stung like crazy. I held my breath, biting my lip so hard I worried I was going to make that bleed too. "Do I need stitches?" I asked him.

"Naw," he said. "It's a bleeder, but it's not that bad."

When I opened my eyes again, Noah was done and the wound on my hand was neatly covered by two Band-Aids.

"Thank you," I murmured.

He grinned crookedly at me. "Any time, Bailey."

To this day, I can't look at a first aid kit without remembering the first time I fell a little bit in love with Noah Walsh.

Chapter 10
PRESENT DAY

The crickets are loud tonight.

That's one of the most annoying things about sleeping in the country—those damn crickets. Some people like the sound of them or at least can ignore them, but I'm not one of those people. I lie awake, my head throbbing, wishing the crickets would shut the hell up.

One night when Noah and I were camping in the wilderness, lying awake in our tent close to midnight, I asked him why crickets were so loud. Noah, who was a Boy Scout for his entire childhood, was always ready with an answer for any question that came up during a camping trip.

"The hotter it is, the louder crickets chirp," he explained to me. "Also, summer is mating season for crickets, and the male mating song is the loudest."

"Fascinating," I said.

He leaned toward me in our shared sleeping bag. "Are the crickets giving you any ideas?"

Ah, sex in a tent. It's been a long time since I've experienced that. Actually, it's been a long time since I've experienced sex period. A really long time.

Great, now I'm being kept awake by the crickets *and* I'm horny.

I get out of bed and shut the window, blocking out the sound of the crickets. The window was providing a nice breeze, but I just can't take any more of the crickets flaunting their superior love lives.

I get back into bed, but now there's another noise filling the room. It's Gwen. And my father. Talking in their bedroom.

I try not to listen, but the walls are paper thin. God, I hope that doesn't mean I'm going to have to listen to them having sex during this trip. I don't think I can handle that on top of everything else.

"…not her fault," I hear my father say.

"Not her fault!" Gwen bursts out. She's not even attempting to keep her voice down—she probably hopes I'm listening. "Whose fault was it then? *Noah's*?"

"No, it wasn't…" My father mumbles something I can't make out. "She's had it rough, you know?"

"I hope you're not suggesting she had it worse than my son?"

"No! That's not what I'm saying!"

Great, they're having a fight over me. After all the horrible things I've done to Gwen Walsh, now I'm going to break up her engagement.

"I'm just saying," my father says, more quietly this time. "Bailey is sorry. I know she is."

There's a long silence. It doesn't sound like Gwen is trying to scratch my father's eyes out, but I'm not entirely sure what that would sound like.

It's ironic that Gwen hates me so much, given how much she used to like me. Then again, Gwen's affection for me paled in comparison to how much my own mother adored Noah. She practically fell in love with him the first time she met him. She couldn't stop talking about him for days afterwards.

Mom met Noah during my freshman year, soon after she finished her chemotherapy. With the worst of her recovery behind her, the first thing she wanted to do was pay her only daughter a visit at college.

I met her at the entrance to the dorm, where Dad dropped her off before going to find a parking spot. I hadn't seen her since before her chemo started and it was a shock. She lost all her hair again and she had a kerchief tied around her head—Mom never liked wigs. On top of that, she was a good twenty pounds lighter than she was before, and she wasn't heavy to begin with.

"Bailey!" Mom's brown eyes lit up when she saw me. "I've missed you so much."

When we hugged, my mother's frame felt so frail in my arms. I wasn't a big girl by any means, and I felt like I could crush every bone in her body if I squeezed just a little tighter.

"There's no elevator," I told her apologetically. "And I'm on the fourth floor."

"I can manage a few flights of stairs," Mom assured me.

Except by the top of the last flight, my mother was looking decidedly pale. She was breathing heavily and all I could think was that this stupid dorm nearly killed her. Why did I let her come up here? I should have insisted we go out somewhere.

"Mom…" I murmured.

"I'm fine," Mom puffed, managing a smile. "Just give me a minute."

We lingered in the stairwell, waiting for my mother's breathing to return to normal. I gripped the railing of the stairs, watching her face, praying this trip wouldn't involve a call to 911.

"Hey, Bailey!"

I whirled around and my chest fluttered when I found myself face-to-face with none other than Noah Walsh, who had officially cemented himself as my Freshman Crush after he patched up my hand. It was a pointless, hopeless crush though. I'd seen Noah bring home several girls over the semester on scattered Saturday nights, and every one of them was far more gorgeous than I could ever hope to be.

"Hey, Noah," I said.

"How's your hand?" he asked.

I held up the hand he'd bandaged for me in his room. "All better."

I glanced at my mother, who was breathing better now. Well enough, in fact, that an appreciative smile curled her lips at the sight of Noah.

Noah looked at my mother, and his eyes widened slightly—almost unperceptively, but I caught it. I knew he was pre-med and he was no dummy on top of that. I'm sure he could take look at her wasted frame and bald head and put it altogether.

"Bailey," he said, "you didn't tell me you had a sister visiting you."

It was the most obvious line in the history of the world. He didn't think my mother was my sister. Not a chance. Hell, my *grandmother* would have been a more realistic guess at that moment. But Mom tittered and blushed in a way that surprised me. Maybe she wasn't falling for his line, but she clearly liked the attention of a handsome, sophomore coed.

"This is my mother," I told Noah. "She's visiting for the weekend."

I'd noticed people often got anxious about touching my mother when she looked this way, but Noah quickly stuck his hand out for her to shake and offered his best smile. "Nice to meet you, Mrs. Chapin. I'm Noah. I live down the hall."

"Down the hall, huh?" Mom said, giving me a pointed look.

"I can really see the resemblance," he added, looking between the two of us. "But you must hear that all the time."

"Not as much as I used to," Mom said as she beamed up at him.

"Anyway," I said regretfully, "my mother had a long trip, so I think we're going to go to my room."

The grin didn't slip from Noah's face. "Well, if there's anything you guys need while you're visiting, just let me know. Like I said, I'm right down the hall."

"Well, aren't you nice?" Mom was so obviously completely smitten.

Noah sprinted down the stairs, taking them two at a time, leaving me standing alone with my mother. She looked down after him, a tiny smile playing on her lips. I'd always thought my mother was immune to the attentions of any man besides my father.

"Wow," Mom breathed, when he was officially out of sight (and hopefully earshot). I expected she was going to say something about how nice he seemed, but instead she said, "He's *hot*."

"Oh, Mom…" I covered my face so she couldn't see my cheeks turn red.

She laughed. "Well, he *is*, isn't he?"

"I don't know," I mumbled.

She smiled that secret smile again. "You're so lucky, Bailey. Only eighteen years old and you've got *that guy* living right down the hall."

At the time, all I felt was frustration that my Freshman Crush was so solidly out of my league. But as it turned out, Noah was only one tragic act away from being mine.

———

I wake up in the morning with Lily's feet staring me in the face.

Lily and I are no strangers to being forced to share a bedroom. We've shared one for the past three years, since Theo took off. And about half the time, at some point during the night, Lily migrates to my bed.

I want to say it's a joy sleeping with my daughter. I do love having her warm little body encircled in my arms, and I'm sure she likes it too, which is why she comes into my bed. But Lily is a very restless sleeper. It's not at all out of the ordinary for her to turn 180 degrees during the night and end up with her feet on her pillow, intermittently kicking me in the face. In fact, when she does have her head on the pillow at the end of the night, I suspect it's only because she did a full 360 turn.

Well, at least her feet don't smell too bad.

I sit up in bed, massaging a crick in my neck. It's not yet seven in the morning—I'm probably the only one awake in this house. But looking on the bright side, that means I can hit the shower before anyone else can get there.

I tiptoe out of bed before Lily wakes up. I grab the towel Noah left for me as well as my toiletries. I nearly bring a change of clothes, but then I figure I can just wrap a towel around myself for the three-foot-long journey back to my room. It will be fine.

The door to the bathroom is shut, but the light isn't on, which is Lily's usual MO. I got her in the habit of closing doors behind her, so she always closes the bathroom door, which drives me nuts because I'm never sure if it's occupied. I open the door to the bathroom, thinking I'll have a little talk with Lily later.

Except as it turns out, the bathroom *is* occupied. By Noah. Who just finished taking a shower.

It's not like I never walked in on Noah just after a shower before. Hell, I've walked in on him *during* a shower many, many times. On purpose. And in a lot of ways, he looks very much the same as he used to back on the day he bandaged my wounded hand. He still has a full head of hair plastered to his skull, although it's shorter than it used to be. He still has those strong, tight muscles in his shoulders, arms, and chest, but that's no surprise since I could see them through his T-shirt earlier. He does have more hair on his chest than he used to, but I suppose that's normal with aging. And... well, let's just say my favorite part of his anatomy is just as I remember it.

But the Noah before me is entirely different than the Noah I used to catch coming out of the shower. That Noah wasn't sitting in a wheelchair. That Noah had two strong, muscular legs sprinkled with golden hair. This Noah has two pale stumps, half the size of what his femurs used to be and half the width, with white scars where the rest of his legs used to be.

"Bailey," he gasps.

"Oh my God," I say. "I'm so sorry!"

I slam the door shut, but of course, it's far too late. If I have earned any goodwill whatsoever in the last day, I have instantly lost it.

Chapter 11
PRESENT DAY

I lie in bed awake for the next hour, the image of what I just saw burned into my brain. It's not like I never saw Noah that way—sitting in a wheelchair, his legs gone. I have. But then it all seemed so surreal, like maybe some hero doctor would rush in and tell us that they managed to save his legs after all. The scars were fresh back then. Now it seems so... permanent. Forever.

When I was a kid, I found a starfish at the beach with my mother, and she told me that if you cut a starfish's arm off, it would grow back. That doesn't happen with people, obviously. Once your legs are gone, they will always be gone.

Even Lily gets out of bed before I do. I absolutely refuse to leave my room until Lily grabs me by the arm and insists that I come out to breakfast. "Noah is making pancakes!" she announces happily.

I'd rather eat mud. Which is a good thing, because I'm sure he'll make sure my pancakes taste like mud.

I put on a pair of my running shorts and pad out to the dining area, where Noah is back on his feet again, fully dressed in jeans, a wrinkled T-shirt, and sneakers, standing at the stove. He glances up when I enter the room, and the look he gives me almost physically hurts. I bet he's sorry he didn't tell me to leave last night.

"Here you go, Lily," Noah says as he sets a plate of food down in front of her.

It's a large pancake that fills the entire plate. He's taken a bunch of blueberries and formed them into eyes, a nose, and a smile. It's a smiley face pancake. Theo would never make Lily a pancake that looks like that. Hell, *I* would never make Lily a pancake that looks like that. Lily actually gasps with delight at the sight of it.

"It's a smiley face!" she announces happily.

Noah smiles. "Glad you like it, Lily."

As Lily chows down on her pancake, she looks at Noah and smiles adoringly. She's so infatuated with him—it's really cute. But that's the way it's always been with girls and Noah.

Lily gobbles up the last of her pancake while Noah gets to work on mine. I don't know where my father and Gwen are, but it's clear they've gone out. It's just the three of us in the cabin. Just me, my daughter, and a guy who despises me.

A couple of minutes later, Noah lays down a plate in front of me that has three pancakes on it. They're not burned or disgusting or anything like that. They look perfect and delicious. He probably put poison in them.

"I'm done, Mommy!" Lily announces, having gobbled up every bite of the smiley face pancake in record time. "Can I go play with my Barbie?"

I don't want Lily to leave. I need her to be the buffer between me and Noah. But she's already getting up and running for the living room, so there's not a lot I can do. We don't do formal dinners in our tiny apartment at home.

Noah sits down across from me at the table, glaring at me like he was just forced to cook pancakes for Hitler. When Lily is out of earshot, he hisses at me, "Ever hear of knocking?"

My cheeks grow warm. "The light was out. I didn't think anyone was in there."

"There's a window in the bathroom," he says. "I was using *natural light*."

"Well, I'm sorry," I say, for what feels like the millionth time during this trip.

Noah glances down at my untouched pancakes. "Are you going to eat those? Or did seeing me in the bathroom make you lose your appetite?"

"Noah…" I want to tell him it's not true, because it's most definitely not, but I know that my words will sound hollow. There's too much bad blood between us. Really, I should just leave now. Except Lily is having such a great time.

Before I can say anything else, Noah stands up abruptly and leaves the room. He goes out on the

81

patio and sits there, staring out at the lake in the distance, probably thinking about how much he hates me.

I hear a ringtone in the distance and realize that someone is calling me. I wonder if it's my father. God, I hope he's getting back soon. I can't take too much more one-on-one time with Noah.

Except when I get to the bedroom, it turns out the caller is Theo. I see his name flashing on the display and consider letting it go to voicemail. It's hard to recall even one positive interaction with Theo since our divorce. I don't know if I can handle him right now.

My relationship with Theo was a direct reaction to my relationship with Noah. Theo was everything Noah was not. Theo was an artist while Noah was hardcore pre-med. Theo was scruffy and grungy, while Noah was relatively clean-cut. Theo was moody while Noah was even-tempered. Theo dropped out of college, while Noah graduated *summa cum laude*.

Theo was the sort of guy I'd always been attracted to before Noah. I met him when I was out with a friend at a bar where he was playing with his band. He had a great voice—raspy and deep. When he buried his face in the microphone, crooning an old Nirvana single, his stringy brown hair falling in his face, I felt something stirring in me that I thought was permanently dead. I came up to him after his set was over and told him how much I loved it.

Instead of thanking me, Theo looked at me with his soulful brown eyes and said, "How come a pretty girl like you looks so sad?"

My mouth fell open. I hadn't thought I looked sad at that moment, but he was right. I'd been struggling with serious depression over the last several years. It felt like he'd looked right into my *soul*.

"It's complicated," I finally told him.

"Maybe you could tell me about it while I buy you a drink?"

"I…" I looked away, down at my sweaty hands. "I don't really… date."

"It's not a date. You just look like you could use someone to talk to."

He was right. I did need someone to talk to. And that night, Theo was an amazing listener. I told him everything. Well, almost everything—I never told him about Noah, which was maybe the most important part of the story. But we ended up talking until the bar closed down, then walked to Times Square and talked till the sun came up.

One year later, I found myself pregnant with Lily. Theo asked me to marry him, and despite growing reservations, I said yes. At the time, I figured it was better than being a single mother.

I figured wrong.

Theo was great in theory. He was sexy and a true artist and great in bed. But in practice, he was a mess. His band was a failure—they could barely book even non-paying gigs and there was constant inner turmoil among the band members. They kept on their coke-snorting drummer way too long, even though he'd routinely not show up for their sets. But Theo wouldn't consider any other career aside from the one he'd always dreamed of, so he took side gigs waiting tables or bartending to pay the bills. That was fine in his early twenties, but not when he was in his thirties and had a wife and child to support.

Also, the long hair was much less sexy when his hairline started to recede. I told him he should consider shaving his head completely, and he blew up at me so violently that I never mentioned his hair again.

I could have lived with all of that though. I could have dealt with the poverty, the moodiness, the bad hair—all of it. But what I couldn't deal with was the other women. When he'd come home sweaty after a gig, smelling like another woman's perfume, that was too much for me to tolerate. Worst of all, he was blatantly unapologetic about it, claiming I'd tied him down too early with a child. As if that broken condom was *my* fault.

I stare down at the phone now, wondering what Theo wants from me. Of course, now that Noah has been reaming me out, my feelings toward Theo are warmer than usual. Theo may be a deadbeat, but at least he doesn't outright despise me. He'd move right back in if I'd let him.

I grab the phone just before it goes to voicemail. "Theo? What's going on?"

"Hey, Bailey." The anger that had been in Theo's voice during our last conversation is gone. Thank God. "I just wanted to say that I'm sorry about yesterday."

"Oh." It's a rare moment when Theo apologizes for something. I should relish it. "That's okay."

"You've never taken Lily anywhere out of the state before," he points out. "I just freaked out."

He was worried, and I can't entirely blame him. If he had taken Lily on a big trip without telling me about it, I would have gone ballistic. Just because he sometimes blows Lily off, that doesn't mean he doesn't love her. He's her father, after all.

"I'm sorry," I say. "I should have told you."

"Where *are* you, anyway?" Theo asks.

I tell him the approximate location of the cabin, best I can. To be honest, I'm not entirely sure where we are. And I'm not about to ask Noah.

"And you'll be back in a week?"

"Yeah," I say. "Lily has school next week so we'll be back for that."

"When you get back," Theo says, "maybe I can take Lily someplace really special. What do you think she'd like?"

"Maybe the Bronx Zoo?" I suggest. Then I regret it, because I know the admission fee is more than Theo can afford. "Or Coney Island?"

"Sure," he says. He's quiet for a second. "And maybe you could come along too?"

I grit my teeth. This is a typical Theo move. He begged me not to kick him out, even though he could never promise to be faithful. Every once in a while, he makes a play to get me back. But I'm too smart for that. "Maybe," I say, just to put him off.

"No pressure," Theo says.

"Listen, I should go," I say. "But… we'll coordinate things when I get back."

"Sure. Have a great trip."

"Thanks."

I hang up the phone, feeling a modicum better. Even if Noah is being a jerk to me, at least Theo was nice for a change. I don't think I could handle being attacked by both of them.

I go back to the dining table to finish my cold pancakes. Noah is back in the living room and he's talking to Lily. She's listening to him intently, her little heart-shaped face beaming with happiness. God, she's got one hell of a crush.

"Mommy!" Lily shrieks when she sees me. She's waving her hands to get my attention even though she's right in front of me. "Mommy, Noah is going to take me to see his boat and then we're going to go get some crabs at the lake!"

"Wonderful." I take a bite of my pancake. Even cold, it's pretty tasty.

"And then, Mommy," Lily continues, "he's going to cook the crabs for our dinner!"

I look at her in amazement. "*You're* going to eat crabs?" Lily subsists primarily on a diet of frozen chicken nuggets and hot dogs with a side of macaroni and cheese. And the chicken nuggets must be shaped like dinosaurs. Or else.

"Noah says he makes them taste really good," she says.

Wow, she really loves him.

I look up at Noah sitting in the living room, remembering when I felt the same way.

Chapter 12
14 YEARS EARLIER

I'm on a date.

It's my first date of college. Even though my crush on Noah Walsh is still very much present, I've resigned myself to the fact that our relationship will consist mostly of waving hello when we pass each other on campus, or maybe some small talk in the hallway. Noah isn't really my type anyway—I've always preferred more artistic guys than clean-cut, athletic, pre-meds.

Derek Malone is more my type of guy.

He's in my Visual Studies course, and he's an art major like me. Long hair, ink-stained fingertips, a goatee. And I like him just as much after our dinner out at an Italian restaurant. We talked about our common class, although less about our visual relationship to nature and culture than we did about how our professor has the strangest, unidentifiable accent. Derek guessed he was French—I thought Russian. It was quite a debate.

As Derek walks me back to my dorm, I wonder if he's going to kiss me goodnight. It will be my first kiss of college—something surely memorable. I wonder if Derek's goatee will feel scratchy against my chin. I wonder if he'll try to slip me some tongue. Or if I'll let him.

"May I walk you upstairs?" Derek asks me as we approach the door to my dorm. The wind is blowing his long, brown hair into his face, and he looks very much the artist. If he were a musician, this could be his album cover.

I smile. "Of course you may."

We make it up to my front door and that's where our date will come to an end. Derek turns to face me, a tiny smile playing on his lips. "I had a great time, Bailey."

"So did I," I reply honestly.

We stare at each other for a minute while my heart pounds in my chest. Is he going to kiss me? I want him to kiss me. If he doesn't kiss me, I'll spend the next week wondering what I did wrong.

But I don't have to worry much longer. Derek leans forward and presses his lips against mine. Derek's tongue probes my mouth just a little more than I would have wanted, but I forgive him for that. It's hard for guys to know the exact right amount of tongue. And bonus points for pulling back at exactly the right moment.

This is the perfect end to this date. All I can think about is when we're going to have our next one.

Except then Derek leans forward and kisses me again. This kiss is more aggressive than the first one, his tongue more probing and insistent. I feel his body pressing me against the door to my room, getting closer than I'd want him to on a first date. Not that I'm a prude, but…

"How about we go inside?" he breathes in my ear.

I shake my head. "Not tonight."

"Come *on*," he whines. "Just for a little while."

Before I can answer, he kisses me again. This time, I don't allow my tongue to respond to him at all. This kiss is most certainly unwelcome. Especially the way he's pressing his body against me so firmly that I can hardly move or breathe. Derek is thin but wiry.

"I'm just sort of tired," I say when he pulls away for air. "I'd like to go home."

"But we're having such a great time," he points out. "And it's still early."

"I think my roommate might be home," I mumble, even though it's eleven o'clock on a Saturday night, which means there's no way in hell Carla's home. She calls me pathetic when she comes home at three in the morning to find me already asleep in bed.

"Why don't you check?"

I swallow. My perfect date is completely ruined. Why is Derek being so goddamn pushy?

"Listen," I say, "like I said, I'm tired, so…"

"But I bought you dinner," he says.

I frown at him. "What is that supposed to mean?"

"It means that maybe you should stop being a cocktease."

I stare at Derek. I can't believe the guy I was thinking was so romantic only minutes earlier is turning into the biggest jerk I've ever met. All I want is for him to leave.

But Derek isn't taking the cue. He pushes me against the door again, kissing me more roughly. That's when I notice that nobody whatsoever is in the hallway. It's Saturday night, and every single person is out with friends or at a party or just *gone*. I'm all alone here with Derek.

I try to shove him off me, but his fingers grab my wrists and further pin me against the door. He's kissing my face and my neck and his body is pressed against me so hard that I can feel his erection. I try to struggle against him, but I can't budge. He's so goddamn strong—at least compared to me.

Shit, what am I supposed to do in this situation? Why didn't I take that campus self-defense course when I had a chance?

I squeeze my eyes shut, hoping he'll get sick of it when he sees I'm not responding, but he doesn't. He's kissing me more roughly while I squirm helplessly under his grip. "Please stop," I beg him.

"Oh, cut it out, Bailey," he says. "You know you want this."

Tears are forming in my eyes. I can't believe this is happening. I can't believe Derek is going to assault me right in the hallway outside my dorm room.

Except before the tears can escape, I feel the weight of Derek's body being lifted off me. At first I think that Derek realized I didn't want his advances and decided to leave me alone. Then I open my eyes and see none other than Noah Walsh throwing Derek against the wall, so roughly that his body makes a resounding thump on impact. Derek tries to make a run for it, but Noah grabs him by the collar and shoves him backwards, pinning him against the wall.

"What the fuck did you think you were doing to her?" Noah practically spits in his face. I can see the anger in his blue eyes—if it were directed at me, I would have been terrified.

"Listen, this is none of your business," Derek says weakly. "Bailey and I were out on a date."

"Do you think I'm a fucking idiot?" Noah releases Derek for a second, then buries his fist in Derek's stomach. Derek doubles over, gasping with pain. Derek might have been able to overpower me, but Noah's both taller and stronger than he is.

"You listen to me, you little shit," Noah hisses at Derek. "If I ever see or hear about you laying a finger on Bailey ever again, I will personally break every bone in your puny little body. You don't touch her, you don't speak to her, you don't even *breathe* on her. You got me, asshole?"

Derek nods, still hunched over and clutching his stomach.

"Now get the fuck out of here," Noah growls at him.

Derek doesn't need to be told twice. He limps off in the direction of the staircase, still holding his belly. He doesn't look back.

Noah turns to me, breathing hard. The fire has left his eyes and he furrows his brow. "Are you okay, Bailey?"

My legs have given way underneath me, and I crouch against the door, trembling. I manage to nod.

"I just…" He glances at his own room. "I was out at a party and came back to grab a bottle of vodka I had in my room, and I saw…"

I don't say anything. I might never speak again.

He looks down at his right hand, as if in amazement. "I never hit anyone before," he breathes.

His blue eyes meet mine, and they are so kind that the tears I'd been holding back all this time spill over. I wipe them self-consciously, as Noah crouches down beside me. This isn't the most comfortable place to be sitting, but he stays there with me while I cry it out. At some point, he fishes a crumpled tissue out of his jacket pocket and hands it to me.

"Do you have your room key?" he asks gently.

I nod and fish around in my purse until I find it. I pass it over to him, and he gets to his feet. He holds his hand out to me to help me stand up—his hand is big and warm and safe. He opens the door for me and leads me inside.

"Go lie down, okay?" he tells me.

"Okay," I murmur.

Noah closes the door behind him while I settle down on my bed. I've never been a stuffed animal kind of girl, but now I wish I were. I want something to cuddle to feel safe.

"You're going to be fine," Noah says gently, kneeling down by my bed.

"What if he comes back?" I manage to say.

Noah thinks for a moment. "I'll stay. As long as you want. Keep guard."

"What about your party?"

He shrugs. "So what? There are a million parties."

"Aren't they waiting for the vodka?"

He shakes his head and laughs. "So they'll just have to make the supplies last a little longer. It's fine."

I look at Noah sitting cross-legged on the ground, leaning best he can against my desk. It looks incredibly uncomfortable. He's watching me intently, an unreadable look in his eyes. I feel a sudden and almost overpowering rush of affection toward him, something far deeper than my Freshman Crush.

"Thanks for saving me tonight," I whisper.

"No problem," he whispers back, his eyes never leaving mine.

The truth is, I can't stop looking at him either.

"You look uncomfortable on the floor," I observe.

He waves his hand and smiles crookedly. "I'm fine."

"You can lie next to me," I say softly. "If you want."

His eyes widen. "Uh… I don't… I mean, you don't need to feel like you have to…"

"I'd feel safer if you were next to me," I say. I'm not sure if that's true. I feel safe with Noah on the floor. But I still want him next to me.

He doesn't have to be told again. He gets up off the floor, slips off his sneakers, and climbs into my bed next to me. His body feels warm and large next to mine. I scoot over to get closer to him, but I can tell he's not entirely sure what to do. Which is weird, considering he hasn't had any shortage of girls accompanying him to his room this year.

I slide into the crook of his arm, feeling safe and comforted by the heat of his body. I rest my arm on his chest, feeling the muscles of his abdomen under my hand. He puts his own arm around my shoulder, gently pulling me closer.

I look up at his face. God, he's sexy. He lowers his head slightly, but I'm the one who bridges the gap. I kiss him first, and despite what nearly happened with Derek, I realize I want this. I want Noah desperately, and I can't hold back another second. It feels so right to be here in Noah's arms. I've never been kissed like this before.

And as he kisses me, the fleeting thought goes through my head that this is the boy I'm going to marry someday.

Chapter 13
PRESENT DAY

Gwen and my father went into town to do some shopping, and my father texts me to ask if we'd like to we'd like to join them for lunch. I wouldn't. But Noah apparently got a similar text and says to me in that flat voice I've gotten used to, "We're going into town to meet our parents for lunch." And that's that.

When we get out to Noah's 4Runner, I notice that there's a new addition: a booster seat in the back. My mouth falls open when I see it.

"When did you get the booster seat?" I ask him.

"I went out and grabbed one after I picked you up yesterday," he says. He frowns at me. "You're really supposed to have a booster seat for kids less than eighty pounds, and I didn't want to put Lily in any danger. Not that I'm not a good driver, and... well, this car is really safe, but still." He looks away. "You never know, right?"

Right.

"Thanks," I say. "I appreciate you thinking of Lily."

Lily is clearly not thrilled by the booster seat when I show it to her while Noah is taking care of something back in the house. "Why do I have to sit in that?" she whines. "Daddy doesn't make me sit in a baby seat."

"It's not a baby seat," I say. "It's a booster seat. For big kids."

"No!" she howls. "It's for baaaaaaaabbbbbbies!"

Just when I'm worried she's going to hurl herself onto the dirt and have a tantrum, Noah emerges from the cabin. He grins at Lily. "Hey there," he says to her, "did you see the new special seat I bought just for you?"

Lily's eyes widen. She looks between Noah and the offending seat. Then, without another word, she climbs into the seat and allows me to buckle her in. This is almost getting ridiculous.

Noah puts on music for the ride into town, and I'm grateful we don't have to attempt to make conversation. In the brief time I've been here, we have yet to have one interaction that didn't include him yelling at me. I'm getting sick of it. I promised my father I'd stay here for a week, but if things don't get better with Noah, I may take off sooner.

Gwen and my father are waiting outside the diner when we arrive. Gwen is holding a big shopping bag and has a beaming face. God, I hope she's not spending all of my father's money—he's barely making ends meet as is. Then again, Gwen has a son who's a rich doctor. She doesn't need my father's meager social security checks.

"I thought it would be nice to eat out," Gwen says. She pats Noah's shoulder, "You deserve a break from cooking for us."

"I don't mind," he says.

The diner is one of those all-American places where you can get a big pile of greasy food. It's just what I feel like right now. Plus, I'm fairly sure I won't be the one paying. I hope not, at least.

There are four steps to get to the front door, and Noah hangs onto the railing as he climbs them very, very slowly. He is the last of us to reach the top, and my father is holding open the door for him. Even though he doesn't say anything, I can tell from the look on his face that Noah hates having the door held for him. When we were together, he would always jump ahead of me to hold doors for me. He even rushed to open the car door for me, even though I would laugh and tell him he was being silly. He liked being a gentleman, especially for me.

It was something I missed when I was with Theo, who wouldn't have thought to hold a door for me in a million years. I mentioned it to him once, when I was missing Noah, and he said, "Uh, I think you're capable of holding a door open yourself." I was, but that wasn't the point.

A pretty waitress greets us at the door. Her nametag reads "Katy," and she's in her late twenties with teased blond hair and too much make-up. She beams at us when we ask for a table for five. "Certainly, honey!" she says with the slightest twinge of a Southern twang. "Any special family occasion?"

Noah smiles crookedly at her. "Sort of." He gestures at me. "Her dad and my mother just got engaged."

I can see the wheels turning in Katy's head. She looks down at Noah's bare left ring finger and puts it all together. "Oh!" she says to Noah. "So you and her... you two ain't married?"

He shakes his head no, and Katy's smile widens.

Way back when, girls used to hit on Noah in front of me. Far more, actually, than guys would hit on me, even when I was alone. Noah's hotter than I am, apparently. In any case, it happened, but it wasn't out of control. However, today, right now, in this diner, Katy's behavior is out of control. Fine—I get that she thinks he's hot, but she's practically slobbering over him as she leads us to our table. I feel embarrassed for her.

Once we get seated, Katy rests her hand on Noah's shoulder. "Now I've got to go take another order," she says to us, but mostly to him, "but I will be right back here in a jiffy to take good care of y'all."

"Thank you," Noah says.

Katy doesn't move her hand. "My, you've got some big muscles there... Do you work out?"

To his credit, Noah looks embarrassed. "Uh, I guess."

"Well, you keep it up." Katy winks at him as she walks away.

Gwen, who is thankfully seated next to Noah so I don't need to sit next to him yet again, says to her son, "You should ask that girl for her phone number, Noah."

"Christ, Mom," he says. "I don't need to ask out every waitress who flirts with me at a restaurant."

"I'm just saying," she says. "She seems really sweet. And she sure seems to like you."

"She sure does," I mutter.

Even though I said the words under my breath, Noah hears me. He raises his eyebrows at me across the table, and I'm worried about what that means.

Katy returns a minute later, and maybe I'm imagining it, but it looks like she's freshened up her cherry-red lipstick during that time. She positions herself right next to Noah. "Now can I get y'all something to drink?"

"I'd love a beer," Noah says, lifting his blue eyes to gaze directly at her. "What do you have on tap?"

"Well, we got Budweiser, Bud Light, Coors Light, Miller Lite, Guinness, and Sam Adams." She ticks them off on her long red fingernails. "Which one would you like, sugar?"

He smiles up at her. "Which one would you recommend… Katy?"

She beams at the use of her first name. "Well, you seem like a Guinness man to me… what did you say your name was?"

"I'm Noah," he says.

She thrusts out her chest, which is already at least a cup-size larger than mine. "Yes, I'd definitely recommend a Guinness for you, Noah."

"Perfect," he says. "Looking forward to it."

So apparently, Noah has taken my comment as a personal challenge. When Katy returns with our drinks and to take our orders, he spends forever making her go through all the specials even though I know he only ever orders burgers at diners.

"Now how are the French fries here, Katy?" he asks her.

She bats her eyelashes at him. "Best in town, sugar."

"Is that so?"

"Well, I guarantee it."

"I don't know," Noah says doubtfully. "I think I went to another place last month that had damn good fries."

"Tell you what," Katy says, "you show me a place in town that has better fries than here, and I'll give you your next meal on the house."

"Maybe I will," Noah says.

"Give me a break," I mutter.

Noah hears me again, but this time, he grins. Congratulations, Noah. You have succeeded in both irritating me and making me extremely uncomfortable.

And maybe a little bit jealous.

Not to be outdone by a waitress with too much hairspray and make-up, Lily tugs at Noah's shirt. "You said you'd take us to the movies."

"Yeah, I did." He nods. "What do you want to see, Lily?"

"*Dogcat!*"

I clench my hands into fists. "Lily, I already took you to see *Dogcat*."

"Yes, but I want to see it again," she insists. "It's my favorite movie!"

I don't see how *Dogcat* could be Lily's favorite movie or anyone's favorite movie. It was literally the worst movie I've ever seen in my life. There are some movies where they try to make it entertaining for the adults who get dragged along to see these films, but I feel like the people who made *Dogcat* weren't even making a half-hearted attempt.

"Maybe Lenny and I could take Lily," Gwen suggests. "I'd love to get to know her a little better."

"Sure," Noah says, clearly relieved to be released from his *Dogcat* responsibilities.

Lily looks around the table, her face crumpling. "But I want Noah to come!" she wails.

Before this can turn into an all-out tantrum, we quickly reassure Lily that Noah will come to the movie and this is in no way a rejection of her. You think two-year-olds throw bad tantrums? You should see my six-year-old daughter when she's at her worst. She screams her head off like we're committing child abuse.

Katy brings out food for Noah and Lily first, then returns with plates for Gwen and my father. My stomach growls as I wait patiently for my own burger and fries to arrive, while everyone else digs into their food like I don't exist. Doesn't anyone at this table have any *manners*?

"I wonder what's taking my food so long?" I ask, craning my neck to spot our waitress.

Noah shrugs as he takes a bite of his juicy burger. "Maybe your food is more complicated?"

"I ordered *literally* the same exact same thing you did!"

"Be a little patient, Bailey," Gwen says evenly. "I'm sure she'll bring it out soon."

I look at Noah, who shrugs again.

Katy is nowhere to be seen. I finally get out of my seat to go search for her because I'm just that hungry, only to return to our table and find her standing with her hand on Noah's shoulder.

"Can I get you a refill of that beer, sugar?" she asks him. "On the house?"

A refill of his beer? *Where's my food*?

Noah smiles up at her. "Better not. I've got to drive."

"Oh, you're so *responsible*!"

I bite the inside of my cheek and take a deep breath, knowing this woman can (and probably will) spit in my food. "Excuse me," I say tentatively, "is my burger coming out soon?"

Katy flashes me an annoyed look. "I'll go check on that for you, ma'am."

Ma'am? Wow, that was low.

Katy brings out my plate from the kitchen a minute later and drops it unceremoniously in front of me. Right away, I can see I got onion rings instead of the fries I ordered. And my burger has no cheese on it. And it seems like the extra time in the kitchen was spent charring my burger to a crisp, but somehow they still managed to make time to let it grow cold.

"What's wrong, Bee?" Dad asks me. "You were so hungry a minute ago."

I eye the unappetizing burger. And the onion rings that will probably give me heartburn. "It's just that…"

I glance at Gwen, who already gave me a hard time for complaining about the burger last night, and is giving me her best "now what?" expression. I can't give these people any further reason to hate me.

"No, it's fine," I say quickly.

While we're eating our meals, Katy comes over to check on how Noah's doing no less than five times. I suspect if I weren't here, Noah would have gotten irritated with her at some point, but each time she comes over, he flirts with her. He tells her the fries are "pretty good," but he's sure he's had better ones in town.

"Well, you'll have to show me before I believe it," Katy says.

He winks at her. "Guess I will."

Gwen is delighted by all the flirting. I don't get it—she can't possibly think Noah really likes this woman. He's clearly doing it to get back at me.

We tell Katy we're not interested in dessert, but she brings over a whopping slice of apple pie a la mode, which she sets down right in front of Noah. "You *can't* have a burger without a slice of pie at the end," she tells him. Despite the fact that my father and I also both got burgers yet were not given free pie. I didn't even get cheese on my burger. I'm lucky I got a napkin.

Noah glances down at the pie. "I'm not really that hungry." He looks over at my daughter, who is practically salivating over the pie. "Can Lily have it?"

At the mention of her name, Lily clasps her hands together. "Puh-leeeeassse, Mommy?"

I know the pie is going to give her a terrible sugar rush, but I'm desperate to seem like a nice person, so I say, "Sure, honey."

Gwen's mouth falls open. "You're really letting her have *that whole thing*?"

I really can't win. I smile awkwardly. "She'll never finish it."

Lily never finishes anything, but damned if she doesn't finish every single bite of that stupid pie. She even licks the plate when she finishes. I keep my eyes on the table, avoiding any judgmental stares.

When Katy brings out the check, Noah quickly waves it over in his direction. "No, Noah!" Gwen scolds him. "You always pay. You let me treat for a change."

"*I* should be the one treating," Dad says. "Noah, you're the one offering your home for us all to stay in."

I keep my mouth shut. *I'm* sure not paying.

Noah plucks the check out of Katy's fingers. "I'm paying. End of story."

"You're *so* generous." Katy smiles at him and pulls a little napkin out of her pocket. She places it on the table next to the check. "I also got something else for you. For later."

After Katy walks away, Noah flips over the napkin to reveal ten digits scrawled in pen. His eyes meet mine, and he smiles.

"She gave you her phone number!" Gwen claps her hands excitedly. "Noah, you're going to call her, aren't you?"

He takes the napkin and shoves it into his pocket. "Maybe."

Lily wrinkles her nose. "You're going to go on a *date* with her?"

"He's not really," I say before I can stop myself.

I probably shouldn't have said that. Suddenly, every adult at the table is glaring at me. If Katy were sitting with us, she'd probably be scratching my eyes out with her long, red fingernails.

Noah raises an eyebrow. "Why not, Bailey? Why can't I go out with her? What would be so wrong with that?"

Great. Now he's probably going to marry that waitress just to teach me a lesson.

"Nothing," I mumble. "Nothing would be wrong with it. You should ask her out. I'm sure you'll have a great time."

"Glad I've got your approval."

Maybe he will go out with that waitress. Maybe they'll really hit it off. Maybe she's his future wife.

And I'm not sure why that idea bothers me so much.

Chapter 14
12 YEARS EARLIER

Noah and I are studying on his common room futon together. He's got his arm around me and a physics book balanced on his legs, while I've got a History of Roman Art book balanced on my knees. We're on a rotating schedule of studying for twenty minutes, then making out for twenty minutes. It's not the most effective means of studying.

Especially if you consider the break we took for Noah to screw my brains out about an hour ago.

Even though Noah and I have been together for two years now, the attraction I feel for him is still almost painful. I thought those feelings would fade after a while, but they haven't. At all. At least not for me. I can't imagine ever liking anyone as much as I like Noah.

"Hey," Noah says, eying me over the edge of his physics book.

I raise my eyebrows at him. "Yes."

He grins at me. "I love you, Bailey."

My body fills with that warm, nice feeling I get whenever he says those words. "I love you too."

"I love you more."

"I love *you* more."

He puts down his book, and starts climbing on top of me. His lips lower onto the area where my neck meets my shoulder. "How about another study break, huh?"

My boyfriend has a *lot* of stamina. Good thing I do too.

The lock turns on the door to Noah's suite. He quickly scrambles off me, although the two of us have equally guilty expressions when his roommate George strolls into the room.

George winks at us, "Am I interrupting something?"

Noah and I exchange looks. "No," I say quickly, just as Noah says, "Yeah."

George laughs and claps Noah on the shoulder. "Don't worry. I'll be out of here soon, so you can have some privacy." He gathers some texts from a bookcase on the wall. "By the way, Noah, I heard the good news! Congrats!"

I can't help but notice the way Noah stiffens.

"What good news?" I ask.

"NYU for med school!" George gathers his books in his arm and punches Noah's shoulder using his free hand. "You smart bastard. Good going."

"Thanks," Noah mumbles.

George walks into his own bedroom, whistling the whole way, completely oblivious to the shitstorm he has just created. I slide to the other end of the couch, staring at Noah. "Were you planning to tell me?"

He scratches at his head. "Uh…"

Here's the thing: Noah's graduating in June. I still have another year left of college (and no idea what to do with my life, but that's a whole other issue). He's been applying to medical schools all over the place, but only Syracuse is anywhere near the college. He hasn't yet been offered an interview at Syracuse. And I know he's had his heart set on a school in the city.

My question is: where does that leave us?

It's a question I've been afraid to ask the boy I truly want to spend the rest of my life with. Because I'm not sure he feels the same way. I mean, I know he loves me. But does he love me *enough*?

"Look," Noah says, "I'm sorry I didn't say anything. I've just… I've been working out what I want to do about everything."

"Have you?"

He nods. "Yeah. It's an important decision. It's the rest of my life, Bailey."

"So…" I take a deep breath. "Do you think you're going to go to NYU?"

Noah chews on his lip for a minute. Finally, he says, "Yeah, I probably am."

Just as my heart starts to sink, he quickly adds, "But that doesn't mean we have to break up. I was thinking that we could… you know, *not* break up."

I raise my eyebrows at him. "And how would that work, exactly?"

He smiles and shrugs. "I'd drive up to see you. You'd drive down to see me. It would only be a year and then we can be together."

"Meaning I'd have to move to the city."

"So?" Noah frowns at me. "You're an artist. Isn't New York City, like, the art capital of the world?"

"I think Paris is the art capital of the world."

He furrows his brow. "So… you're saying that after you graduate, you want to move to Paris?"

"*No*." I sigh. "I'm just saying that if you expect me to follow you to New York, I'd expect a little more of a commitment from you."

"More commitment?" he repeats. "What are you talking about? I'm not some guy you just met. We've been dating for *two years*!"

"I know, but…" This argument isn't going to a good place. "Look, we're dating, but it's not like we're engaged or anything."

"Engaged?" Noah's blue eyes become huge. "Are you *kidding* me? I'm only twenty-one years old! You really expect us to get *married*?"

His words sting. It doesn't surprise me, but it hurts nonetheless. My father proposed to my mother in college, after all. And Noah has been very serious about our relationship. He's taken me to two semiformal dances, he's met my parents and I've met his mom, and we spend all our free time together.

"No, I don't," I say. "I don't expect us to get married. But likewise, you can't expect me to follow you to Manhattan."

Noah sighs and drops his head against the futon. "Shit, Bailey. I don't want to lose you, but… I'm not ready to get married yet. I'm *not*."

"I understand," I murmur.

I understand. I really do. Noah is right—he's only twenty-one years old and doesn't want to rope himself into a commitment. I knew it was what he was thinking all along. Yes, he loves me and we have amazing sex. But I'm sure he can find another girl with whom he can check off those boxes just as well. Guys who look like Noah and want to be surgeons don't want to be tied down with their college sweetheart for the rest of their lives. I get it.

But I have to admit, there was a part of me that was hoping he'd be willing to make that commitment. Hoping he'd decide he was never going to find anyone he loved as much as me, and he couldn't let me go. The fact that he isn't willing to propose makes me think that he believes he might find someone better than me someday.

And if that's the case, I can't plan my life around him.

Noah is graduating today.

It makes me sick to think about it. No, that sounds bad. I'm happy for him—I truly am. But at the same time, graduation means that Noah will go to New York City and spend the next four years making new friends at NYU and meeting new girls who will soon replace me. I already hate these new girls.

We won't even have the summer together. Noah just finished the last of his vaccinations and is flying out to Africa next week to help dig a well in Gambia. That's what he's doing with his last summer before med school—digging a freaking *well*. He says it's really important, that the people in the town don't have clean water, et cetera, et cetera. He's not doing it to pad his resume—he genuinely cares about this cause. So I would have felt like a monster if I begged him to stay in the states to hang out with his girlfriend when there are dehydrated little Gambian children who need clean water. Although I'm not entirely sure why they can't dig their own damn well.

Wow, I sound like such a bitch. But it's only because I can't stop thinking about how much I'll miss Noah.

Noah looks painfully handsome dressed in a crisp white shirt with a blue tie. He got his hair cut very short for his medical school interviews and he seems to be keeping it that way. It makes him even more conventionally good-looking than he was before, but I miss the shaggy hair he used to have. Maybe because the whole thing feels like a sign that he's moving on.

Without me.

I'm helping Noah tie his tie. I watched a video about how to do it, so I'm doing it for him. I loop one end of the tie over the other, watching his Adam's apple bob. I'm inches away from his face, and I can't help but notice how nice he smells. He started using a new brand of aftershave lately. I love it, actually, but it also makes me sad. Noah's changing. He's going to move on.

"There," I say as I tighten the knot on his tie. I brush off imaginary lint on his shirt. "Perfect."

Noah turns to examine himself in his bedroom mirror. "I wouldn't say *perfect*."

"Pretty good for a first try!"

He smiles crookedly. "That's a little different than 'perfect,' isn't it?"

I let out a huff. "What's the difference? You're going to be wearing a cap and gown anyway."

Noah looks down at the black cap and gown lain out on his bed and shakes his head. "It's a million degrees out. I'm getting out of that stupid gown the first second I can."

"Well, I think the tie is fine," I say.

"Fine!" he snorts. "So we've gone from 'perfect' to 'pretty good' to 'fine.' You're worrying me, Bailey."

What I really want to say to him is, *Why are you obsessing about a stupid tie when we're probably never going to see each other after this?*

Except he doesn't care. Not really. He's already moved on. He mentioned a graduation party his mother is throwing for him in a few days, and only half-heartedly invited me. *If you feel like it.*

In his head, I'm already his ex-girlfriend. And it makes me so depressed, I can't even think straight.

I deeply regret our conversation earlier in the year. I wish I hadn't laid down an ultimatum. *Marry me or break up.* Clearly, he's not ready to get married, and now I've backed myself into a corner. He's already got it in his head that we're breaking up, and he's made peace with it. If I suggested doing the long distance thing at this point, he'd probably say no.

He's the best thing I ever had, and I lost him because of my own stupidity. I will never meet another guy I like as much as Noah. I'll never meet someone who races to open doors for me, deeply cares about the welfare of children in Gambia, and makes me knees weak when he kisses me. There's only one Noah Walsh in the world, and I blew it.

"*You* look perfect," I correct myself. "That was what I meant."

Noah smiles and puts his arms around my waist. "You look perfect too."

Just not perfect enough.

I swallow a gigantic lump in my throat. "So… when do you have to go?"

"Pretty soon." Noah looks down at his watch. "Actually, I need to get out of here any minute now."

"Oh." This is it. The end.

"There's just one thing I need to do before I go." He turns away from me and reaches into the top drawer of his desk. I don't see what he pulls out of it, but then a second later, he's on the ground. He's on his knee. He's taking my hand in his and…

Oh my God, he's asking me to marry him.

"Bailey," he begins.

I turn away from him. I'm already crying. I can't seem to stop. I might never stop.

"I love you so much, Bailey," he goes on, "and… hey, stop crying."

"I can't," I manage, wiping my eyes with the hand he isn't holding.

"Look, I know this isn't exactly what you wanted," he says, "but I love you and I want to be with you forever. So… will you marry me?"

I look down at the ring. It's very simple—a plain silver band with a tiny diamond another woman might have laughed at. But I know Noah's hurting for money, what with his med school tuition looming on the horizon, so the fact that he managed a diamond at all makes me cry even harder.

A crease forms between his brows. "You're not saying anything."

"Yes!" I practically yell the word. Thank God he didn't do a public proposal because I'm sure my response would have been on YouTube, embarrassing me for decades to come. "Of course, yes."

Noah gets back on his feet. He places the ring on my shaking finger, made all the more difficult because he's shaking too. We grin dumbly at each other and then kiss for several minutes. I can't seem to let go of him.

"I thought you weren't ready to get married," I say when we finally separate for air.

"I want to be with you," he says firmly. "That's all that matters."

"It can be a long engagement," I say, and he laughs. I mean it though. I don't need a wedding right now—just knowing that Noah and I are going to be together forever is all I need.

Chapter 15
PRESENT DAY

I would have liked to stay in town a little longer, but Noah says he's got to get back to empty his crab trap, and my father and Gwen say they need to get back to take a nap. Which I assume is code word for "sex." I don't want to think about it.

Lily is really excited about the crabs, the same way she's excited about nearly everything Noah does or says. I thought she'd be thrilled to have some one-on-one time with him, but when they're getting ready to go down to the lake, she bounces into my bedroom and says, "You ready to come with us, Mommy?"

I look up from my sketchpad. I've been drawing Katy the Waitress and I quickly turn the page so Lily won't see. I don't know what's wrong with me. Especially because I made Katy look quite hideous.

"Um," I say, "I think I might stick around here. You can go with Noah yourself."

Of all the bad things I can say about Noah right now, I definitely trust him with my daughter. If there were a maniac firing a gun around the lake, I haven't the slightest doubt he'd throw himself in front of the bullets to save her. That's the kind of Boy Scout he is.

"Noah said you should come," Lily says.

I frown. "He did?"

She shrugs. "He said, 'We're leaving. Go get your mom.'"

He probably thinks I wouldn't want her to go without me, which is understandable. I put down my sketchpad and head out to the living room, to tell Noah I'm staying behind, but he's already at the door, waving the two of us through.

"Come on," he's saying. "Let's go! Let's go!"

"Um…" I look down at my bare feet. "I'm not wearing shoes, so…"

He looks at me like I'm a moron. "So put on your shoes. Come on, it's getting late. I want to empty the trap."

I don't want to start arguing, so I put on my sandals. As I'm heading for the door, I notice a crumpled napkin lying on top of the garbage bin. The napkin has a phone number on it.

So he isn't going to call Katy after all.

There's a bucket on the patio, which Noah picks up and hands to Lily. "This is how we're going to carry the crabs," he tells her. "How about you carry it there, and I'll carry it back."

"I can carry it back!" Lily insists.

"It's going to be a lot heavier on the way back," he says. "Also, the crabs are going to be alive and I don't want one of them to pinch you." He glances up at me. "Your mom would kill me."

Lily shoots me an accusing look. I think she likes him better than she likes me.

Before Noah steps off the patio, he picks up a simple black cane that's leaning against the side. Up until now, he seemed capable of walking without a device with no problem. So it's surprising to see him pick up that cane. His eyes meet mine for a second, as if daring me to comment. I don't.

Lily is another story.

"What are you using a cane for?" she speaks up. "That's for old people."

He grins at her. "*I'm* old."

"No, you're not," she says. Then she amends, "Well, you're a *little* old. Like Mommy. But you're not very old."

"Aw, thanks." He looks down at the cane. "I'm using it because there's no pavement here and it helps me keep my balance."

"Why do you need help keeping your balance?"

Noah hesitates for a second. "See, Lily, the reason I sometimes have trouble balancing is because I have bionic legs."

Lily frowns. "Bubonic legs?"

He smiles crookedly. "No, *bionic*. Like, robot legs."

She looks down at his legs, then back up at his face. Her own face breaks out into a smile. "No, you don't! You're foolin' me!"

"I do," he insists. He glances at me, then he picks up the right leg of his pants to reveal the narrow metal rod that's now where his shin would have been. Then he picks up the other side of his pants to reveal the same exact thing. Lily's blue eyes turn into saucers.

"Are you a robot?" she breathes.

Noah laughs. "No, I'm not. But I do have robot legs."

"That's so…" I hold my breath, waiting to hear what Lily's going to say. "That's so cool!"

And then she looks up at him in a way that makes me think she loves him even more than she did a minute ago. After all, not only is he handsome, but he's also a *robot*. Which is better, somehow.

We follow Noah down to the dock where the crab traps are set up, and there are also a bunch of moderately sized motor boats tied up.

"Which boat is yours?" Lily asks Noah.

He points down the pier at one of the smaller white boats. There's room in the front of it for two people to sit, then room in the back for another two or three people. It's far from being a yacht, but it looks like it would be fun to ride around in that boat. Not that I would suggest such a thing.

Lily claps her hands together. "Can we go for a ride on it?"

Noah squints up at the sky. "It's getting late. How about tomorrow? We can fish a little if you want."

Great. Stuck on that boat for hours fishing.

The thought of it brings back memories. I glance over at Noah, wondering if he's remembering too. But he won't look at me.

We walk down to the end of the pier where all the crab traps are set up. Noah leans his cane against one of the poles supporting the pier, and he bends on one knee to pull the trap from inside the water. It's basically a huge cage filled with live crabs. They're crawling around inside, crazy to get out.

"So this is the fun part," Noah says to Lily. "We have to get them out of the cage."

Noah actually holds onto the cage for support to get back on his feet, which seems dangerous to me. Once he's standing again, he lifts the cage in the air, opens a little door on the side, and starts shaking it out over the bucket. One by one, the crabs fall out of the cage into the bucket.

"Crabs!" Lily squeals. "Look, Mommy! They're crawling everywhere!"

Oh my God, they are crawling *everywhere*. They're squirming and trying to climb out of the bucket, and are just generally horrifying. I edge away from the bucket.

Noah raises his eyebrows at me. "You okay there, Bailey?"

"Fine!" I say, too loudly.

When the bucket is about half-full, Noah shakes the rest of the crabs out into the water to release them. Then he drops the empty trap back in the water. He starts to pick up the handle of the bucket, but then hesitates.

"Hey, Bailey," he says. "You know, it would *really* help me out if you could carry this bucket." He gestures down at his cane. "My balance isn't very good."

He's lying. That bastard is lying. I can see it in the smirk on his lips. He's not even pretending not to be lying. He just wants me to carry these stupid crabs because he knows I'm absolutely terrified of them. Well, I can play that game too.

"No problem," I say. I pick up the bucket of crabs and immediately they all start shifting. One of them somehow climbs on top of its friends, and manages to scale the side of the bucket. I scream as it jumps ship and scurries across the pier.

In my defense, Lily screams too.

Of course, she's *six*.

Noah laughs like he's never seen anything so funny. He holds onto the side of the pier as he carefully leans forward and picks the crab up off the ground. He holds it by its shell, so that its writhing

125

limbs don't pinch him. He drops the crab back in the bucket as I shudder.

"I really appreciate your help," he says to me, all wide-eyed.

Screw you, Noah. These better be the best crabs I ever tasted.

———

I don't know if they're going to be the best crabs I've ever tasted, but they certainly smell good. The aroma of them travels into the bedroom and distracts me from the book I'm reading. My stomach growls insistently.

Right on cue, Lily comes into the bedroom and flings herself on the bed beside me. "Mommy! Dinner's! Ready! In! Five! Minutes!"

I don't know why Lily sometimes feels a need to emphasize every word she says.

"Okay." I close my book. "It smells really good."

"I know!" Lily licks her lips. "Noah's a really good cook."

"Uh huh," I mutter.

Lily leans her chin thoughtfully on her hand. "Maybe you should go out on a date with him."

I nearly choke on the drool that's been accumulating in my mouth since I started smelling the crabs. "A date? With Noah?"

"Yeah!" She grins at me. "If you and Noah got married, then we could come here all the time and he could cook dinner for us."

Riiiiiiight.

"I don't think Noah wants to go out on a date with me," I say. Actually, that's not true. I *know* that Noah would not want to go out on a date with me in a million years.

"I think he might," Lily says.

Um, what does *that* mean?

"Why do you say that?" I ask carefully.

"I don't know." She shrugs her skinny shoulders. "He keeps looking at you whenever you're not looking."

I don't know exactly what to make of that information. But I'm certain he's not looking at me because he's hoping for a date. More likely, he's glaring at me and wondering how to tell me he wants me to leave.

Chapter 16
11 YEARS EARLIER

Noah is late.

He's usually late, if I'm being honest. He usually shows up about half an hour after the promised time, all full of apologies and kisses and good sex. Noah's never been great at being prompt, so I can't fault him. I'm sure he means to get on the road at the right time, but then gets distracted by something on the computer, or caught up studying for a test, or who knows. It's fine. Considering he's driving nearly five hours just to see me, I can't get too angry.

Today, however, he's two hours late. Actually, more than two hours. We're closing in on three hours past the time he was supposed to arrive at my dorm. During the last hour, I've gone from angry to worried. Even though I try not to call him when he's on the road, I've dialed his cell phone three times. No reply.

It was snowing yesterday. I told Noah the roads might not be safe, but he insisted it was fine and he wanted to see me. God, I hope he's okay.

Just when I'm about to completely lose my mind, my cell phone rings and I see Noah's name flash on the screen. I pick up the phone, ready to give him a piece of my mind for worrying me so badly, when I hear a female voice on the other line.

"Bailey?" the voice says.

"Yes?" I reply. My stomach has twisted back into the knot that had loosened slightly when I first got the call.

"It's Gwen," the woman says. "Noah's mother."

Gwen Walsh. I've met her a handful of times since Noah and I have been together. She's a nice woman, and she seems to like me a lot. She seems like she'll be a good mother-in-law.

"Hi, Mrs. Walsh," I say, because I can't quite bring myself to call this middle-aged woman by her first name.

"Bailey," she says, and her voice breaks on the words. "Bailey, I'm at the hospital. Noah… he's been in an accident."

This horrible, cold sensation overtakes my entire body. I'd tried to tell myself that it couldn't be true, that Noah was fine. But all along, I knew it. He never would have kept me waiting this long without a call. Never.

A lump forms in my throat. He's dead. I know it.

"I just got to the hospital," Gwen tells me. "But… I didn't see him. They said he's in emergency surgery and that he's in critical condition and…" Her voice breaks on the words, and she can't go on.

My knees go weak. I grip the phone, sinking down onto my bed. "What hospital?"

Gwen names a hospital about two hours away from me.

"Is it all right if I come?" I ask her.

"Of course it is," Gwen sniffles. "Bailey, he loves you so much. That's why when they gave me his phone, I called you right away because I knew you'd be worried." She takes a shaky breath. "When he wakes up, he'll be happy to see you there."

If he wakes up. "I'm on my way."

———

I make it to the hospital in an hour and a half. My hands are trembling the entire way, but I keep my foot jammed on the gas pedal. I realize it would be ironic for me to get into a car accident and die while coming to see Noah after his accident, but I can't help myself. I need to get to the hospital. I need to see him.

Gwen gave me instructions on how to find the waiting area where she's keeping vigil until Noah is out of surgery. I have no idea what kind of surgery he's getting. It could be absolutely anything. I try not to think about it too much, considering the last thing I need is to start getting faint right now.

I find Gwen sitting in a plastic chair in the waiting area, her strawberry-blond hair disheveled, looking ten years older than the last time I saw her. There's a pile of magazines on the table next to her, but she's just sitting there, staring straight ahead, her eyes red and swollen. When she sees me, she stands up.

"Bailey!" she cries.

Then she hugs me. She hugs me even though *I'm* the reason Noah got in this accident. He was driving out to see *me*.

In the middle of our hug, Gwen starts sobbing hysterically. "They won't tell me anything." She pulls away from me to wipe her eyes. "For all I know, he could be…"

I swallow hard. "If it were really bad, they'd tell us, right?"

"All they said was that he was critical." She looks in the direction of the door that leads to the operating rooms. "They said he lost a lot of blood."

Lost a lot of blood. I sink into one of the cheap plastic chairs. I can't think about this. I have to believe he's going to be okay. He'll pull through this. He's so young—he *has* to.

And then I'm crying too. We're both crying and hugging. And praying Noah will be okay.

It's another forty minutes before a man in his forties in a surgical cap and scrubs emerges from the back room. He has a grim look on his face. I look over at Gwen, who is getting ready to cry again. My eyes are just as swollen as hers, and I feel them welling up too.

131

"Mrs. Walsh?" the man asks. Gwen nods. "I'm Dr. Hoffman."

I can't help but think of Noah's dream to become a surgeon. I wonder if this surgeon realizes this about the boy he was just operating on. Probably not.

"So we got him stabilized," Dr. Hoffman says.

Gwen's eyes spill over with tears. "You did? You mean he's okay?"

Dr. Hoffman hesitates. "It's still early to know for sure, but he's most likely going to pull through."

My knees feel weak with relief. Noah isn't going to die. He's going to be okay. Thank God.

"That's so wonderful," Gwen sobs as she grabs onto Dr. Hoffman's arm. "Thank you so much, Doctor! Thank you for saving my son."

The surgeon's expression is still grim. "You have to understand though, Mrs. Walsh, his injuries are very severe."

Gwen frowns. "But you said he's going to live."

Dr. Hoffman sighs. "Yes, but…"

"I don't understand," Gwen says. "Is he some kind of vegetable…?"

"Nothing like that," the surgeon says quickly, although Gwen is still wary. "We scanned his brain and there was so sign of bleeding—nothing to indicate a significant brain injury. He did have a lot of blood in his lungs though, which is why we had to place a chest tube and we're keeping him sedated and intubated for now. The major trauma, unfortunately, was to his lower extremities."

Gwen shakes her head. "His…?"

Dr. Hoffman puts his hand on Gwen's shoulder. "I'm sorry to tell you this, but we had to amputate his left leg above the knee. He had already lost a tremendous amount of blood through his femoral artery and by the time we got him to the table, the leg wasn't salvageable. There was nothing we could do."

Gwen's mouth falls open. I understand exactly how she's feeling. Five minutes ago, all I cared about was that Noah would live. But hearing this new piece of information is a punch in the gut. He lost his leg. He will never, ever be the same after this.

"Also," Dr. Hoffman adds. There's an "also"? Shit. "There were multiple fractures in his right leg as well. He had an open femoral shaft fracture, which means the bone went through the skin, and he unfortunately lost quite a bit of skin. He had a tibial shaft and tibial plateau fracture. He also has a trimalleolar ankle fracture. We placed an external fixator, but he's looking at an extremely long recovery time for that leg."

"But at least it's still there," Gwen says.

Dr. Hoffman is quiet for a moment. "Right. It's still there."

I can hardly listen to any of this. I'm trying my best not to imagine all these injuries, but even so, there are spots dancing before my eyes.

"Can we see him?" Gwen asks.

The surgeon nods. "We're going to be moving him to the surgical ICU. You can see him down there."

Part of me is hoping Dr. Hoffman will say I can't go in because I'm not immediate family. I'm not his wife—I'm nothing. But I know Gwen wants me with her, and nobody is trying to stop me. I'm just not sure I can handle seeing Noah like this. The thought is making me feel like I'm going to throw up.

I follow Gwen down the hallway to get to the surgical ICU. I can't stop shaking. My whole body feels cold and horrible. She glances over at me. "Don't worry, Bailey," she says. "Noah got through his dad leaving us in the middle of the night, and he's going to get through this. We're going to get him back."

The surgical ICU is quiet, which makes sense considering it's two in the morning. There's a woman manning the front desk, who gently asks us who we're coming to see. "My son was just brought here," Gwen tells her, in a voice stronger than I've heard since I arrived. "His name is Noah Walsh."

There are no separate rooms here, only hospital beds. Three of them are occupied, and from afar, I couldn't say which of the patients is my fiancé. They all look the same—a million tubes coming out of them, bandaged up, barely alive.

It brings back memories of my mother. When she was at her worst. When we thought the cancer might win.

"That's him!" Gwen grips my arm.

She's pointing to a bed at the end. Of the three patients, Noah looks the sickest. As we get closer, I see he's got a tube coming out of his throat, taped to stay in place. He's wearing a hospital gown with only a sheet half-heartedly covering the parts of him that aren't injured. I count at least three tubes coming out of his body and draining off the side of the bed.

"Oh, Noah!" Gwen cries out. She runs to his side, grabbing his hand in hers. She reaches out to stroke the side of his face, at the stubble growing there. He doesn't even flinch. "Noah, your mother is here. I'm *here.*"

The nurse at the desk, watching the entire encounter, speaks up, "He's very sedated right now. He's not going to respond to you."

But Gwen doesn't care. She keeps whispering to him and stroking his hand. As for me, I try my best to focus on Noah's face. Amazingly, his face seems to have sustained very little damage. He's got an abrasion on his cheekbone, but other than that, he looks fine. Well, aside from the tube sticking out of his mouth, pushing air into his rising and falling

135

chest. Looking at his face makes me feel like he really might be okay.

But my eyes get drawn like a magnet to his legs. His right is clearly badly injured. It has pins sticking out of it both above and below the knee, with rods connecting the pins. If he were awake, I'd have to imagine it would be extremely painful. Everything is wrapped in gauze, but I can see the blood oozing out under the gauze.

And then there's his left leg. Or the absence of it. Where his leg used to be, there's only nothing. His left leg ends abruptly, mid-thigh, swathed in bandages. I see crimson staining the bandages. Dark, dark crimson. So much of it.

So much.

And that's when I pass out.

———

It's embarrassing. More than embarrassing—it almost sends me to the emergency room. The nurse saw me starting to go down and managed to catch me before I hit the floor, and then she started fussing over me like I was one of the patients. She ended up giving me some apple juice while I sat in a corner, feeling horrible about the fact that the sight of my fiancé made me faint.

Gwen decides to spend the night at the hospital, dozing in a recliner by Noah's bed. I offer to stay too, but it's a relief when she insists on paying for a hotel room for me nearby. "Come back in the morning," she says. "When you're feeling better."

As if I've got some sort of bug that knocked me out.

In the morning, I take my time. As much as I love Noah, the thought of seeing him like that again makes me queasy. But it's not like I can leave town and not come back until he's better. Especially since the doctor promised his recovery would be a slow process.

It's mid-morning by the time I make it to the surgical ICU. I've braced myself for the worst, but when I arrive at the small unit, I get a surprise: Noah is awake, the tube out of his throat.

The head of the bed is raised so he's partially sitting up. He has dark circles under his eyes and he's very pale, but he's most definitely alive. Gwen is next to him, looking exhausted but still smiling. There's a white sheet covering his lower body, making a strange-looking tent over the pins and bars in his right leg, then falling flat over where his left leg would have been.

When Noah sees me, his face breaks into a tired half-smile. "Bailey," he says. His voice is hoarse. "We thought you took off."

He's joking. He has no idea how close he is to being right.

"He took out the tube in his throat himself early this morning," Gwen tells me. "They were going to wait another day, but as soon as the anesthetics wore off a little, he pulled it right out."

"It was uncomfortable," Noah says.

Gwen pats his arm. "I'm just relieved you're awake and okay."

Noah leans his head against his pillow and sighs. "Yeah, that's relative."

Gwen looks between the two of us, then stands up from the chair where she's spent the night keeping vigil. "Let me give the two of you a little privacy. I'll grab some food from the cafeteria."

With Gwen out of the way, I slowly make my way to the empty seat that she had occupied. It's better if I'm sitting. Just in case.

Noah rolls his head to look at me. He sighs and shakes his head. "I'd say you look worse than I do, Bailey, but I'm not sure that's possible."

"You look fine," I say, too quickly.

"Do I?" He raises his eyebrows at me. "I heard about your little spill yesterday. The nurse blabbed."

"Oh." My cheeks grow warm. Why would someone tell him that? I thought I'd keep that secret from him till one of us was in the grave. "Well, you know how I am."

"Yeah," he mutters.

I squeeze my hands together. Aside from seeing his mangled limbs, this was the part I'd been dreading—finding out how my usually upbeat fiancé would react to something beyond horrible. And now he knows I couldn't even stand the sight of him last night. "I'm sorry," I murmur. "It wasn't… I mean, it was just hard to see…"

Noah is quiet for a long time. Long enough that my stomach starts to churn and I'm certain he hates me. When he finally speaks, he says, "I threw up."

Huh? "What?"

"When I first saw them," he says. "My legs. I looked at them… what's left of them… and I… I threw up." He gestures down at them. "That's why this sheet is here. I couldn't stand to look at them."

I feel a new rush of sympathy for Noah—at least I can go to the hotel and not think of what's going on here, but he can't escape it. Ever. I reach out and grab Noah's hand off the bed. He slides his fingers into mine, and squeezes my palm.

"This is really fucked up," he sighs in that hoarse voice.

I squeeze his hand. "It's going to be okay."

"Says you."

"Don't worry," I say. "Even if I faint every day, I'm going to be here with you through this whole thing."

He manages a hollow laugh. "I think at some point, you might get desensitized. Hey, maybe after all this, you'll decide to go to med school."

Well, that's impossible. But I make a vow to get past my phobias and be here with Noah through this entire ordeal. He needs me. I'm not going to let him down.

Chapter 17
PRESENT DAY

Noah's crabs with Cajun seasoning were the best crabs I've ever tasted, even though it was a lot of work digging out all that meat. Lily loved them too, to my surprise. I'm pretty sure she only tasted them to impress Noah, but then she couldn't stop eating them. Lily's palate is really being expanded—maybe when we get home, I can convince her to try some new things. Like chicken nuggets that *aren't* shaped like dinosaurs. Maybe *circular* chicken nuggets.

After dinner, my father and Gwen go out to take a walk. They offer to let me come along, and I'm torn between not wanting to be a third wheel on their romantic midnight stroll and not wanting to be stuck in the cabin alone with Noah (and Lily, who doesn't want to budge from the couch). I finally decide to stay behind.

It ends up being the three of us in the living room. Noah is reading in an armchair, Lily is flopped on her back, staring at the ceiling, and I'm sketching on my sketchpad. I almost started drawing Noah just out of old habit, but I stopped myself. I'm drawing Lily instead. Because it's not like I don't already have twenty billion sketches of my daughter during every moment of her life. I've even got a sketch of her using the potty stashed away somewhere.

"Mommy?" Lily's voice interrupts me as I'm adding definition to her hair. Lily's reddish-brown hair is easy to draw because it's very straight and fine.

"Yes?" I ask, even though I know what's coming.

"Mommy, I'm booooored!"

Lily is incapable of saying the word "bored" without drawing it out over several syllables.

"What about your new doll?" I say.

"I'm bored of that," she says. She plops down on the couch next to me and frowns. "I wanna watch TV."

I look around the room. "I don't know if Noah has a TV."

Noah pulls his eyes from his book to regard us briefly. "I don't."

I give her a pointed look. "See?"

Lily scrunches up her little face at Noah. "How come you don't got a TV?"

He doesn't even lift his eyes this time. "Because they rot your brain."

"We have *two* TVs at home," Lily informs him. "My favorite show is Spongebob Squarepants. It's usually on all day on Saturday." Please stop talking, Lily. "But I also like Gumball. And The Thundermans. And Ben Ten. And Unikitty. And My Little Pony. And Teen Titans Go." Please, Lily. "And Henry Danger. And School of Rock." For the love of God… "And I used to like Princess Sofia, but I don't really have time to watch it anymore."

"I can't imagine you would," he murmurs.

"Look, there's nothing wrong with a little TV," I say.

He raises his eyebrows. "A *little*?"

"Hey, she's *my* daughter, and if I want her to watch TV, she can watch TV!"

A wry smile plays on his lips. "Not here, she can't."

Good point.

I can see Lily is revving up for a tantrum, so to circumvent it, I quickly say, "Lily, why don't you grab the extra sketch book from my luggage? There are some of your crayons in there too. We can draw together."

I can see Lily thinking it over, deciding if this is acceptable. She must be trying to impress Noah with her obedience, because she skips off to our bedroom to retrieve the book. When she returns, she's got the sketchbook, but not her crayons.

"The crayons are in the side pocket," I tell her.

"No, Mommy," Lily says. "I want one of your special pencils. I want to do a *nice* drawing, like you."

I can't suppress a smile. Usually Lily just likes to color, but occasionally she does express interest in learning how to draw. I pull a fresh pencil out of my

143

pack and hand it to her as she sidles up next to me on the couch.

Lily leans her head against my shoulder as she works on her drawing. I get distracted from my own drawing as I watch her create a picture of a princess I'm almost entirely certain is Queen Elsa from *Frozen*. It's only recently that I've been able to identify Lily's artwork more specifically than "woman" or "dog" or "green blob monster."

"I'm not good at drawing feet," Lily comments as she draws the woman's shoes at right angles to the body.

"Well," I say, "the trick is you want to draw them just slightly at an angle to the body."

She looks at me blankly.

"Here, let me show you." I turn a page of my sketchbook and quickly sketch a picture of a girl. I draw her feet slightly slanted to the side as Lily watches in fascination. "Like this."

"Oh!" She smiles happily and goes back to work. And she actually draws Queen Elsa a pretty good pair of feet.

I look up from my daughter and see Noah is no longer looking at his book. He's watching us, an unreadable expression on his face. But when he notices me looking, he quickly drops his eyes and goes back to his book.

It's funny—I always thought Noah never had much interest in me until that night he punched Derek in the stomach. But after we'd been going out a few weeks, he admitted he'd been thinking about me long before that.

"It was right after you cut your hand on that glass," he told me. "I was jogging back to the dorm after playing basketball, and I saw you sitting in the grass, leaning against a tree. You had your sketchbook out and you were drawing a picture of the campus. You were so focused—you had no idea I was even there."

I smiled at him. I had no idea he'd been noticing me at the same time I'd been noticing him.

"I watched you draw for a little while." He smiled crookedly. "The picture you were doing... it was amazing. You were capturing all these little details that I never even would have noticed on my own. I couldn't stop watching you, to be honest."

Of all the things I've missed about Noah, one of the things I missed most was the way he looked at me when I was drawing.

Chapter 18
PRESENT DAY

I wake up to the smell of bacon and eggs.

I haven't woken up to the aroma of cooking food since I was in high school and my mom made me breakfast on the weekend. Even back when I was married, Theo was hopeless in the kitchen. I was lucky if he brewed a pot of coffee in the morning.

I follow my nose into the kitchen, where Noah is scraping scrambled eggs onto a plate for Lily. He's got his own plate with a similar portion of eggs, and I see he's also given them each two pieces of bacon. My mouth is watering—how come bacon never smells this good when I make it?

Lily digs into the eggs with gusto, despite the fact that she's spent the last three years refusing to eat anything for breakfast besides frozen waffles from the toaster oven.

"These eggs are so good!" she exclaims.

Noah grins at her. "That's because I got them from a magic chicken."

"No, you didn't!" Lily says. "There's no magic chicken."

"Uh huh, there is. I climbed up a beanstalk and stole it from a giant."

She bursts into giggles. "That's Jack and the Beanstalk!"

146

"Hmm. I'm pretty sure that story is called Noah and the Beanstalk."

Lily laughs hysterically, spraying little chunks of egg all over the table. He's good at getting her to laugh. Then again, making a six-year-old laugh isn't exactly challenging. She thinks this show on YouTube about an orange who befriends a pear is the height of comedy.

I clear my throat. "Hey," I say.

Noah looks up and the smile slides off his lips. "Oh. Hey."

I force a smile of my own. "Are there any more scrambled eggs left?"

"No, we ate 'em all." He raises his eyebrows at me. "Why? You want me to make some for you?"

"Um…" The smell of eggs is tantalizing, but the last thing I want is Noah slaving over the stove for me. I don't need to give him another reason to resent me. "That's okay. I'll just have some cereal."

"You sure?"

"Uh huh." I nod vigorously as I pull a box of Cheerios from the cupboard. "I like Cheerios a lot. It's got lots of fiber. Good for the bowels."

Oh God, did I just say that? Did I really talk about my bowels in front of Noah? The aroma of those eggs must have scrambled my brain.

"Noah's going to take us swimming today, Mommy," Lily tells me as she happily chews on a mouthful of eggs.

I glance at Noah, who is nodding at her. My heart sinks. "Lily, honey, I didn't pack bathing suits for us."

Lily's face falls. "Why not?"

"Yeah, why pack *bathing suits* for a trip to the *lake*?" Noah mutters under his breath.

I ignore his attitude as I sit down with my Cheerios and milk. I like Cheerios as much as any adult possibly could (and they *are* good for the bowels), but anything would be a letdown after smelling those eggs. "I didn't realize it was going to be so warm in April."

Lily's lower lip starts to tremble. "But I want to go swimming…"

I hold my breath, praying she likes Noah too much to throw a huge tantrum right in front of him.

"Don't worry, Lily," Noah says brightly. "I'll take you and your mom out to a store today and we'll buy you some bathing suits. Sound good?"

I groan inwardly. Bathing suits are expensive. Even though Dad paid for Lily's Amtrak ticket, my own ticket still set me back a lot. I don't want to shell out forty bucks for two bathing suits when we've got perfectly good bathing suits at home.

I'm not sure how to explain that to Noah though. He's a doctor, so I'm guessing the cost of a bathing suit isn't something he worries about.

"Better not," Lily says thoughtfully, before I can say anything myself. "It's too 'spensive."

I cringe. I hate that I stress about money so much that my six-year-old immediately thinks of the price tag when Noah brings up buying new clothes. But it's the reality of my life. I'm a social worker single mom with a deadbeat ex-husband. So.

"It's just bathing suits," Noah says.

"No," Lily says firmly. I'm not sure whether to hug her or tell her to shush. Maybe both. "Mommy says new clothes are too 'spensive."

Noah glances at me, a crease forming between his eyebrows. After a moment, he turns back to Lily with a smile on his face. "Well, good thing I'm paying then."

Great. Now I'm a charity case on top of everything. This trip is getting better and better. "Noah, you don't have to…"

He glances at me and his eyes briefly meet mine. "Don't make a big thing of it," he mutters. "Really."

I'm about to protest again, but Lily has leaped out of her chair, whooping with excitement at the idea of a new bathing suit and getting to go swimming in the lake. I can't deprive her of this—

despite what Noah probably thinks, I'm not some kind of monster.

But I'm not going to let him pay for the bathing suits.

———

My father texts me that he and Gwen went to some golf course for the day. If he had offered to let me and Lily tag along, I would have jumped at the chance, but he didn't. They just left without telling us. So it looks like it's going to be just me, Noah, and Lily. Together. All freaking day.

Noah drives us to a shopping center in town where there's a Marshall's. I usually buy most of Lily's clothing at consignment sales, and short of that, Walmart. I could get a bathing suit for Lily for five bucks at Walmart. Marshall's isn't exactly Prada, but it's going to set me back.

The parking lot at Marshall's is surprisingly full. Most of the spots in the vicinity of the front are taken, which means we'll be parking in no man's land again. I spot a handicapped spot right by the entrance and, remembering the wheelchair symbol on Noah's plates, I point it out: "There's a handicapped spot."

I thought I was being helpful. But it's very obvious from the way Noah's eyes darken that I've said the wrong thing yet again. "I'm not parking there," he says. "That spot is for someone who *needs* it."

"But…" I sputter. "You have the plates…"

He doesn't answer for a moment, his eyes back on the lot, searching for another spot. He finally says, "I only use them when I need to."

I don't know what that means, but I certainly know better than to dig further. I'm already on Noah's shit list times a hundred. Better not make it worse. But in all fairness, he *does* have the plates. It's only natural to wonder why he'd have them if he never, ever uses them.

Lily skips the entire way from the car to the store, her cute little pigtails blowing in the slight spring breeze. We hold hands as she skips, although I get the feeling she'd rather be holding hands with Noah.

We find the swimwear section of the store, and that's where the fighting begins. Lily wants a bikini. And I'm not talking about a two-piece bathing suit that is a shirt and suit bottom. She wants a full-on string bikini that has little triangles that barely cover her nipples and will reveal the entirety of her belly. Honestly, I don't know why they even *make* bathing suits like that in size 6T. Whoever designed these suits is depraved.

"Can I help you?" asks a salesgirl.

I turn my head and see a girl in her twenties with a nose ring and a cute, black bob. She's wearing a nametag that says Nina. I've been to many Marshall's in my life and this might be the very first time *ever* that a salesgirl has approached me to offer assistance. I mean, they don't work on commission, so why should they?

But it's pretty obvious why. She's looking right at Noah. And I suspect she's taken notice of the fact that he's not wearing a wedding band.

"We're just looking at bathing suits," he explains.

"You're buying a bathing suit for your daughter?" Nina asks sweetly.

He hesitates. "No, um… she's not my daughter. She's… we're friends."

"Oh!" Nina's dark red lips widen in a smile. "Well, how nice of you to tag along then."

God, this is getting ridiculous. Is this going to happen every place we go? He's not *that* good-looking. Well, okay, maybe he is. But still.

I clear my throat loudly. "*I* could use some help, actually."

The girl shoots me an annoyed look, but does manage to help me find bathing suits in my own size. Unlike Lily, I am all about the one-piece suit. I don't need Noah catching a glimpse of my C-section scar. Or noticing the way my belly simply will not go flat anymore, no matter how little I eat. I already know Noah's chest is just as perfect as it was when we were in college—I don't need to feel any worse about myself right now.

I manage to talk Lily into a less risqué suit, and the two of us go to the dressing room to try them on. Nina is unabashedly talking to Noah when we march off with our suits, and she's still with him when we come out again. And she's got her hand on his arm. I'm sure she's working out a way to give him her number, if she hasn't already.

Lily goes running to Noah and practically shoves her new bathing suit in his face. "Look! It has monkeys on it!"

He grins down at her, turning away from Nina. "So it does."

"Can I buy it?"

He nods. "Sure, let's go to the cashier."

Nina looks like she has more to say, but Noah has already turned away from her and is leading us to the cashier. The girl's face falls, and her lip juts out in a pout. Better luck next time, Nina.

I don't know why the lines are so long at Marshall's in the middle of the day. We're supposed to be in the middle of a recession, so it's not clear why everyone else except me has lots of money for shopping. Noah picks the first line, which clearly isn't the shortest of the lines.

This is typical Noah. When there's more than one line, he always gets in the first one he sees, without even *trying* to figure out if there's a shorter line. I got worked up over it countless times, and Noah's even-tempered response was always, *What's your big hurry, Bailey?* And then he'd kiss me or do something else to make our waiting time much more tolerable.

Well, I'm not going to say anything this time. We'll just wait in this stupid long line. Even though there definitely won't be any kissing action.

"Noah?" Lily says. She's practically bouncing with excitement over her new bathing suit.

"Uh huh?"

"Was that your girlfriend?"

Noah looks down at her and laughs out loud. "No, it wasn't."

She looks at him thoughtfully. "Do you have a girlfriend?"

I let out a breath I didn't realize I was holding when he replies, "Nope."

"Why not?"

He shrugs. "I don't know. I just haven't met the right woman yet, I guess."

She cocks her head at him. I'm bracing myself for her to ask him if she could be his girlfriend. It seems like the kind of thing she'd be thinking about, judging by her hero worship of him so far this week.

"Mommy *never* has a boyfriend," she says instead.

Oh God, that's much worse. So much worse.

Noah lifts his blue eyes to look at my face. Based on the heat I'm feeling, I'm guessing my skin is the color of a ripe tomato. "Is that so?" he says.

"Yep," Lily says. "Never."

Why are you selling out your own mother this way, Lily? *Why*?

"Never?"

She nods solemnly. "She never even goes out on dates."

I can't meet Noah's eyes as I mumble, "I go on dates sometimes."

Lily looks plainly shocked. "You do? When?"

"When you're with Daddy," I lie.

Lily considers this. "Daddy has lots of girlfriends," she finally comments.

Oh Jesus. Why is this goddamn line moving so slowly? Noah has really outdone himself in choosing this line. This is the slowest line *ever*. Is everyone in this store paying with checks or pennies or something?

"Lots of girlfriends?" Noah repeats.

She nods. "Yep. There's a new one every month!"

Noah's eyes meet mine. "Wow," he says, "that ex-husband of yours seems like a real gem."

I avert my eyes, craning my neck to check out the line next to us. "Maybe we should switch lines."

"No, we're fine," he says evenly.

"We're not moving at all!"

He shrugs. "What's your big hurry, Bailey?"

Forget it. We're staying in this line. Probably until Lily graduates from college. At least Noah doesn't say anything further about Theo's many, many girlfriends, several of whom undoubtedly existed while we were still married.

Now that Lily has revealed every embarrassing secret in my life (at least, the ones she knows—she is unaware of my vibrating secret in the drawer near my bed at home, otherwise we'd definitely be discussing it now), it's finally our turn to pay. I checked the price tags of the two swimsuits, and determined with tax, I'll end up paying around thirty-five dollars. It's not ideal, but I don't want Noah to feel like he has to pay for me. I'll never live that down.

I whip out my credit card only seconds after Noah has gotten out his. I push his arm out of the way. "I can pay for the suits," I tell him.

He shakes his head at me. "Bailey, I told you not to make a big thing of this."

I don't drop my hand holding the credit card. "I can pay."

"Don't be so goddamn stubborn."

The cashier looks between us. Yes, he's right—I'm stubborn. He already knows that about me. That's where Lily gets it from.

"You can pay for lunch, okay?" Noah murmurs. "I told Lily I was buying the suits, so just let me buy them."

He's got me there. I drop my hand and let the cashier take his card. Good thing, because it ends up being well over forty dollars. I never said math was my best subject.

Chapter 19

PRESENT DAY

After we finish up at Marshall's, it's nearly time for lunch. I figured we were going to hit up another diner, but instead, Noah pulls onto the drive-thru line of a Taco Bell. I couldn't have been more shocked if he drove off a cliff.

"You hate Taco Bell," I say to him.

"I don't think you're any kind of authority on what I hate or don't hate." He cranes his neck to look at Lily in her booster seat. "What do you say, Lily? You like Taco Bell? Wanna head for the border?"

"Yay!" Lily cries, even though I haven't ever been able to talk her into going to a Taco Bell in the city. When I offered it to her, she said she "hates tacos," even though I'm certain she's never had a taco in her entire life.

I'm no idiot though. I know why we're eating here. I recognize we could probably buy everything on the menu at Taco Bell for what Noah paid for our bathing suits.

"You don't have to eat here just because it's cheap," I mumble.

"I'm not," he says as he pulls forward on the drive-thru line. "I like Taco Bell. *Yo quiero* Taco Bell."

I roll my eyes. "Stop it."

"What's wrong, Bailey?" he says. "*No quieres* Taco Bell?"

I don't dignify that with an answer.

"Anyway," he says, "I'm going to get the most expensive thing on the menu. I'm going to get a steak… quesadilla."

He doesn't get a steak quesadilla. He gets two tacos that cost a dollar combined. I get the same. Lily hems and haws because she really doesn't want tacos, but when Noah tells her to order a quesadilla, she obliges. The whole meal costs six dollars and change.

We eat in the car, which is something I haven't done in ages. Noah and I used to do that. We'd take road trips together all the time, and we'd pull off the highway to grab drive-thru fast food, which we'd always eat in the car. "It's more private in here," he'd tell me, as he'd lean forward and kiss me. Yes, a lot of meals did end with a make-out session. We could never keep our hands off one another.

"So what did you think of Taco Bell, Lily?" Noah asks her.

Lily chews thoughtfully on her processed quesadilla. "I like McDonald's better. Do you know McDonald's?"

He laughs. "Yeah, I've heard of it."

She takes another bite of congealed cheese and cardboard-texture tortilla. "Noah?"

"Uh huh?"

"Can we go visit McDonald's farm?"

He flashes her a perplexed look. "McDonald's… farm?"

"McDonald's farm!" She sings, "Old McDonald's had a farm, ee-i-ee-i-o!"

"Oh!" He laughs again. "Well, it's not… there are farms out here but… I mean, they're not affiliated with…" He pauses thoughtfully. "Have you ever been to a farm, Lily?"

"Nope!"

He raises his eyebrows at me. "Never?"

"We live in *Queens*," I point out.

"Yeah, but…" He frowns, trying to comprehend the fact that I don't have the funds or transportation to get my daughter to a farm. And God knows, it's not like Theo ever had any interest. "So… we can go to a farm today, if you want. Right now. There's one about fifteen miles from here. I buy milk there sometimes."

Great. More time in a car with Noah. But then again, he's been fairly well-behaved today. Maybe it will be fine.

"And on that farm, will there be pigs?" Lily asks.

"Yep," Noah says.

"And on that farm, will there be sheep?"

"I think so."

"And on that farm, will there be cows?"

"Sure."

160

The next fifteen miles in the car involve Lily singing *Old McDonald Had a Farm*. Over and over. And over. I ask Noah if he'd like to turn on the radio but he gives me a look and says, "Lily's singing." So I just have to listen to it.

As we get closer to our destination, I find that I'm getting weirdly excited. I haven't been to a farm in… I don't know how long. We turn off the main road onto a dirt path, and I can tell by the tempo of Lily's singing that she's excited too. There's a white fence that surrounds acres of grass. Even grass is something I don't get to see much of unless we're at the park.

Noah pulls his 4Runner onto an even more uneven path, leading us down a road to where there are a couple of dusty barns and a large pen with animals pacing around. Lily bounces in her seat, shrieking, "Mommy, I see a cow!"

I glance at the main barn, looking for a sign. "Is there an admission fee or…?"

"No, nothing like that," Noah says. "They know me. We can just check out the animals—no big thing. There's also an ice cream stand."

I crane my neck to get a better look at the animal pens, barns, grass, and numerous trees. This is so different than what I see in my daily life in Queens. I haven't been to a place like this since…

Well, since I was dating Noah.

"Can we pick apples?" I ask.

He frowns. "Apples?"

I nod. "Yes, like from the trees?"

A smile twitches at his lips. "It's *April*, Bailey. Spring. You know how stuff gets planted in the spring and then has to grow and ripen?"

"Oh, right," I mumble, feeling dumb.

"But," he adds, "you can come back here in September for apple-picking."

I stare at him in surprise. "You… you want us to come back here? To visit?"

He throws the car into park, avoiding my eyes. "Sure, why not? Lily seems to be having a good time."

Without another word, he gets out of the car. Except the second I get out myself, I can see how uneven the ground is here. It's much worse than around his cabin, and he needed a cane over there. Noah holds onto the hood of the car as he makes his way to the trunk.

"Are you okay?" I ask him.

"Fine," he grunts as he pops the trunk. He pulls his cane out from inside while I help Lily get out. She makes a beeline straight for the pen of animals, but I hang back to make sure Noah doesn't need help. He's more stable with his cane, but I can tell it's still difficult for him to walk here. I remember how he used to love to go hiking, but it's clear something like that would be hard—if not impossible—for him now.

162

He's walking very carefully over to where Lily is fawning over some baby goats. He hits a dip in the dirt, and his knuckles turn white as he struggles to keep his balance. He stops for a moment while I step closer to him, one arm outstretched in case he really does fall.

"Are you okay?" I ask again.

Noah lifts his blue eyes to look at me. "Bailey, don't ask me if I'm okay again unless you see me sprawled on the ground. *Okay*?"

I nod. Sheesh.

The door to one of the barns on the side opens, and a woman steps out. She's about the same age as Noah's mother, with white hair scraped back into a bun. Her eyes light up when she sees Noah, just like every other female between the ages of one year and death.

"Noah!" she calls out, waving her hand.

He stops walking, looking relieved to have an excuse to take a break. "Hi, Peggy."

"You didn't have to get out of your car," she says to him. "I would have brought some milk out for you."

"No, it's okay," he says. He nods at me and then at Lily in the distance. "I brought…"

The woman, Peggy, looks me up and down, and a smile quickly spreads across her lips. "Oh!"

He shakes his head. "No, they're not… remember how I told you my mother's getting remarried? She's her fiancé's daughter. They're visiting for the week."

The smile doesn't leave Peggy's face. "Oh," she says again. She thrusts out her hand to me. "I'm Peggy."

I take her hand, and when she gives me a squeeze, I feel the deep callouses on her palm. "Bailey," I say. "And that's my daughter, Lily."

"Ooh, I love those names," Peggy sighs. "Very earthy."

"Lily's never seen a goat," Noah explains to Peggy.

"Yes, she has," I protest. At the Central Park Zoo.

"Well." Peggy rubs her hands together. "Let me give her the grand tour then."

I don't know how, but we manage to spend the next two hours at this little farm. Lily gets an experience that I'm certain very few of the kids in her kindergarten class in Fresh Meadows will ever have. Peggy lets her feed the goat and the sheep, sprinkle out feed for the chicken, and she even—no joke—gets to milk a cow. For two hours, Lily is a little farmer, and when I see the way her face glows with happiness, I don't ever want to leave. Even though being around Noah is stressful, I definitely want to come back here just to go to this farm again. And actually, Noah isn't

164

too bad at all right now. He's grinning as he watches Lily experience all the cool stuff on the farm. Once he even smiles in my direction, although he looks away the second I catch him doing it.

We end our afternoon on the farm with Noah buying us all ice cream from the farm store. The ice cream is so delicious and creamy that I'm convinced every ice cream I've ever had in the past has been synthetic garbage.

By the time we head back to the car, I've almost forgotten about the fact that Noah hates me. Or that in spite of that one smile, he's barely said two words directly to me all afternoon.

We head back home in the afternoon. Within five minutes of driving, Lily has been lulled to sleep by all the fresh air and food she's eaten. Her head sags against her shoulder, some drool slipping adorably from her lips. Noah turns the radio down to low, Kelly Clarkson's voice just barely audible from the speakers.

There's something surreal about this scene. For a moment, I imagine another life—one I could have had, where I married Noah instead of my deadbeat ex-husband. I imagine Noah is Lily's father, and he's driving his wife and daughter home from a fun day we spent as a family at the local farm. And when we get back home, Noah will make us dinner on the grill, and we'll tuck Lily into her bed. And then Noah and I go to bed. Together.

But of course, that's so far from reality, it's ridiculous. Noah is not Lily's father. Her father is a man who can't be bothered to make time to see her most weekends. And Noah hates me so much, he can barely bring himself to speak to me.

I really screwed things up.

"Thanks for taking us there," I say softly, breaking up the silence in the car.

"Yeah," he mutters.

"Lily enjoyed it," I add. "We don't get to do stuff like that very often."

Noah is quiet for a moment. At first, I think he isn't going to respond at all, but then he says, "Does he pay you child support?"

"Um, *what*?"

"Your ex. Does he give you child support for Lily?"

If someone else had said that, I would have told them to mind their own damn business. But I'm skating on thin ice already with Noah. "Why do you ask?"

"Why do I ask? Because you were having a panic attack over buying a couple of bathing suits at Marshall's. So I'm thinking he's not giving you much—or any—money."

I look away from him, at the blur of grass outside the window. I don't want to make excuses for Theo, but I also don't want to admit I was dumb enough to get knocked up by a guy who doesn't support his kid.

"Maybe he should spend less money on his girlfriends then?" says Noah.

My face burns. I don't care what Noah has hanging over me—I'm not going to have this discussion with him. "This isn't any of your business."

He takes his eyes off the road for a moment to glance at me. "You're right," he says quietly. "It's not. After all, I found out you were getting married from fucking *Facebook*."

I lower my eyes, looking down at my lap. "I'm sorry."

"Why are you sorry? It's not like I was expecting an invitation."

"Yes, but…" I pick at a loose thread on my shirt, which turns out to be looser than I thought. The whole thing might unravel if I'm not careful. "I should have called you."

"You think so?" He stops at a red light and raises his eyebrows at me. "What would you have said, exactly? 'Hey, Noah, just thought you should know: I found this great guy I'm marrying. He's a musician, and you know I'm into those artsy types. Oh, and he's got two legs, and you know how much I like *that*…'"

Oh God. This conversation has gone downhill fast.

"I'm sorry I said anything," I mumble. "I just… I wanted to thank you for a nice afternoon. I didn't want to fight with you again."

Noah doesn't say anything right away. I hold my breath, steeling myself for his next attack.

"You're welcome," he finally says.

And we don't speak again for the rest of the drive back.

Chapter 20
10 YEARS EARLIER

"Noah's not doing well."

Whenever I see Gwen Walsh's number pop up on my phone, I know it's not going to be good news. Gwen never has good news for me lately. Noah's not doing well… that's old news. Tell me something I don't know.

"The skin graft they did last week isn't taking," Gwen continues.

That's new information, but not surprising. This is Noah's third skin graft and his sixth surgery. He has experienced every complication there is—skin grafts failing, bones not healing, infections with microorganisms that require me to put on a yellow gown every time I visit him in his hospital room.

"He's getting really depressed," she says. Getting? I haven't seen Noah smile in two months. "He's in so much pain but he keeps refusing the pain medications because he's worried about… you know, he doesn't want to be like his father. But it's hard to see him suffering so much."

"Yeah," I mumble into the phone.

I'm sitting alone at the desk in my single room in the dorm. I'd been waiting to be a senior so that I could have a single all to myself, but now I wish I had a roommate. I have friends I can talk to and I can call my mother, but there's nothing quite like a roommate.

I'm lonely.

"I know he'd love to see you, Bailey," Gwen says. "It would really give him a lift."

When Noah first got injured, it was right before my Christmas break. I was able to spend two straight weeks with him without much hassle. Now is a different story. He's been transferred to a hospital in New York City, and it's a five-hour drive for me. I have my classes to think about, and my grades have plummeted recently. I can't just pop over there.

That said, the distance isn't the only reason I haven't been to visit much.

Still, it's been three weeks since I've seen Noah. Actually, close to a month. We've talked on the phone, but it isn't the same, especially since he's in so much pain that doing practically anything, including talking for more than a short period of time, is difficult for him. Gwen's right—he should take the pain meds.

"I'll come this weekend," I tell her before I can change my mind.

"Oh, that's wonderful! He'll be so happy."

Noah won't be happy—that I'm certain of. I'm starting to wonder if he'll ever be happy again.

———

Every time I see Noah, he looks worse.

When I walk into his hospital room, passing by his roommate (a big, fat guy who Noah told me snores like a chainsaw), I find him lying in his bed, like he's been every day for the past four months. He's hardly been out of bed at all during that time, thanks to his goddamn right leg.

Noah looks exhausted. There are vivid purple circles under his blue eyes and his dark blond hair has become greasy and disheveled. Any trace of humor or playfulness on his face has completely vanished. He's absolutely miserable.

I look down at the source of his misery. The pins sticking out of his leg are long gone, replaced with various rods and screws under the skin. His leg is lying exposed on top of the sheets, red and swollen to twice the size it ought to be, partially swathed in various bandages. And of course, next to that leg is the flattened sheet where his other leg should have been.

"Bailey." He doesn't smile when I walk into the room. "So nice of you to stop by."

My face burns. I know he's not trying to be a jerk—he's just worn down by the pain and surgeries. I have to remind myself of that.

"You know," I say evenly, "I just drove five hours to get here."

Noah sighs and shifts in bed to boost himself up. He grimaces because any movement at all of his right leg is agony for him. "I know," he says. "I'm sorry, Bailey. I know it's not easy for you to get here. It's just that… it hasn't been a great day."

I raise my eyebrows at him. "Anything you want to talk about?"

"The fucking skin graft." He shakes his head. "It's failing. *Again*. Everything keeps getting infected. I'm so goddamn sick of this."

I grab the chair across the room and pull it over so that I'm next to his bed. I sit down and take his hand in mine. His is clammy.

"I'm in so much pain, Bailey." He winces at the words. "Every minute of every day. I can't take it anymore. I can't even *sleep*."

"What about the pain meds?" I say.

"*No*." He shakes his head again. "You know my dad was an alcoholic and I don't want to go down that road. Anyway, they don't even really help that much."

"But if you're in that much pain…"

"I said *no*."

Noah is glaring at me now. He's so unhappy that it's difficult to even have a conversation with him. But really, if it were me, I'd take the pain medications. Anything would be better than dealing with the pain he seems to be experiencing.

The tension is broken when a tall, gray-haired man in a white coat enters the room. I recognize him as Noah's plastic surgeon, Dr. Hill. He recognizes me and smiles in greeting. But overall, he has that same grim expression I've come to expect from every doctor who enters Noah's room. Why can't any of them have *good* news for us?

"Hi, Noah," Dr. Hill says.

Noah nods in response, not looking thrilled to see his surgeon.

"And…" The surgeon regards me. "Bailey, right?"

"That's right," I say.

"So, Noah," Dr. Hill says. "I think we need to have a talk about your leg. Is it all right to talk in front of Bailey?"

"She's my fiancée," he says. "I'd like her to hear anything you have to say."

"Okay." Dr. Hill nods. He's supposedly one of the best plastic surgeons in the city for skin grafts. That's what Gwen told me anyway. "So as you know, the latest skin graft is not doing well. I think it's safe to say that it's failing."

Noah nods. I can see him gripping the sheets of his bed.

"We can wait a little longer and try again," he says. "But here's the thing, Noah. You've been in the hospital for… what? Three months? This leg is not doing well and it's not just the skin graft. And I can see how much pain you're in."

"Yeah," he mumbles. "I can handle it though."

"I'm sure you can," Dr. Hill says. "But I'm wondering to what purpose we're doing all this. We fused your right ankle so you have almost no movement there. You have a lot of nerve and muscle damage in your leg. Even if all the bones heal and we get a skin graft to take, that leg is never really going to be functional. Not in the way you're going to want it to be."

Noah nods, not looking entirely surprised. I'm sure all this was said to him before.

"You're always going to need a cane to walk, at best," Dr. Hill says. "You'll never be able to run. You're likely always going to have some degree of discomfort in that leg. It will always hold you back."

Noah's face is turning red. "Yeah. I know."

"And you're only… what? Twenty-three?"

"Twenty-two."

"What I'm trying to tell you, Noah," the surgeon says, "is that I think your best bet might be to consider amputation."

Noah's mouth falls open. "You mean… take off my other leg?"

Dr. Hill nods. "At this point, I think we've done everything we can to save it. You can either spend another six months in the hospital and *maybe* end up with a leg that doesn't work very well, or do an amputation now and be out of here in a week or two."

Noah's face reflects how I'm feeling right now. How could they suggest amputating his leg? That's his *leg*, for God's sake.

"I can see this is a shock to you," Dr. Hill observes. "But if it were me, that's what I'd do. You'll walk much better without that leg."

Noah swallows and looks up at the doctor. "If I were to agree to this, where would you...?"

"We'd have to take the knee, unfortunately," Dr. Hill says. "The worst skin loss was above the knee, so if we're going to do it, we'd have to go proximal to the injury. But we'd be able to give you a long enough limb that you could easily fit a prosthetic. The prosthetic knees they have now are incredible."

"Yeah," Noah mumbles. He lowers his eyes. "I... I've got to think about this."

Dr. Hill nods. "I understand it's a big decision. But if you do this, we could have you home and walking again before you know it. And your pain would be significantly reduced, if not gone entirely."

I can see that last statement has gotten Noah's attention. Of course it has. He's been in horrible pain for months, to the point where I think he'd accepted it was something he'd have to live with for a long time.

The surgeon leaves the room, and now Noah and I are alone. He's staring ahead at the wall, his eyes glassy. I wonder what he's thinking.

"That was… intense," I finally say.

Noah snaps out of his trance, blinking his eyes a few times. "Yeah. It was."

I look down at Noah's right leg, wrapped in layers of gauze from his mid-thigh down to his calf. It still makes me a little queasy. "Are you actually considering it?"

He doesn't answer right away. He leans his head back against his pillow, staring at the ceiling now. "I don't know. Maybe. Yeah. I think I am."

My stomach sinks. I don't want him to do this. As much as I hate seeing him in so much pain, going through surgery after surgery, I hate the idea of him losing his other leg too. I would love Noah if he had no legs, but…

God, I can't keep thinking about this. I'm starting to hate myself. Anyway, it's his decision.

Noah rolls his head over to look at me. "What do you think?"

"I…" I bite my lip. "I don't know. It's your decision."

Don't do it.

"I need to think about it," he says.

But I know my fiancé. We've been together for nearly four years. I know how much he's suffering. I know what he's going to decide.

Chapter 21
PRESENT DAY

It's hard to sleep.

After getting back to the cabin, Noah immediately left to go out on his boat, and he didn't offer to take the two of us with him. Gwen and my father bring back some steaks from town, which Gwen attempts to cook on the grill. Noah comes back soon after they've charred two of the steaks into hockey pucks, and saves the rest of them from suffering similar fates.

He doesn't say one word to me through the whole meal.

I thought that I'd drop off right to sleep after all the fresh air and food and no TV to keep me awake. But instead, I'm now lying in bed, staring at the cracks on the ceiling. They're not even interesting cracks. They don't look like faces or horses and airplanes. They just look like cracks.

Part of the problem is that Lily is in bed next to me, tossing and turning in her sleep. She's already started to rotate—she's currently about thirty degrees counter-clockwise. Soon her feet will be in prime position to kick me in the gut.

Ugh, I'm never going to fall asleep.

I struggle to sit up in bed. I rub my eyes, wondering if I should read in bed or surf the web on my phone with the sparse signal we get out here. Or maybe I'll steal some food from the fridge. It's such a luxury to be in a house where there's something in the fridge besides ketchup and a carton of milk.

I stumble into the hallway, which is very dark. After living in an urban area, it's strange to see how dark it is out in the country. It's practically black outside my room until I get out to the kitchen, where I notice someone has turned on the dim light over the oven. It turns out I have company in my late-night kitchen raid.

Noah is here.

Great.

Except now he's sitting in that same wheelchair I saw in the bathroom. He's wearing a T-shirt and boxer shorts, and I can see the tips of his stumps poking out from the ends of the shorts. I thought he used his prosthetics all the time so I'm surprised to see him using the wheelchair around the house.

"Um, hi," I say.

Noah's eyes widen at the sight of me. That's when I look down and notice I forgot to put my own shorts on—I'm wearing a tiny tank top and my bikini-cut panties. Well, at least I don't have a thong on.

"Oh," I murmur. "Shit, let me… cover up."

"Don't bother," he says before I can run off. "It's not like it's anything I haven't seen before."

I shoot him a dirty look, then race back to my bedroom to grab my shorts. Maybe he's seen it all before, but he saw a younger, tighter version of it. Once I'm in the bedroom, I consider not coming out again, but I figure that will just give Noah more ammunition to hate me.

When I get back in the kitchen, Noah is fiddling around with his phone at the table. He looks up when I come in and his handsome features are outlined in the glow of light from his screen. "I told you I didn't care," he says.

"Well, I did."

He glances down at his legs. "Does that mean you want me to cover up too? Am I making you sick here?"

I turn away from him so he can't see how my face is getting pink. "Stop it."

Noah glares at me for a good minute before he looks away too. He grabs the wheels of his chair and pushes himself over to the fridge. "You want ice cream?"

"What kind?"

"Is there some kind you *wouldn't* want?"

He's right. I'd kill for any brand, variety, or flavor of ice cream right now.

Noah pulls a container of Neapolitan ice cream out of the freezer, reaching with his right arm while he hangs onto the wheel of his chair with his left. I see his stumps tremble slightly as he stretches, even though I'm trying my best not to stare. He gets the ice cream down and then just stops, looking frustrated.

"The bowls are up on top," he says. He shrugs apologetically. "Usually if I'm alone, I just eat right out of the container."

"I don't mind doing that."

"Maybe *I* mind."

Fine. If that's how he wants to be, I'll play his game. He wheels back to give me room to retrieve the bowls from the cupboard. While I'm doing it, he finds an ice cream scoop and spoons in one of the drawers. He portions out the ice cream, giving me only vanilla and strawberry. My two favorites—I've never been a fan of chocolate. I'm sure it won't be as good as the ice cream on the farm, but it looks pretty damn good right now.

"This cabin could be a little more accessible," he says, shaking his head. "I only bought it last year and I don't have the money to make any changes right now."

"But you…" I bite my lip, wanting to ask but being afraid of angering him again. "You're usually not in the wheelchair… right?"

He's quiet for a moment, eating a bite of chocolate ice cream. "I'm not really supposed to be on the prosthetics more than nine or ten hours a day.

Any more than that and I'm in pain. So usually I use the chair in the evening."

"Oh." Aside from now and that time I busted in on him in the bathroom, I haven't seen Noah once without his prosthetics. He's got to have spent over fourteen hours in them today.

"I'm using the prosthetics more now, obviously," he says. "Mostly because I don't want to freak out your kid."

"Lily?" I frown. "What are you talking about? She won't get freaked out."

"Won't she? Her mother sure as hell did."

I take a large bite of ice cream. Too large—it's agonizing as it melts in my mouth. But I'm grateful for the pain right now.

"You know," I say quietly, "*you're* the one who invited me here, Noah. It's not like I forced my way in. I'm trying my best to be civil to you, but you get in every possible jab you can. What do you want me to say? That I feel awful about what happened? I do. I feel awful." I take a shaky breath. "But there's nothing I can do about it except apologize. I'm trying my best. And *you* are being an asshole."

I'm certain he's going to hurl another insult at me, but instead, his shoulders sag. "You're right," he says quietly. "I'm being an asshole." He runs his hand through his dark blond hair, which emphasizes how short it is compared to the way he wore it in college.

"I thought I'd be okay seeing you, Bailey, I really did. I have a good life—I'm happy. And I thought it was that whole thing about how living well is the best revenge, you know? But now that I'm actually seeing you, it's like... the last ten years never happened. And everything just came rushing back..."

"I know what you mean," I murmur.

To my surprise, Noah holds out his hand to me. "Truce?"

I reach out to shake his hand. Despite the fact that he was just eating ice cream, his hand feels warm and large in mine—the way it always did. "Truce," I say. "And I promise you, Lily won't freak out if she sees you in a wheelchair. She's not like that. She's not like... me."

Noah looks down into his bowl of ice cream. "I have to disagree. She seems a lot like you."

I laugh. "You're the first person to ever say that. Everyone thinks she looks just like my ex-husband."

He shakes his head. "She has your eyes."

"Um, no. Hers are blue and mine are brown."

"It's not the color." He looks thoughtful. "It's the intensity. The way she looks at things. It reminds me of you. And when she was drawing last night, she did the thing with her tongue you always do."

"The thing with my *tongue*?"

"Yeah. You stick your tongue out when you're drawing."

"No, I don't!"

"Yeah, you do." He grins. "Just a little bit. Like this."

He sticks his tongue about two millimeters out of the side of his mouth. I roll my eyes.

"She'll probably be an artist like you wanted to be before you gave up, for some reason." He cocks his head. "Why did you give up anyway, since we're asking the uncomfortable questions?"

I look down at my ice cream bowl. The vanilla and strawberry have melted to make a pinkish soup. I stir it with my spoon. "It's a long story."

He looks around and shrugs. "It's not like I have anywhere else to be right now."

I bite my lip. This isn't a story I tell very many people. I never imagined it would be one I'd tell him.

"After I… after we broke up," I begin, "after that, I just couldn't…"

I lift my eyes and see he's looking at me intently. There's no anger in his eyes anymore—only concern.

"I couldn't draw anymore after that," I say in a gush of words. "Not for a long time. Every time I picked up a pencil, I just felt… I kept thinking about you and I couldn't focus. Drawing made me happy, and I felt like I didn't deserve to be happy anymore after that."

His eyebrows bunch together. "Bailey…"

"I thought maybe as a social worker, I could do some good." I look back down at my pink soup. "Penance, you know?"

He's quiet for a moment. "Well," he finally says, "at least you didn't become a nun."

Despite everything, I laugh. I can't say becoming a nun was ever on my radar. I felt bad, but not *that* bad.

"Anyway, how come you didn't become a surgeon?" I ask him. "Wasn't that *your* dream?"

He looks at me like I've completely lost my mind. "Didn't I just tell you that I can't be on my prosthetics more than ten hours? How do you think I would manage to get through a surgical residency?"

I remember the first time Noah met my father, Dad grilled him about his future career. Noah was usually fairly confident about himself, and I'd never seen him so nervous as when he was trying to impress my parents.

"So you want to be a surgeon, do you, Noah?"

"Yes, I do. I always have."

"It's a hard life. You know that, don't you?"

"I do."

"Lots of hours. Physically demanding. You have to be on your feet for the whole day."

"I'm in good shape."

"But you might not always be. What about when you're an old man like me?"

185

Noah had laughed and so did I. He was twenty years old, played basketball three times a week, and swam five times a week. He was in perfect physical condition. Neither of us could envision that ever not being the case. We had no idea that only two years later, everything would change.

"Oh, right," I mumble. "I'm sorry."

"Just…" Noah shakes his head. "Could you *please* stop saying you're sorry? Okay? You're making me feel like I'm some kind of charity case you're doing social work for."

"Okay, I'm sor… er, I'll try not to say it anymore."

He lets out a long sigh. "I think I'm going to head to bed, Bailey. It's been a long day."

He pulls away from the table, and wheels himself in the direction of his bedroom. His biceps tighten with each push of the wheels and he pauses only briefly to smooth out his boxers over his stumps. They're just barely long enough that I can see the ends of them through the shorts—the surgeon told Noah he'd leave him enough of his limbs so that he'd be able to use prosthetics. That was what was important at the time.

I keep staring after Noah as he wheels himself down the hall, the muscles of his back tightening under his T-shirt. I watch him the whole way, and after he's gone, I think about him. I think about his

186

handsome face, his short but tousled dark blond hair, his blue eyes, his lean and muscular upper body, and even his pale white stumps.

God, it's been a long time since I've lusted after Noah Walsh.

Chapter 22
PRESENT DAY

Gwen calls us in the morning to tell us that she's purchased five tickets for the afternoon showing of *Dogcat*. I distinctly remember stating that we had already seen *Dogcat* and that we were never, ever going to see it again. But it's hard to get too angry when I see how excited Lily is.

"*Dogcat* is my favorite movie in the whole world," she tells Noah while we're eating cold cut sandwiches for lunch.

Lily's favorite movie is always the last movie she's seen. Every time she sees anything, it's suddenly the greatest movie ever. But I'm worried. If she sees *Dogcat* a second time, will that cement the movie as her favorite movie of all time *forever*?

"What is this movie about, anyway?" Noah asks me as he bites into his turkey sandwich on wheat bread.

"It's about a cat," Lily explains to him. "But then the cat becomes a dog. Except he wants to be a cat again. And also? He fights crime."

"Does he?" Noah looks like he's suppressing a laugh.

"Yes, he does," Lily says. "Like he saves a whole family of frogs from a burning building."

Noah frowns. "Why is there a family of frogs living in a building?"

Lily frowns back. "Where else would they live?"

"It's an alternative universe," I explain to Noah. "Where instead of people, animals are essentially in charge of the planet." I think there was also some sort of lesson in the movie about taking good care of the planet, but the message was lost in the awfulness that was *Dogcat*.

Noah is smirking. "I can't wait."

We drive over to the theater to meet Gwen and my father. Gwen is holding another shopping bag and this time she pulls out a dress that she bought for Lily. It's bright pink with a lacy skirt—beautiful but completely impractical. I can't even imagine an occasion where Lily will be able to wear this dress. But of course, Lily loves it. She loves it so much that I have to promise her to take her to the bathroom as soon as we get into the movie theater so she can put it on.

"I'm so happy you like it, sweetie," Gwen says. "You should have at least one nice thing."

My face burns. Lily has nice things. Well, *some* nice things. I mean, it's not like I can afford to buy her tons of frilly, impractical dress just because.

Noah notices the look on my face. He frowns at his mother and says, "Actually, I think Lily has on a really nice outfit right now."

189

Lily glances down at the outfit she's wearing, clearly skeptical. It's a short-sleeved rainbow-colored shirt with black stars on it that she paired with pink shorts. It's a completely unremarkable outfit I threw into the duffel bag when I was randomly shoving in clothes for our trip. I wouldn't call it "really nice." It's acceptable. It's clean, at least.

"Of course she does!" Gwen says quickly. "Lily *always* is dressed in nice outfits. And of course, we're all so excited to see this *Dogcat* movie."

Gwen might hate me, but at least she's sucking up to my daughter.

However, Noah sticking up for me—*that's* a new development.

"I'll buy the popcorn," Noah offers. He looks at me. "What do you guys want?"

Lily nearly explodes from happiness. "Popcorn! Mommy never lets me get popcorn! It's too 'spensive."

Here we go again. My daughter knows the words "too expensive" all too well, even if she can't quite pronounce them.

Noah grins. "Well, this is a special occasion because your grandpa just got engaged. So you get to have popcorn."

Lily runs around in a happy circle. Literally.

Noah looks at me again and furrows his brow. "So to drink… she wouldn't have soda, right?"

I snort. "Why? You think she needs more sugar? Water is fine, thanks."

Gwen takes Lily to the bathroom to help her put on her new dress and I'm left alone with my father, while Noah gets in line to buy the popcorn. I notice the girl at the counter immediately starts flirting with him. And I can tell he's flirting back. Not that there's any reason he shouldn't.

"So it looks like you and Noah are getting along okay," Dad says.

"We had a truce," I say, and wince at how dumb that sounds.

Dad smiles. "That's good to hear. I knew it would be okay, once we were all settled in."

"Yeah," I mumble.

"Gwen was surprised at how upset he seemed when you showed up," Dad adds. "She said that he… well, obviously he's done well for himself, in spite of everything. She said he never even talked about you. Not since right after."

"Oh." I don't know why that comment leaves me feeling cold. It's not like I wish Noah had been obsessing over me for the last ten years. But at the same time, I feel sad to discover he never even thought about me. I sure thought about him. I always wondered what he was doing. If he became a surgeon. If he was married. If he had a little girl of his own.

But I never checked on Facebook to find out if it was true. I knew how painful it would have been to find out Noah was really taken.

Noah comes off the line carrying three bags of popcorn and three empty cups for drinks. He's limping more than usual due to the strain of everything he's holding, and he looks like he's about to drop everything. "Little help here?" he calls.

Dad comes over to take their popcorn and drink, while I grab Lily's smaller bag of popcorn and the cup I'll probably fill with water (or lemonade, if she really insists). With impeccable timing, Lily emerges from the bathroom with her impractical new dress on. It's so frilly that she looks more like she's going to a wedding than seeing *Dogcat* for the second time. She runs right up to Noah to show him.

"Do you like it?" she asks.

"I love it," he says very seriously. "Just be careful not to spill anything on it."

Lily nods solemnly, her blue eyes wide.

We all fight over who's going to sit next to Lily. Well, I don't fight too hard, considering I got to sit next to her the first time we saw *Dogcat*. Lily wants to sit next to Noah, and her choice is to sit between him and me, but Gwen wants to sit next to Lily as well. After some intense negotiations, Lily ends up between Noah and Gwen, with me on the end next to Noah.

"Be careful," I whisper to Noah. "Lily may make a move when the lights are down."

Noah laughs. "Don't worry. I've got lots of experience fending off female advances. Even six-year-olds."

I'll just bet he does.

As the lights dim though, it's not Lily I'm thinking about. It's Noah, inches away from me, in this dark theater. I can just barely smell his aftershave and it's making me want to rest my head on his shoulder to get closer. After all, the last time Noah and I were in a dark theater like this together, his arm was around my shoulders, keeping me close to him. And if the movie was boring, we'd start making out. Or maybe just because we felt like it. Every activity was an excuse to make out with each other.

It was never like that with any other guys. Not even with Theo.

"Hey," I hear Noah whisper as the opening credits to *Dogcat* start rolling on the screen. "I didn't know Robert DeNiro was in this movie."

"Yeah," I whisper back. "He does the voice of some mob boss parakeet that *Dogcat* has to take down."

I can make out Noah smiling in the dark of the theater. "Wow, all-star cast."

"Yeah, I wish they'd spent the money making the movie not suck."

Noah stifles a laugh. He shakes his bag of popcorn in my direction. "You want some popcorn?"

"Nah."

"You sure? I got a large."

I shake my head. "It will make me too thirsty."

He raises his eyebrows at me. "I also got a large drink."

Sharing a drink. That means drinking from the same straw. I stare at him in the dark.

"I don't have cooties, Bailey," he whispers.

He's looking at me in a way that makes my heart speed up. This is definitely the most excited an adult has ever been during a viewing of *Dogcat*.

"Fine," I whisper back as I take a handful of popcorn.

He's just sharing his food with me. There's no reason to make more of this than it deserves.

Chapter 23
10 YEARS EARLIER

As I'm driving to Noah's mother's apartment in Brooklyn, I have a sick feeling in the pit of my stomach. I try to distract myself with music, but even Adam Levine's voice isn't enough to make me feel better.

Two weeks ago, my mother broke the news to me: her cancer was back for Round Four.

She'd known for several weeks, but she didn't want to tell me because I was going through "so much right now." I resented that she wouldn't tell me something so important. But at the same time, the news nearly broke me. Between Noah's accident and her cancer, my emotions are going through the ringer. I'm one stubbed toe away from a complete meltdown.

I came home two days ago, just in time for my mother's first chemo session. She was throwing up all night last night. At first, she could make it to the bathroom, but then I brought her a bowl to retch into while I tried to get rid of the smell of vomit from the bathroom. Dad sat with Mom in her room, putting cool compresses on her forehead.

I can't take much more of this. The hardest thing in the world is watching someone you love be sick. And it feels like that's become my entire existence.

Because of my mother, I've been neglecting Noah. I only saw him once right after his surgery, when they took his other leg off at the mid-thigh. I couldn't stay too long because I had exams to get back for, but I spent some time with him when he was in a post-anesthetic haze. At one point, he grabbed my arm and said, "I made a mistake, Bailey. I can't believe I let them take my leg."

Noah's sick. Mom's sick. I had to keep my eyes pinned on Noah's face the whole time I was with him to keep from passing out. I'm horrible at dealing with this. I wish I could be strong for them.

But I can't. I can't do it anymore. I've got bags under my eyes, and even though I showered before I left the house, I swear I still smell like the vomit I cleaned from the bathroom. I'd probably throw up myself, except I couldn't keep down any food this morning.

As I drive across the Brooklyn Bridge, my eyes are drawn to the blue-gray water below. For a moment, I'm seized by the irrepressible urge to swing the steering wheel right so the car will fly right off the edge.

God, why am I thinking these things? This couldn't be healthy.

They were able to discharge Noah only a week after the second surgery, something I knew he was thrilled about. Also, he told me his pain was significantly better—he was able to sleep through the night again. He's been going to physical therapy, although he's still far from the point where they'll be able to fit him with any kind of prosthetics. The last time we talked on the phone, he said to me, "I did the right thing. I'm so glad to be out of that goddamn hospital. It was *killing* me, Bailey."

I find parking a block away from their building. It's an old building, but it does have an elevator, which is a good thing since Gwen Walsh lives on the fourth floor. I don't know how Noah could make it right now, considering he can't walk anymore.

I stand in front of their apartment door for a good minute, unable to make myself knock. I'm so tired. I can't deal with Noah being ill and in pain anymore. I can't have another fight with him about why he should be taking his pain meds. The thought of it makes me want to crumble into a little ball.

I tell myself that Noah's okay. He's out of the hospital. His pain is better. He's *okay.*

Except he's not really okay. He'll never be okay again.

Before I can drive myself crazy a minute longer, I knock on the door. Gwen is the one who opens the door. She's wearing a dress stained with brown splotches and her hair is falling out of its bun. The second she sees me, she cries out, "Bailey!" And she hugs me. The longest hug ever. It makes me hate myself even more.

When she pulls away and looks at me, the smile on her face falters. I avert my eyes, knowing if I see a flash of sympathy, I may very well burst into tears.

"You've lost some weight," she says, unnecessarily.

"A little," I lie as I move past her into the apartment. I'm afraid to even step on a scale anymore. It was hard enough to eat when it was just Noah who was sick, but now it's impossible. Food tastes like cardboard. I had to buy a belt to hold up some formerly skintight jeans that have now gotten baggy.

"And how's school going?"

Another loaded question. I can't tell Gwen Walsh I'm failing three of my classes. It was humiliating enough to tell my parents. So instead, I force a smile. "Great."

Before we have to make further small talk, I see him. Noah. Easily twenty pounds lighter than he was before the accident, still with purple circles under his eyes but lighter than last time. He's got a T-shirt on, but it isn't wrinkled and sweaty like the ones I always saw him wearing at the hospital. It's fresh and clean, right out of the wash. And he's sitting in a wheelchair—a hospital-grade chair with the leg rests removed as he obviously has no need. He's wearing a pair of his old shorts, which would have reached his knees before, but now just lie flat at the ends. He's still clearly not back to his old self, but better than I've ever seen him.

"Bailey," he says.

I wave to him awkwardly. I should probably come in for a hug. Yes, that's what I should do. So I walk over to him and we hug and it's awkward.

"Um," Noah says. "Do you want to… um, go in my room?"

I glance at Gwen, who is beaming at the two of us. Not a lot of privacy in here. "Sure," I say.

I've been in Noah's room a few times since we've been together. It's a typical guy's bedroom—creaky wooden desk, single bed pushed against the wall, a bookcase with books arranged haphazardly on the shelves. I finger a book called *Netter's Atlas of Human Anatomy*.

"Are you going back to med school?" I ask.

Noah looks at me in surprise. "Yeah, of course I am. I just… well, not *yet*. But I'm going back."

"But…" I look down at his legs.

"Christ, Bailey," he says. "I'll have prosthetics in a few months. And even if I didn't, there are doctors out there who use wheelchairs."

"Right. I'm sorry." I try to smile. Noah seems so much better than he was, almost like the old version of himself again. Maybe it's all going to be okay now.

He'll get his prosthetics, he'll go back to school like he said—everything will be fine.

I wish I could believe that.

Noah cocks his head at me. "It's okay. Look, I know all this is… a little weird. But… I've missed you so much." He smiles shyly. "Do you realize this is the first time we've been completely alone together in four months?"

My eyes widen as I realize what he's saying. The two of us haven't had sex in four months. Hell, we haven't even kissed beyond just pecks on the cheek. He hasn't seemed even remotely interested in either, but the way he's looking at me now, it looks like the surgery that took his leg may have given him back his libido.

Thank *God*. Maybe the old Noah really is back.

I smile nervously. "So, um, what do you want to do about it?"

He squeezes the edge of his wheelchair cushion, looking just as anxious as I feel. "I guess I should, um… transfer to the bed?"

I nod and step back to give him room. He scoots himself forward a little in his chair, so that his shorts ride up so they're no longer covering his amputated limbs. I can see the scars on the ends of his legs—pale on the left, which was done months ago, and angry red on the right. He puts one fist on his bed and holds his wheelchair cushion with the other hand, rocking

200

back and forth a couple of times. He heaves a breath, then tries to move himself from the chair to his bed.

Except before he can make the move, his chair slips backwards. He goes tumbling to the ground with a terrifying thump.

"Fuck!" Noah yells. "I forgot to lock the wheels!"

I bend down next to him, my hands shaking the way they were last night while I crouched next to my mother as she was relieved the contents of her stomach into the toilet. He's clutching his right stump, which is oozing blood from the incision that had appeared to be closed moments earlier. Actually, it's quite a lot of blood.

Quite a lot.

"Shit," he mutters. "It opened up again. Fuck."

I swallow hard, averting my eyes. "Are you okay?"

"Yeah, but…" His voice trembles. "Do you think you could run to the bathroom and grab me some gauze from below the sink? There's a bunch of it down there."

"What about getting off the floor?" I say. I don't want to have to lift him, but I can't see how else he'll get back in his chair.

"I just want to get this cleaned up, okay?"

"But—"

"Bailey, can you get me the goddamn gauze please?"

And now I'm seeing spots in front of my eyes. I figure I should get him the gauze just so I can leave this room and not have to look at all the blood anymore. "Okay," I whisper.

Noah leans back against the dresser, letting his eyes flutter shut. He's still clutching his injured right stump with his hand. "Thanks, Bailey. I… I'm sorry this happened. It… it's not how I wanted to spend this afternoon with you."

"It's not your fault." I force a smile as I straighten up. "I'll go get the gauze."

"Thanks." He reaches his fingers out to me, and I give his hand a quick squeeze. His palm is clammy and blood ends up smeared on my fingers.

I start to leave the room, but I'm unsteady and my foot catches on the chair that wheeled backwards. I knock it over, going down with it, my knee cracking hard against the floor. I feel a flash of white-hot pain in my kneecap that makes me gasp aloud.

"Bailey?" His eyes widen. "Are you okay?"

"Fine," I manage, even as I feel the tears rising to my eyes.

I try to get to my feet, and my knee groans with pain. Noah's wheelchair is toppled over next to him. He reaches over, trying to right it with his arms, his stumps trembling with the effort. It's obviously not easy for him.

"Let me help you," I say.

"No." He holds up a hand to keep me away. "I've got it."

"It's easier for me to…"

"*No.*"

My eyes meet Noah's. I see the pain in his blue eyes and have to look away. It's almost as bad as my throbbing knee.

"Just get the gauze," he sighs. "Please, Bailey."

I nod silently. I leave Noah's room with the door cracked open and slip into the bathroom right next door. He said the gauze was right below the sink. I crouch down, the stench of old urine emanating from the bowl. My stomach turns. I can still smell my mother's vomit.

I find the gauze packages lined up below the sink. My knee screams with pain as I rest it on the cold tile floor. I slide down onto my butt and roll up the leg of my jeans. Great—I'm bleeding. Not as much as Noah was, but not an insignificant amount. I take one of the pieces of gauze and rest it against my skinned knee, swallowing my tears.

I can't do this anymore. I can't be here for Noah while I'm taking care of my mother. I can't. It's killing me.

I can't fucking do it anymore.

I straighten up, letting my pants leg fall back down to cover my wound. I leave Noah's bathroom, but I don't bring him his gauze. Instead, I go into the living room, where Gwen is reading on the couch. She looks up in surprise and smiles at me. "Everything okay, Bailey?"

I silently pull the ring off the fourth finger of my left hand and place it on the nearest bookcase. I leave the apartment without answering her or saying good bye.

———

I get back to my car in half the time it took me to get from my car to the apartment. I slip into the drivers' seat, stick my key in the ignition, and take off like I just robbed a bank. I don't know why. It's not like Noah is going to be chasing me down.

I make it nearly to the Brooklyn Bridge before my cell starts ringing. I see Noah's name on the screen and nearly let it go to voicemail. But I can't do that to him. The man is my fiancé—at least, he was. I had planned to spend my life with him. I owe it to him to answer the phone. So I pull over, flip it open, and answer, "Hello?"

"Bailey?" He doesn't sound angry, only confused. "Where did you *go*?"

"I, um…" I swallow a lump in my throat. "I'm in my car."

"Your *car*?" His voice rises several notches. "So you just… left?"

I wince, only partially from the pain in my knee. "Sort of. Um, are you okay?"

"Yeah," he says. *No thanks to you.* "My mom helped me. She… she got me bandaged up, and… well, she helped me back into my chair. So…"

"Oh," I say. "That's good."

There's shuffling on the other line—Noah's mother is saying something to him. He must have put down the phone for a second, because I can only distantly hear his voice say, "She did *what*?"

His mother must have found the ring.

When he returns to the line, the confusion is coupled with an anxious edge to his voice. "Bailey," he says, "did you leave your engagement ring on the bookcase?"

"Yes," I admit. "I did."

There's a long silence. "Can you tell me what the fuck is going on?" he finally says.

"I…" I take a deep breath, knowing what I'm about to say can't be taken back, but plowing ahead anyway. "I don't think I…"

I can hear him breathing on the other line. "What?"

Tell him, Bailey. Tell him the truth.

"I can't do this anymore," I whisper.

"Do what? What are you talking about?"

My voice is so tiny, it barely makes a sound: "Be with you."

I hear Noah suck in a breath. "*What*?"

"I need a break," I say. "From us. I'm sorry. I love you, Noah, but… I'm overwhelmed. I can't deal with it anymore. I *can't*."

"Holy shit," he breathes. "You're *dumping* me? *Now*?"

"I'm not dumping you. I told you—I just need a break."

"A *break*?"

"I'm sorry," I say again, my voice trembling. "This is all… it's too much for me."

"Too much for *you*?" he repeats. "I fucking *lost my legs*, Bailey. Both of them. I'm in a *wheelchair*. I'm…"

"I'm really sorry." I sound like a broken record, but it's all I can think to say. "I just can't come over anymore. We could talk on the phone if you want. If you need someone to talk to or anything like that, I promise that I'll—"

"Fuck you," Noah says.

I've never heard him say those words before. Not to anyone, but especially not to me. Before this moment, I couldn't have conceived of it.

I bite my lip. "Noah, I'm sorry."

"You think I don't know what this is about?" And now I hear that anger that I'd expected when he first called me. His voice is thick with it. "You liked me when I was whole, but now that I'm crippled, you're not attracted to me anymore."

"Noah, *no*."

"Bullshit."

"My mother is sick," I whimper. I didn't want to tell him about it, compounding his own problems, but I need him to understand. "She needs me right now—"

"Wow," he says. "You're using your *mother* as an excuse. That's low, Bailey."

"It's not an excuse," I try to tell him, but it's clear he's not listening to me. He doesn't believe a word I have to say. All he knows is I'm abandoning him when he needs me. "Please, Noah. You have to understand…"

He laughs bitterly. "No, I understand. Believe me, I understand."

"Listen…" My hands are shaking so badly, it's hard to hold my phone. "I'll call you…"

"Don't." His voice burns daggers into my chest, even through the phone. "I never want to speak to you again. Ever."

"Noah…"

But the line is dead.

———

I cry all the way back to Queens.

I'm still sobbing when I park my car two blocks away from my parents building. Then I cry during the walk home, still limping on my bad knee. I'm the girl on the street sobbing her eyes out. Everyone is looking at me, trying to figure out if they should say something comforting or just leave me alone. In the end, they leave me alone and I'm glad.

By the time I reach my parents' apartment, my eyes are sore and my face is pink and swollen. I have an ache in my right temple that's turning into a throbbing pain and my knee is on fire. I thought I'd feel relief when I told Noah I couldn't be there for him anymore, but I don't. I feel much worse.

But at the same time, I don't want to go back to him.

I assumed Mom would be lying in bed resting, and I'd been hoping I could sneak off to my bedroom without anyone noticing. But Mom is sitting on the couch when I limp in, and her eyes lift when I walk into the apartment.

Mom looks much worse than Noah did. The purple circles under her eyes are as deep as they've ever been, and she's pale like a sheet. It's hard to look at her like this. But she's my mother, and I will do for her what I couldn't do for Noah. Now that I don't have him in my life anymore, I can give her my all. She needs me more than he does.

"Bailey." Despite her own appearance, her eyes widen at the sight of my face. No wonder people were giving me a wide girth on the sidewalk. "What happened? Is… is Noah okay?"

No, he's not. Thanks to me.

"We broke up," I manage. And the tears start all over again.

Mom takes me into her arms. She hugs me tight to her, stroking my hair the way she did when I was a little kid and I had fallen off the monkey bars. Even though she's very weak, the hug still feels warm and good. Like everything could be all right again. Maybe Mom will beat the cancer again. Maybe in a few months, Noah and I can make a go of it again. If he's willing to forgive me.

"I can't believe Noah would break up with you," she murmurs. "After all you've been through together."

I pull away, wiping my eyes with the back of my hand. "Actually," I say, "I ended it with him."

Mom stares at me in surprise. And disappointment. "You dumped him? *Now*?"

My face burns. "Mom, I just… I couldn't do it anymore…"

"You dumped him one month after he had his leg amputated?" Mom is staring at me like I'm worse than Hitler. I *feel* like I'm worse than Hitler right now. "What did you say to him?"

209

I can't bear to repeat it. Even thinking about it makes me hate myself.

"It was just too much for me," I whisper. "I couldn't… not with everything going on with you. I just *couldn't* anymore."

"Don't use *me* as an excuse for abandoning him," she says, which is eerily similar to what Noah told me. "I've got your father. I'm fine, Bailey."

"You're *not* fine!" I burst out. "You need me! *Everyone* needs me! And I just… I couldn't be there for him anymore. I had to end it."

Mom is quiet. I wish she'd tell me she understands. She's always done that before. It's not like I've never done stupid things before in my life. Or even mean things. I'm not a perfect person. I've never claimed to be.

"If it had happened to you," she says, "Noah would have been there for you till the end. No matter what else was going on in his life."

"Well, he's a better person than me," I say bitterly.

"You've always been strong for me," she reminds me. "And I've been sicker than he is."

"But you're my mother."

She brushes hair from my face. "He would have been your whole life."

Would he? Even when Noah and I were engaged, somehow I never believed it would end in marriage. I

210

knew there was something that would get in the way of having a happily ever after. After all, that's how my life has been. And that's how *his* life has been.

I just never knew that something would be me.

Chapter 24
PRESENT DAY

Now you hate me.

That's okay—I hated me. I was horrible to Noah. I know it. I knew it then and I know it now. It was one of the darkest periods of his life, and I made him feel awful about himself. I was selfish.

After that, every time something bad happened to me, I was glad for it. I welcomed it. It felt like penance for what I did to Noah. I couldn't draw anymore. Every time I picked up a pencil, I felt a dark, horrible feeling in my stomach. I gave up art and started a career in social work, hoping to make up to the world the awful thing I had done.

Then a year later, my mother lost her final battle with breast cancer. She fought valiantly but lost Round Four. My mother, the person I loved more than anyone else in the world, was dead. Finally, it felt like I had paid my dues to the universe.

Not long after that, I met Theo. I started drawing again. I let myself move on.

After *Dogcat* finally ends, Gwen and my father say they're going out to dinner. Someplace nice. Lily crinkles up her nose. "I wanna go to McDonald's!" she cries.

"We went to the farm just yesterday," I remind her.

"Not the farm." Lily shakes her head at me like she can't believe I'd think something so dumb. "The food place. I want a Happy Meal."

"Lily," I say patiently, "we can go to McDonald's back in Queens. We're going out to a nice restaurant tonight. So you can show off your pretty new dress."

"McDonald's!" Lily insists, tears welling up in her eyes. "Happy Meal!"

I look at my father and Gwen. They both shrug.

"Is there a McDonald's in this town?" I ask Noah.

"Are you kidding me?" He rolls his eyes. "Yes. There is. And it's got a play area or something like that."

"Play area!" Lily squeals, despite the fact that she's dressed more appropriately for a ballroom.

McDonald's used to be one of my favorite places to eat, but I may have outgrown it recently. Don't get me wrong—the food tastes really good. But an hour later, I feel it sitting in my stomach like a big ball of lead. Especially those crispy, delicious French fries.

Unfortunately, going to McDonald's and not ordering French fries is an exercise in futility. I settle on a small fries and pair it with an Artisan Chicken Sandwich, which at least is grilled chicken rather than fried. We go to the back of the restaurant, where there's an outdoor play area, and Lily takes exactly one bite of her chicken nugget before running off to play.

Noah sits next to me at a table, eyeing my food appraisingly. "An Artisan chicken sandwich, huh?"

"What's so wrong with that?" I say.

He shrugs and grins. "I don't know. What makes it 'Artisan,' exactly?"

I look down at my sandwich. Even though it's supposedly grilled chicken, it still looks incredibly greasy. "Because it's, you know, prepared in a healthier, better way."

Noah whips out his phone and fiddles with it. "So the definition of 'Artisan' for a food is 'made in a traditional or non-mechanized way using high-quality ingredients.' So how exactly does that describe a mass-produced sandwich that comes from *McDonald's*?"

I shake my head. "Aren't you hungry? Can't you order some food that I can make fun of?"

"I had a bunch of popcorn," he says. "Anyway, I'm going out later to eat."

I raise my eyebrows at him. "Oh? Like, going into town again?"

He hesitates. "I've got a date."

Noah has a *date*? For some reason, that information hits me like a punch in the stomach.

"Is it with that waitress?" I ask.

He smiles crookedly. "No, somebody else."

Sheesh, he's got a busy social life. I shouldn't be surprised though. Everywhere we go, women are

215

hitting on him. Unlike me. I haven't been out on a date in about a year.

"So…" I take a sip of my Diet Coke. "Is it a first date?"

Noah looks like he's contemplating telling me that it's none of my damn business, but instead he says, "Second date."

So it's a new relationship. It's a pre-relationship. Second date… I wonder if she knows his secret.

"She knows," Noah says before I can dare ask.

"Huh?" I say innocently.

He rolls his eyes. "You were wondering if she knows I'm a double amputee. The answer is that she does. I don't let it get to a second date without telling them—there's no point."

I stick a French fry in my mouth. These things are so bad for me, but damn, are they good. "And she's okay with it?"

"We're going out on a second date, aren't we?" He snatches one of the fries off my plate and pops it in his mouth. "She's a nurse, so… you know."

"How did you meet her?" I don't know why I'm asking him so many questions, especially when I don't really want to know the answers. I don't want to know about Noah's love life.

"At the supermarket," he says. "We were waiting in a long line and we just got to talking."

Yes, I'm sure she thought to herself, *Wow, that guy ahead of me in line is hot. Let me try to talk to him.* And imagine her delight when she discovered he's a doctor too.

"Well, you sure have a busy social life," I comment.

He flips his palm back and forth. "So-so." He takes another fry from my tray. "After we broke up, it took me a really long time to get up the nerve to ask a woman out again. I figured any girl would be disgusted when she found out."

I lower my eyes. "I… I'm sorry."

He shrugs. "Believe me, I hated you at the time. But I got over it, especially when I found out it wasn't true. Okay, some of them run for the hills like you did. But some are fine with it. Varying degrees of fine."

I look across the table at Noah, wishing I was that nurse out on a second date with him. That I had a fresh start so I could tell him how I find him incredibly sexy without him laughing in my face.

Noah isn't looking at me though. He's watching Lily, who is climbing some sort of play structure that hovers over a sea of multicolored balls. "So you went and married a musician, huh?"

I quickly avert my gaze from him, in case he notices I'm staring. "Yeah. But that's long over. Obviously."

"I knew you always liked that type." He smiles crookedly. "Was he in a punk rock band or something?"

"He's actually a really talented guitar player and singer." I don't know why I feel a need to defend Theo. Especially after how awful he was to me.

"I'll bet." Noah takes another fry. "Did you actually think he was going to be a rock star?"

"No," I admit. "Not really."

"Did *he* think so?"

"He *still* thinks so."

"Oh, *that* type," Noah laughs. "If you didn't think he was all that, how come you married the guy?"

I wave my hand at Lily. "You're looking at the reason."

He looks genuinely surprised. "You got knocked up? You're kidding. You were always so anal about birth control. You had an alarm on your phone to remember to take your pill."

I glare at him. "Condoms break sometimes. What do you want?"

"You were using a condom?" He raises an eyebrow. "How long were you with the guy when it happened?"

"A year," I mumble.

"And you were still using condoms at that point?"

I sigh. "Look, he's was in a band. You know how it is."

Noah shakes his head. "I don't, actually. I never cheated on you once the whole time we were together. I've never cheated on *anyone* before."

"I made a bad decision." I look at Lily writhing around in the ball pit. "At least one good thing came of it."

Noah reaches out and takes another of my fries. I swat at his hand. "Would you quit stealing my fries?" I scold him. "I only got a small."

"Yeah, but I'm hungry," he complains.

"I thought you were full on popcorn."

"Guess not." He grins. "Maybe I'll go get my own fries."

"Don't you want to be hungry for your date?"

He winks at me. "I don't think she's all that concerned with what I eat."

He gets up and goes back into the McDonald's to get more food. I wish he weren't going on that date. But even if he didn't, it wouldn't change the situation between the two of us. It's just as well.

Chapter 25
PRESENT DAY

"Wake up, Mommy! Wake *up*!"

"Muh?" I say. I feel Lily's little body crawling into the bed next to me, then on top of me. God, she's getting heavy.

"Noah says wake up," she says in her most bossy voice. "We have to go fishing."

I stayed up too late last night. Noah left for his date at a quarter to eight, looking almost painfully handsome in a blue dress shirt and khaki pants that reminded me of what he wore on our first date. He winked at me when he left and said, "Don't wait up."

But of course, that's exactly what I did. I was especially horrified when it hit midnight and Noah still wasn't back yet. I finally heard him coming in at half past twelve, then had to scurry back to my bed, to make sure he didn't realize I'd been waiting up for him.

Of course, Gwen didn't seem the least bit upset that her son still hadn't come home when she was getting ready for bed. "Does he usually come home this late?" I asked, trying to sound casual.

"How should *I* know?" She frowned at me. "He's an *adult*. I don't make him call me when he gets back to his apartment."

At that point, I realized I was making a fool of myself and decided to shut the hell up.

Considering how late Noah got home, I'm surprised he woke up so bright and early. But then again, he always was a morning person. That's why he said being a surgeon would suit him. But it didn't work out that way.

"Why don't you go fishing without me?" I suggest to Lily.

"*No.*" Lily shakes my arm. "It won't be any fun without you, Mommy."

Well, that's sweet. I thought with her hero worship of Noah, she wouldn't have minded going with him alone. Glad she hasn't forgotten about her old mom.

Except just when I'm thinking how great my kid is, she adds, "That's what Noah said."

Hmm.

"Also," Lily adds, "he said to wear your bathing suit."

"Is Noah wearing a bathing suit?" I ask.

"He's wearing swim shorts." Lily's eyes are wide. "You can see his robot legs. They're *so* cool!"

This I've got to see.

After I shower, I put on my modest bathing suit and toss a simple blue sundress over it. Noah always told me he liked me in blue, but that's not why I wear the dress. At least, I don't think it is. And that's not why I put on makeup either.

I mean, some days I feel like wearing makeup. Today is one of those days. It's totally unrelated to spending the day with Noah.

Noah is in the living room, showing his fishing equipment to Lily. He's kidding himself—she'll never have the patience for fishing. But what catches my attention is the fact that this is the first time I've seen him in shorts since I've been here. He's sitting, so I can see the calf-sized metal protruding from the legs of his shorts, then the computerized hinge that makes up his knee joint, leading to a slightly widened metallic royal blue shaft that ends with his sneakers. Lily's right—they *do* look pretty cool.

"Finally!" Noah says when he sees me. He pushes his hands against the couch to provide leverage to stand up. "We've been waiting forever for you to be ready, right Lily?"

Lily folds her hands across her chest and nods angrily.

Since the path to Noah's boat isn't paved, he grabs his cane to help him balance. He holds the tackle box in his other hand and puts Lily in charge of holding the fishing pole. "We're going fishing," Lily announces happily.

"And when that gets boring," Noah says, "I'll take us to a place where you guys can swim."

I smile, thinking back to the first time I ever got on a boat with Noah. It was when we were dating about three months. He took me out to Lake Erie and rented a rowboat, then rowed us to a secluded spot where we could go fishing. When he opened his tackle box filled with fishing supplies, I told him it looked like a sewing box. He made a face at me. "You're being really emasculating by calling my tackle box a sewing box," he said.

He showed me a little red ball from his tackle box that really looked like something that should be in a sewing kit. "This is a bobber," he told me. "It floats in the water, which keeps the bait in place and also will tell us if we've got a bite."

He threaded the bobber through the fishing line, then he pulled out a hook. He tied an elaborate knot at the end of the line, before digging out his can of worms that was to serve as bait. I had to look away as he pierced the worm with his fishing hook.

Then we waited.

While we waited, we talked. I'd dated several guys before Noah, but he was the first one that I felt like I could just sit on a boat and talk with for hours on end. It always felt like we never ran out of things to say to one another. I told him things I'd never told anyone before, like my dreams of becoming a famous artist one day and my certainty that it would never, ever happen. And he confessed things to me that I knew were hard for him to talk about. He told me I was the first person he'd ever been able to open up to about his father.

I brought a sketchbook along, and while we talked and fished, I sketched. At first I was drawing the lake and the trees around us. But then I drew Noah. I captured the curve of his lips, his strong jaw, and the shading around his eyes. It was actually a very good likeness.

"You're looking at me funny." Noah squinted at me across the boat. "Like you're studying me."

"I'm drawing you," I told him.

He laughed. "Really? Can I see? Or should I not look?"

"Sure. Take a look."

Noah carefully crossed the boat to sit next to me on a bench barely wide enough for my own hips—it was a snug fit with the two of us. He looked at the drawing and raised his eyebrows.

"Wow," he said. "You really think I'm that good-looking? No wonder you like me."

I rolled my eyes. Noah was just messing with me—he knew how hot he was. He had to when girls were constantly throwing themselves at him. But he only seemed to have eyes for me.

Noah pulled the sketchbook out of my hands and started kissing me. Nobody else was in sight, so I allowed him to slide his fingers up my shirt, under the awkward bulge of my life preserver. Even though we'd been together three months, we still hadn't had sex yet. I was ready.

And right now, on this lonely rowboat in the middle of the lake on a warm spring day, with Noah's arms around me and his lips on mine, I couldn't imagine a more perfect moment for our first time.

"Noah," I breathed in his ear. "Do you have a condom?"

He pulled away, his brow furrowed. "A condom?"

I nodded.

He grinned crookedly. "*This* is when you're asking me for a condom? When we're on a tiny rowboat in the middle of nowhere?"

I shrugged and returned his grin. "The heart wants what it wants."

"It sure does." Noah looked around the expanse of water, frowning. "I don't have a condom, no. And to be honest, I'm scared if we had sex on this boat, we'd capsize and drown."

"Oh."

He picked up the oars from inside the boat. "I'll have us on shore in twenty minutes, and I've got a condom in my car. You hang on, okay?"

I nodded again. So much for fishing.

Noah rowed so quickly that it would have been funny if I wasn't feeling the same urgency as he was.

225

By the time we get back to shore, we were ready to rip each other's clothes off. But Noah had to tie up the boat, and then we had to find a place to park where we wouldn't get arrested for indecent exposure. He drove around for ten minutes, diving deeper into the wilderness, until we pulled onto an empty dirt road that looked like it doesn't see much (or any) traffic. He pulled off to the side just in case. Then he popped the glove compartment.

"Emergency condom," he said, holding up the little square package. He nodded at the backseat. "We'll probably be more comfortable back there."

Once we moved to the backseat, Noah started kissing me far more aggressively than he was in the car. But then he abruptly pulled away from me to gaze into my eyes. "Bailey," he murmured.

"What?" I said.

"I love you," he said. It was the first time he'd ever said it to me. And he said it very solemnly. Like he really, really, really meant it. He later confessed it was the first time he'd ever said that to a girl.

"I love you too," I said. Like him, it was the first time I'd ever said that to a boy. And I really, really, really meant it. I couldn't imagine ever feeling this way about anyone else.

As Noah kissed me, I could only focus on how wonderful it felt. When he tugged down my shorts, he didn't rush a thing. He touched me down there until I shivered with pleasure. When I was dripping wet, he put on the condom, and crawled on top of me.

His eyes stayed with mine the whole time, as he ran his fingers through my hair. He kissed me as he touched me with the tips of his fingers, until it felt like a balloon burst all over my genitals, spilling lovely feelings everywhere. A moment later, he gasped and collapsed on top of me.

"Jesus," I said as I wiped sweat from my forehead. "That was… *wow*…"

"Bailey Chapin," he said in a reprimanding voice. "That wasn't your first orgasm, was it?"

It most certainly was. The one boy I'd been with before Noah was my date on prom night, who had no clue or interest in bringing me to climax—I only slept with him so I wouldn't graduate high school as a virgin. I'd tried touching myself in the past and it always left me cold. I tried reading so-called erotic stories but none of them were able to make me feel half as turned on as when Noah kissed me. He was stimulating nerve endings I didn't even know I had.

"It was," I admitted.

"Wow," he said. "I'm the *man*."

I laughed and kissed him again.

"I love you," I said to him.

"I love you more," he replied with a grin.

———

I'm not sure if I've even been in a motorboat before. I'm a city girl, after all. Since Noah and I broke up, I could probably count the number of times I've walked on grass, much less gone hiking. But I have to say, I love riding in Noah's motorboat. I love the feeling of the wind whipping my hair around my face, the smell of the lake, and the sounds of Lily squealing with delight in the back seat.

When we get to a quiet, isolated spot, Noah pulls out his bucket of worms. This one is basically a container of squirming dirt. Lily is fascinated by it.

"Where'd you get them?" she asks.

"I dug them up myself this morning," he tells her.

Even though the worms are distasteful to me, there's something sexy about the thought of Noah digging up worms from the ground.

"Do you want to put them on the hook yourself?" he asks her.

"Yeah!" Lily says, because even at six, she is far braver than I am.

Noah digs around in the dirt and pulls out a squirming little worm. "The thicker end is the head and that's where you want the hook to go through," he explains.

He hands the worm to Lily, who immediately drops it on the floor. She giggles as he picks it up and she tries again.

"If you hit the head a few times with the hook, that usually gets it to stop moving," he tells her.

It takes a good five minutes, but Lily finally manages to pierce the worm with the hook. Noah threads it through a few more times, then holds the hook up in the air. "Do you want to say a few words in honor of this worm's sacrifice?"

Before I can roll my eyes, Lily calls out, "Yeah!"

"Okay." Noah looks at the worm thoughtfully. "Dear worm, thank you for helping us to catch a fish. We couldn't do it without you. Your sacrifice is much appreciated."

"Amen," Lily adds.

"Amen," Noah agrees.

Oh Lord.

Noah lets Lily try casting off the line, but since she can't get it to go more than a few feet from the boat, he ends up doing it himself. And then it's time to wait. Fortunately, Lily brought a coloring book and I brought my sketch pad. Noah hasn't brought anything, but he seems content to lean back in his seat, listening to the quiet music playing on the boat's radio. Even Lily seems to be enjoying the silence.

"So how was your date last night?" I comment to Noah, after we've been sitting quietly for about fifteen minutes.

He looks up at me in surprise. He seemed to be in some sort of trance, staring at the water. "Oh. Um, it was okay."

Before I can stop myself, I blurt out, "You got back kind of late."

He raises his eyebrows at me. "Not that late."

I glance back at Lily, to see if she's listening. She seems to be very busy coloring in Rapunzel's hair. "It was after midnight."

He chuckles. "So… what? Were you waiting up?"

"I *happened* to be up."

Noah shifts his legs. I see the hinges on his knees moving like computerized machines. "I think it was just after midnight. That's not so late for a date."

I'll have to take his word for it. As Lily pointed out, my social life is not exactly jumping.

I continue sketching, not looking up at him. "So was it a good date?"

He shrugs. "Sure."

Before I can stop myself, I blurt out, "Will you go out with her again?"

"I don't know. Maybe. Why are you so interested?"

My cheeks grow warm. I don't know why I started asking him about his date last night. What's wrong with me? It's like I've reverted to being twenty years old again. This is such an inappropriate conversation.

"Never mind," I say and go back to my drawing. That's another thing about this trip—I haven't done this much sketching since I was in college.

"What are you drawing?" Noah asks me.

I shrug.

He winks. "Is it me?"

I roll my eyes. "Don't be so full of yourself. I'm drawing the lake."

He leans over to take a look at what I'm drawing. He watches me for several minutes, as if fascinated by my sketching.

"You missed your calling," he murmurs.

I shrug again.

Noah jerks his head in Lily's direction. "Also, I don't understand why she's got a coloring book. That's so uncreative. She was so happy when she was drawing in your sketchbook the other night. That's what she ought to be doing."

"She likes coloring books."

"Lily," Noah says. My daughter looks up and smiles. "Don't you want a page from Mommy's sketchbook so you can draw whatever you want?"

"Yeah!" Lily says with so much enthusiasm, you'd think he'd offered her a trip to Disneyland instead of a blank piece of paper.

I rip out a page from my sketchbook and pass it back to Lily. She gets right to work on her drawing. I've never seen her concentrating so hard, except during that bad bout of constipation when she was three. He's right—she does stick her tongue out of the side of her mouth when she's concentrating.

"Look how inspired she is!" Noah says.

Yeah, yeah. She's probably drawing a flower or something like that. He's getting a little overenthusiastic.

After a minute, Lily holds up her paper and declares, "Done!"

Noah plucks the paper from her hands. He studies it for a minute, his brow furrowed. "Wow, Bailey, Lily did a really good job on this picture. She's really talented."

I roll my eyes. "Do you even know what a six-year-old's pictures are supposed to look like?"

"Do *you*?"

"I know better than you do."

I pull the paper out of Noah's hands. It's a drawing of two people who seem to either be holding hands or perhaps are Siamese twins connected at the arm. It's probably the former, because there's a heart between them. And she drew the feet perfectly, just like I showed her the other day.

"What is this?" I ask Lily.

"It's you and Noah out on a date," Lily says.

I nearly choke. I look at Noah, whose blue eyes have gotten really wide.

"Lily," I say carefully. "Noah and I aren't actually going to go out on a date."

Lily screws up her face like she's going to throw a mid-lake tantrum. "Why not?"

"Because," I say. I glance at Noah, who doesn't look like he's going to give me any help on this one. "Noah is already going out on a date with another woman."

"But he doesn't really like her," Lily says. "He said he wasn't even sure he was going to ask her out again."

Oh no. Lily was doing that thing where it seems like she's not listening at all, but really, she is. On Noah's part, he seems to be suppressing a laugh. Ha ha, very funny.

"Lily," Noah says. "Do you want to hear the real truth?"

Lily nods intently. I'm listening carefully too.

"Your mom and I actually did go out," he says to her. "A really long time ago."

"On just one date?" Lily asks.

Noah hesitates. "Maybe two," says the man I nearly married. "Anyway, it turned out that your mom felt we weren't right for each other. So we stopped going out on dates."

Lily's lower lip juts out. "But why didn't Mommy like you? You're much nicer looking than Daddy."

Oh God. Noah can't hold back his laughter anymore. Thanks a lot, Lily.

"Is that so?" he says. "Well, that's really good to know." Then he stage-whispers to me, "Apparently, your ex-husband is really ugly."

I smack Noah in the arm. He looks at me in surprise, maybe because it's the first time I've touched him since I arrived here. I didn't even realize what I was doing—I'm just so used to being touchy-feely with him. It's odd to be sitting here next to him, but not be able to touch him or kiss him.

My life preserver is starting to feel really tight.

"I! Wanna! Go! Swimming!" Lily declares, apparently tired of our reminiscing. "I hate fishing. It's so boring."

"You got it, kid," Noah says. He pulls the fishing line in from the water, then turns back to the steering wheel. He punches his prosthetic leg down on the gas pedal, and we're off again.

Noah finds an area where the water isn't too deep. He says I'll probably be able to stand, but Lily won't. Dad took Lily to the community pool a lot over the summer, so she's actually gotten to be a decent swimmer, but I still make her keep on her life preserver just in case.

Lily splashes around in the water for a bit, happily swimming laps around the boat. I'm not really swimming much—just floating on my back and enjoying the warm water. Noah stays on the boat, leaning back in his seat like he was when we were still fishing.

"Noah!" Lily calls to him. "Come swim with us!"

Noah glances at me. "Uh, I don't know. I think I'm just going to chill on the boat."

"No!" Lily whines. "It's no fun if you don't swim with us. You already got your trunks on!"

He looks like he's struggling with an internal debate. Finally, he says, "Okay."

I quickly figure out why Noah was hesitant to get in the water. It's clear that he can't get his prosthetics submerged in water. So before coming in the water, he has to remove them. I watch him pull up the leg of his right shorts and fiddle with what looks like a little white circle. He grips his upper prosthetic, gives it a yank, and it pops free. He puts his leg down on the floor of the boat, then pulls off what looks like a rubber sock. He repeats the process with his other leg.

This is the closest I've gotten to looking at Noah's bare legs since that day in his bedroom right before I destroyed him. The scars are still there, but very old. The limbs aren't swollen like they were, and the skin hangs loosely around his thigh bone. Before I can look too closely though, he pulls down the legs of his shorts to completely cover his stumps.

He edges to the side of the boat that Lily isn't on, then hoists his butt onto the edge of the boat. I doubt I'd be able to make a move like that without my legs helping me, but he's much, much stronger than I am. Without hesitating, he swings his limbs over the side of the boat, then dives into the water, legs-first. He goes under for a second, then emerges with his hair plastered to his scalp. He shakes his head to clear the water from his face.

"The water's nice, right?" I say.

Lily is too short to stand in this water, and Noah is too without his prosthetics. He hangs on to the side of the boat. "Yeah, it's great. I'm glad I came in."

"Me too," I say.

Noah narrows his eyes at me, but then dives back into the water and starts swimming around the boat.

Noah is a really strong swimmer—I can tell right away. The two of us both liked to swim back in college—it was something we used to do together. I would have thought that the loss of most of his legs would have slowed him down but it hasn't. There's a buoy in the distance, and Noah swims to it and back in no time at all.

"Do you still swim a lot?" I ask him when he returns.

"Five miles three times a week," he tells me, wiping water from his eyes.

I'm embarrassed to admit that the only swimming I do is when I splash around the community pool with Lily. "Way to make me feel out of shape."

He shrugs. "Well, you have a kid. I've got lots of free time."

"Can I swim out to the floaty thing, Mommy?" Lily asks, pointing out at the buoy.

I squint at it. "No, that's too far."

"Noah did it!"

"Yes, but he's an adult, isn't he?"

Lily looks to Noah for support but he shakes his head. "Your mom's right—it's really far." He cocks his head thoughtfully. "But you know what might be fun? If your mom raced me to the buoy."

Lily claps her hands excitedly. "Yes! Race!"

I glare at Noah. "I don't think that's a fair race."

"You're right—it isn't," he says. "Your legs are longer than mine. I should get a head start." He looks at Lily. "But we're only going to race if you get back in the boat first."

"Why?" Lily says.

"Because you can't be out in the water yourself when your mom and I are distracted," he explains. "That's how kids get hurt. I'm a doctor—trust me."

It probably would have taken me two hours to convince Lily to get back in that boat, but when Noah tells her to do it, she scrambles back up there without question right away.

The race is a surprisingly big deal for the next several minutes. We decide Lily is going to do the countdown to our race, which she performs with great relish: "Three… two… one… GO! GO!" And then, "Go, Noah!"

My own daughter isn't even rooting for me.

Noah and I are even for the first several yards, but he quickly manages to overtake me. I see him taking long strokes with his arms, as his stumps intermittently kick in the water. I'm swimming as fast as I can, but I'm really out of practice and my stamina has gotten terrible. After he's gained some distance on me, I can see him intentionally slowing down. It must be painful for him to swim so slowly.

He reaches for the buoy at the same time I do. Noah comes up from the water and I can see the droplets glistening in his eyelashes. "So who won?" he asks.

"I think it was a tie," I say. "Except I'm pretty sure you let me win."

He grins. "You think?"

We float there a minute, and I'm acutely aware of the fact that Noah's bare chest is less than a foot away from mine. He's looking straight at me and

I can't seem to look away. I don't know what's going on here. It's been ten years since we've seen each other, but it feels like we're twenty again and still in love. I feel like I could reach out and touch him, and everything would be back the way it used to be.

And I want it so bad.

"Mommy!" Lily hollers. "Swim back! Race back!"

Noah raises his eyebrows at me. "Shall we?"

I nod, the spell broken. It's not like Noah and I are going to start making out in the middle of a lake in front of my daughter anyway.

We swim around a little more after that, but after another half hour, Lily says that she's tired and we decide to head back. Noah getting out of the water is slightly more of a challenge than getting in—he has to grab on to the edge of the boat so that it tips in his direction, then hoists his body up until his butt is on the side of the boat. Then he swings his legs around so that he can drop down into the driver's seat.

We all dry off with the three fresh beach towels Noah brought along. Lily wraps hers around her like a cape, with only her little face peeking out—she's never as cute as when she's fresh out of a pool or the bath. Noah towels off his short hair quickly, then his muscular upper body, then goes to work more carefully on his stumps. The scars where they removed the rest of his legs look so faded and dimpled compared to what I remember from years ago.

I can't help but notice the way Lily is watching him with fascination. She's seen his prosthetics before, but this is probably the first time she's seen him without them. I hope it's not too weird for her. Then again, Noah can do no wrong in her eyes.

"I think," he says, "that I'm going to need another ten minutes or so to dry off before I try to get my prosthetics back on."

"I want to go back, Mommy," Lily says in a tiny voice.

Noah glances at Lily, then back at me. "Look, Bailey, I can't drive this boat without my prosthetics on. Do you want to do it?"

I look down at the boat's controls in horror. "No. I really don't."

"It's not that hard. It's like driving a car."

"I haven't driven a car in four years."

He sighs. "Okay, I don't want you to get us all killed." He grabs the towel again and goes to work trying to at least get his right leg dry. After a minute, he picks up that rubber sock, and rolls it carefully over his stump to cover it completely. Then he grabs his right prosthetic from the floor and pulls it over the rubber sock. He has to pull himself up into a standing position to pop it into place. He leaves the left one off.

240

The drive back to the harbor is mostly silent. Lily sits in the back, huddled in her towel, and the wind feels colder now that my hair is wet. When we make it back, Lily scrambles to her feet and practically trips in her haste to get out of the boat.

"You coming?" I ask Noah.

He hesitates. "Nah. I think I'm going to see if I can get a little fishing done. Maybe I'll catch something for dinner."

I expect Lily to whine for Noah to come with us, but she doesn't. She can't wait to get back to the cabin, walking as fast as she can go in her little pink sandals. She stays huddled in the towel the whole time, even though it's not that cold. And then when we get back to the cabin, she sits down on the couch in the living room, still huddled in her towel. She doesn't say a word, her little face white. It's odd behavior for Lily. God, I hope she didn't get sick from the water. Or seasick.

I bet she's seasick. I'm probably going to be cleaning up vomit in a minute.

I sit down next to Lily and gingerly put my arm around her narrow shoulders. "Are you okay, sweetie?"

Lily looks up at me. But instead of throwing up, her face crumples and she bursts into tears.

"Lily, what's wrong?" I ask. Not that it takes much for Lily to cry. She's been in tears over getting a

241

SpongeBob Band-Aid instead of a *Frozen* Band-Aid. But this seems different, somehow. She seems genuinely upset.

Lily sniffles and wipes a big glob of snot on the back of her hand, but she doesn't say anything. Apparently, she's going to make me drag this one out of her.

"Lily," I say again, "please tell Mommy what you're upset about. Did you hurt yourself?"

She shakes her head no.

"Do you… feel like you're going to throw up?" (I still feel like it's a good bet.)

But she shakes her head no again. Thank God.

"Is it…" Christ, parenthood is full of so many mind games. "Is it something that happened on the boat?"

Lily nods. Okay, that's progress.

"Did you get water in your nose?"

Another no.

"Does it…" I frown. "Does it have something to do with Noah?"

Lily is quiet. Bingo.

"Sweetie, please tell me," I say. "I promise whatever you say, I won't tell him. I *promise*."

She looks up at me and a fresh wave of tears floods her eyes. "Mommy, what's wrong with Noah's legs?" she says in a teeny tiny voice.

Oh. How did I not figure that one out? I was so busy ogling Noah that it didn't even occur to me how scary it must have been for Lily to see something like that for the very first time. She didn't notice when we were in the water, but when he was drying off, it was right in her face. It sure scared the hell out of me when I first saw it, and I was *twenty*.

"Lily," I say carefully, "I thought you knew that he had those robotic legs."

She wipes snot on her hand again, then wipes it on the sofa. Oh well. "I *knew*, but…"

I get it. She probably thought Noah's real legs were *inside* the robot legs like it was a robotic exoskeleton. Or… who knows? Whatever she'd been imagining, it wasn't those scarred stumps.

Now that I think of it, I bet Noah recognized that Lily was traumatized by what she'd seen. That's why he got us back fast and left us to go fishing.

"Listen, Lily," I say. "Noah… he was in a bad accident many years ago and… and his real legs were badly hurt. So they decided to replace them with the robot legs. You know, like with Luke's hand in *Star Wars*. Or Anakin's hand in *Star Wars*."

I am so glad right now that I introduced Lily to *Star Wars* as it is our only source of reference on amputees.

"But they look…" Lily lowers her eyes. "They look *weird*, Mommy."

243

"Only because you're not used to seeing them," I say. "The first time is always scary, right? I mean, remember how scared you were the first day of kindergarten? And then you ended up loving it!"

"I hate kindergarten, Mommy!" Lily yells. "Ms. Nelson is always mean to us, and she never gives me any stickers to fill up my sticker chart, and she keeps taking my playtime minutes away!"

Oh right.

"Just trust me," I say. "It probably won't scare you as much next time you see it. I mean, they're just legs, right?"

Lily squeezes her hands together in her lap. "Could that happen to me? What if someone took my legs off?"

"It won't happen to you, Lily," I assure her, although it's a lie. After all, who would have thought that my tall, handsome fiancé would end up having both his legs amputated?

Noah doesn't get back for several hours. It's nearly sunset when he comes back into the house with his tackle box, now wearing a pair of old blue jeans to replace his swim trunks. I'm sitting on the couch playing with my phone while Lily is out with my father and Gwen, taking a little hike. Noah plops down next to me on the sofa, smelling like the outdoors.

"So how did you calm down Lily?" he asks me.

"Uh, what do you mean?"

He rolls his eyes. "She was freaked out when I took my prosthetics off. I told you she would be."

"Okay, fine. She was a *little* freaked out." I'm not going to tell him she cried. "But she's over it." I add, "Really.

"That's good," he says. "Because I've been spending far too much time on my prosthetics the last few days, so after dinner, I'm taking them off for the rest of the night."

"She'll be fine." Hopefully she won't cry again.

He nods. "Want a beer?"

"Oh my God, yes."

He gets up and grabs two Millers from the fridge. He hands me mine and then twists the cap off his own beer. He takes a long swig before he drops his head against the sofa. "Tired," he murmurs.

"That's what you get for staying out so late with that woman you didn't even like," I tease him.

He smiles crookedly.

I attempt to open my beer, but the cap isn't budging. All it does is make angry red grooves in my palm. "Is this twist-off?" I ask.

"Didn't you just *see* me twist off my cap?"

I examine my beer. "I think this one is defective."

He winks at me. "Give it here, woman."

I pass my beer to him and he twists it open so easily that even though I'm a woman, it's slightly emasculating. He passes it back to me and I take a long swig. I sigh contentedly. It's nice sitting here next to Noah, drinking beers together. I could do this for hours. Although I'd probably be pretty drunk by that point.

I groan when I hear a knock at the cabin door. "That must be my dad and Gwen with Lily," I say. "They probably forgot the key." Noah starts to get up but I shake my head at him. "I'll open it. You got the beers."

I twist the single lock Noah's got on the door, and throw the door open, bracing myself for Lily to run into my general groin area. But it's not Lily. It's someone completely different. Someone completely unexpected.

It's Theo.

Oh no.

"Theo?" I manage to say.

I can't believe my eyes. What is my ex-husband doing here, two-hundred miles away from his home? He didn't just wander into the neighborhood.

He looks like he's been driving all day based on the circles under his eyes. Theo is five years older than I am—in his late thirties now—and he's starting to look his age. There's a deep groove between his eyebrows and the lines around his eyes are there even when he isn't smiling or laughing. It's probably a reflection of how much he drinks. And the receding hairline doesn't help matters. He's still attractive in a grungy sort of way, but the shit he's pulled with me over the years has completely killed any sexual feelings I might have had for him.

"Hey, Bailey," Theo says. "I came to see Lily."

I know Theo can't see Noah where he's sitting on the couch and I'd like to keep things that way. I want to get rid of Theo quickly. "I told you—we're staying here just for the week, then we'll be back," I say. "You didn't have to drive down here."

"You took Lily here without telling me last weekend," he says. "I was supposed to see her last weekend."

"Well, *you* were supposed to give me a child support check last month," I point out.

"Again, Bailey?" He frowns, his hands squeezing into fists. "You really don't want our daughter to see her own father just because I'm short on funds? You're better than that."

I sigh. "Look, Lily isn't here. She's… out with my father right now."

Theo looks relieved. "You mean you came here with your dad?"

"Yes," I say, aware that it isn't the full truth.

"Oh." Theo grins sheepishly. "I, uh, I guess I assumed you came here with some guy." He ducks his head down. "I guess I got… you know, jealous…"

"Who's that at the door, Bailey?"

Noah has impeccable timing. Just as I'm getting Theo calmed down, the appearance of another man— especially one who looks like Noah—makes my ex-husband's eyes grow wide and fill with fury. Despite how much he's cheated on me, Theo is not good at dealing with his own jealousy.

"Who's *this*, Bailey?" Theo demands to know. "He doesn't look like your *father*."

Noah narrows his eyes at Theo. He steps toward the doorway, a menacing look on his face. "I own this cabin. Who the fuck are you?"

"I'm Bailey's husband," Theo shoots back.

"*Ex*-husband," I correct him.

Theo waves his hand like it's an insignificant distinction. "I can't believe you, Bailey. *This* is the guy

248

you're messing around with? This prettyboy isn't even your type."

Noah just snorts. He already knows he's not my type. The time for him to be bothered by something like that has come and gone. "Listen, why don't you get lost? Bailey obviously doesn't want you here."

Theo grits his teeth. "You gonna make me?"

"I'd be happy to make you." Noah curls his right hand into a very visible fist. He's got a couple of inches on Theo, as well as quite a bit of weight—all muscle. He's really strong, but I've only seen him throw a punch once ever—the night Derek got fresh with me. I doubt he wants to fight now, but he probably recognizes that the threat of it will frighten Theo. And it does.

"Look," Theo says to me, "I don't want any trouble from Abercrombie and Fitch here."

"Abercrombie and Fitch!" Noah bursts out, looking down at his worn, baggy blue jeans and T-shirt I'm pretty sure he's been wearing since college based on the holes at the seams.

"Where's Lily?" Theo presses me.

"I told you, she's out with my father," I say. "I don't know how soon she'll be back."

"I'll wait," he says.

"Not in my house, you're not," says Noah, who's not helping the situation *at all*. "I want you out of my house, and I want that piece of shit car of yours off my property. *Now*."

Noah's still got his hand balled into a fist, so Theo decides to listen to him. He backs away from the doorway, his eyes still on mine.

"Theo," I say quietly. "I promise we'll be back in a few days. I'll bring Lily over to you, okay?"

Theo nods. I'm relieved that it looks like he's going quietly, although you never really know with Theo. He says to me, "And next time, don't bring Lily somewhere without telling me."

"Maybe if you were a half-decent father, you'd know where your daughter is," Noah mutters under his breath.

I can tell Theo hears him, but he decides not to respond. It's probably better for Theo's self-esteem to avoid a pissing contest with Noah. At least, considering he doesn't know about Noah's secret.

Chapter 27

PRESENT DAY

Years ago, Noah tried to show me how to fillet a fish, but I couldn't watch. He teased me about it for days, but then agreed from then on, he'd fillet any fish he caught. At the time, we thought we'd be sharing many fish together. But it didn't work out that way.

Noah fillets the fish he caught today and cooks them up for dinner. Lily eats up every bite, having regained much or all of her hero worship. But I notice that Noah waits until I'm getting Lily in bed at eight o'clock to take off his prosthetics.

After Lily is asleep, I decide to make myself useful by cleaning up the kitchen. I figure the least I can do to pay for a free week in the country is to wash some dishes. I've finished the last of them when Noah wheels into the kitchen. "You don't have to do that," he says to me.

I turn around, wiping my hands on my jeans. "Too late."

This is the first time I've seen Noah sitting in his wheelchair in the light of day. It's very different from the one he'd been sitting in that day I broke his heart in his mother's apartment. It's a narrow, sporty-looking chair with a low backrest and the wheels tilted out at the base. He's put on a pair of shorts and folded the ends over his stumps. He rubs his right leg and winces.

"You okay?" I ask as I settle into a seat at the kitchen table.

He nods. "Yeah. My right limb is… not great. It's all that hardware and shit they put in it before they did the amputation. Phantom pain, muscle pain, bone pain—I've got it all. I wish they had just taken it off to begin with—I would have been better off."

"I guess." Losing both his legs at once would have been a lot to handle.

"The truth is," he says, "even nine or ten hours on the prosthetics is sometimes more than I can handle. Around my apartment, I only use my chair. And I probably do about a quarter of my ER shifts in my chair." He grins. "You should see the look on the patients' faces. Especially the ones who are already drugged out of their minds."

"I'll bet." I watch him rub his right leg again. "You need something for that? Ice?"

He hesitates. "That would be great, actually. There's an ice pack in the freezer."

He's got one of those blue gel ice packs in the freezer. I pull it out and he rests it on the end of his leg. He lets out a sigh. "Okay."

"You shouldn't wear your prosthetics for Lily's sake," I say. "She's okay with whatever. I mean, she's a kid. They can adjust to anything."

"It's not entirely for *Lily*."

His eyes meet mine and I have to look away.

"Well, whatever the reason," I say. "You should do what's comfortable for you."

Noah leans back in his wheelchair. "Okay, good to know." He raises his eyebrows at me. "Ice cream?"

I laugh and grab what's left of the Neapolitan ice cream from the freezer. We don't bother with bowls this time and just eat directly from the container. Noah asks me questions about my job as a social worker and I tell him some of the more interesting stories. I leave out one of the most intense stories I've had in the last year, about the double-amputee client I had who didn't open the door to the house when I knocked, so I circled his house until I found an open window, climbed inside, and discovered the man passed out in his bedroom, toxic from being in kidney failure. I got him to the hospital and he survived, but it was definitely above the call of duty for me—I just had a really bad feeling that something was wrong.

But that guy was old and sick. He'd lost both his legs because of diabetes and he was barely able to take care of himself. I did the best I could to get him home but he didn't have family and ended up in a nursing home.

But I stick to the funny stories, like about the Jamaica client I have who always pulls me into her apartment to serve me a feast when I come to visit. And Noah tells me stories about some of the patients he's had in the emergency room that have me cracking up.

"So it was Christmas Eve," Noah is telling me, "and I'm thinking it's going to be a super quiet shift. I actually went to the call room and got to lie down for twenty minutes before getting paged back to the ER. It's this twenty-year-old girl who came in with her boyfriend with the chief complaint of rectal itch. At eleven o'clock on Christmas Eve, she came to the ER for rectal itch. I asked her how long it was going on and she tells me six months. I was like, you've *got* to be kidding. I was sure there had to be something else going on, like they stuck something inside her during sex that they couldn't get out, and didn't want to admit it because they were embarrassed."

I giggle. "Does that happen a lot?"

He nods. "Oh yeah. All the time."

"Like what sorts of things do they stick up there?" I ask.

"Honestly, it's usually a pencil," he says. "Then a piece of it breaks off and they can't get it out. The worst was a light bulb that broke. *That* was a mess."

I cringe at the idea of a broken light bulb inside my nether regions.

"But this girl was legit," he says. "It turned out she really was just there for a chronic rectal itch. On Christmas Eve!"

I cover my mouth to suppress a laugh because I don't want to wake Lily. I'm mid-laugh when Gwen and my father pass by the kitchen, both of them looking incredibly amused. "We're going to turn in," Gwen says to us, "just wanted to let you know."

"Oh!" I look down at my watch and realize that somehow two hours have flown by. That always seemed to happen when I was talking to Noah. "Um, well, goodnight."

I watch them walk down the hall to their bedroom. Noah leans in and murmurs, "I'm trying not to think about what's going on in there."

"I know," I groan. "I'm happy they've found each other, but… it's my *dad*. I just don't want to picture it."

"It's probably worse for them to picture *us* having sex," he points out.

For a moment, I try to wrap my head around the idea that Lily will have sex someday. I can't do it. I'm not even going to try. It's just not going to happen.

Noah looks down at the empty ice cream carton between us. "Hmm, looks like I'm going to have to buy more ice cream."

"Oh God." I shake my head. "That was pretty full, wasn't it?"

"That's okay," he says. "You can afford it. You look like you've dropped fifteen pounds since college. Don't they still have food in Queens?"

"I've been busy and poor. More of the latter than the former."

Although it isn't entirely funds that's stifled my appetite lately. After all, I've always managed to feed Lily well on a budget. It's more like… my life is so far from what I wanted it to be at this point. It's always on my mind. And I'm the sort of person who stops eating when I'm depressed.

There's a pounding at the front door that makes both of us jump. Noah looks down at his watch. "It's almost eleven o'clock. Who the hell is that?"

"Bailey!" I hear a voice yelling from the other side of the door. "Open up, Bailey!"

Shit, it's Theo. Drunk.

"Don't open the door," Noah says. "I'm going to call the police."

"No, please don't," I say. "He does this sometimes, but… he's harmless. I don't want him to get arrested because of me."

Noah stares at me. "You let him get away with this shit?"

"Look, I'll just…" I stand up from the table. "I'll get rid of him. It's fine. Just don't provoke him and he'll go away."

"Bailey!" Noah yells as I stride over to the front door. But he doesn't know Theo. I do. He needs to be soothed and then he'll go away. He's never been physically violent with me—he's never hit me. He's not that kind of person.

I throw open the front door and Theo is standing there, his long hair and clothing disheveled. He smells like beer. Obviously he's been drinking and it occurs to me now that he must have driven here drunk. The thought of it makes my stomach turn.

"Bailey." He sways in my direction, and I take a step back. "We need to talk."

"We can talk tomorrow," I say calmly. "When you haven't been drinking."

"All I had is two beers," Theo says. Ha.

"I told you," I say. "Go get a hotel and sleep it off, and we'll talk tomorrow. I'll call a cab."

I try to lead him out to the patio, but he won't budge. "I want to talk to you *now*," he insists. He takes a deep breath. "Bailey, this whole thing is fucked up. You going off to Maryland without me. Fucking some loser jock. This isn't right."

"Okay." I'm still trying to keep my calm. At least Theo isn't shouting. "I promise you, we'll talk about all that tomorrow."

Theo is swaying at the door, but he's still not budging. I wrack my brain, trying to think what I can do to get him out of here when Noah wheels up to us, his blue eyes full of rage. "Listen, buddy," he says. "Bailey's asking you nicely to go. You need to leave."

Theo looks down at Noah. I can see his drunken brain trying to process that the fit young guy he saw earlier is now sitting in a wheelchair. He takes in Noah's lack of legs, his eyes slowly widening.

"Holy shit," Theo says. "You're that asshole from earlier who's sleeping with my wife." He looks up at me. "Bailey, you're really fucking *him*?"

"I'm not fucking *anyone*," I say, which is the painful truth. "His mother is marrying my father, and that's why I've been staying here this week. So we can all get to know each other."

"Jesus Christ…" Theo looks between the two of us for a moment, then bursts out laughing. "Oh man, I really thought that you were fucking a guy with no legs, Bailey. I was out of my mind with jealousy… over *him*."

I can see Noah's eyes darken, but he backs away from us and doesn't say a word. I'm itching to defend Noah, but there's no point. Theo is drunk. I can't talk to him when he's like this. The best thing to do is get him in a cab and send him to a cheap motel to spend the night.

"Now that we've got that sorted out," I say, "I'm going to call you that cab."

At first it seems like he might go willingly, but then Theo shakes his head. "No, Bailey. Look, this whole thing has made me realize I still have feelings for you. I'm not ready for our marriage to be over."

"Our marriage *is* over," I point out. "We're divorced."

Theo reaches out to take my hand, but I pull away. "Come on, Bailey. I know you still have feelings for me too. And we've got Lily to think about."

He must be drunker than I thought if he really thinks I'd consider taking him back after all the shit he put me through. This is just what I want—a husband who can't pay the bills, who gets drunk every weekend, who *drives* drunk, who leaves me hanging on a moment's notice. There was a time when I might have forgiven Theo, when I might have believed he could reform, but not now. It's far too late.

"I'm sorry, Theo," I say. "I really need you to leave."

This is the time when Theo usually takes off to find another girl he can hook up with, but right now, he isn't budging. Maybe because out here, he doesn't have his usual list of ladies lined up to take my place. Or maybe he really has had a change of heart about us. Either way, I want him out of here.

"Bailey…" He tries to take my hand again, but when I pull away, he grabs my arm instead. "Please, let's just talk about this."

I try to shrug him off, but he's got a death grip. Noah's been quiet in the background, letting me deal with this, but when he sees Theo touching me, he wheels right up to us. He keeps his fists on his wheels.

"You need to let go of her right now," Noah growls. "And then get off my property."

Theo blinks at Noah as if he'd forgotten he was there. "Excuse me, but this is my wife, and I'll do whatever I want."

"*Ex*-wife," I correct him as I successfully twist my arm out of his grasp.

Noah wheels closer, right up to Theo. "Get out. *Now*."

My heart is thudding in my chest. I can't believe this is happening. I'm sure if Theo were sober or Noah had his prosthetics on, Theo would be doing the logical thing and making himself scarce. But he's still not budging.

"Fuck off," Theo spits at Noah. "This is none of your business, man."

"It's happening in my house, so it's my business," Noah retorts.

"Don't make me hit a guy in a wheelchair," Theo says. "Because you're being an asshole right now."

Noah snorts. "Yeah, like *you'd* have any chance of taking me down."

I've never seen Theo throw a punch before, but there have been a couple of times he's come home

260

bruised and bloody after a fight broke out at a bar. Somewhere he'd been playing a set or maybe somewhere he'd been hanging out. I never saw the other guy, but Theo always looked bad. I got the sense he wasn't excited about starting fights.

But he must have had more to drink than I thought, because Theo's fist flies through the air, aimed at Noah. Noah doesn't seem the least bit surprised, and he's ready for it. He catches Theo's fist easily in his left hand, pulls him forward, and buries his fist in Theo's gut. Theo doubles over, gasping for air. I remember Noah hit that guy Derek the same way, but it looks like he hit Theo a lot harder. Theo actually crumbles to the ground, clutching his belly.

"If you get out of here now," Noah says, "I'll spare you the humiliation of getting your ass kicked in front of Bailey."

Theo looks up at Noah with watery eyes. He looks back at me, as if in appeal, but I just shake my head. I watch as he literally crawls back out the front door. He limps out to his car and climbs inside, and that's when Noah slams the front door shut.

"I'm calling the cops," he says. "He's drunk and I don't want him driving around here."

There's no point in pleading Theo's case. I don't want Theo driving around drunk either.

Noah makes the call while I go sit on the sofa, trying to process what just happened. My hands

261

won't stop shaking. I look at my arm where Theo was grabbing me, and I could see red marks he left behind.

"I wanted to fucking *kill* him." Noah wheels up in front of me. I can still see the anger in his eyes. "It took a lot of self-restraint to let him walk out of here."

I lift my own eyes to look at Noah. "Thanks for helping me."

"No problem," he says. "I always do, don't I?"

We stare at each other. It's like the moment earlier today in the water, but now we're alone, with nobody watching us. I'm not sure who leans forward first, but a second later, my lips are pressed against Noah's, and his arms are around me pulling me closer to him. It's been ten years since I kissed Noah Walsh, but it almost feels like not even a day has passed. It's like coming home.

"I missed you so much," I whisper when we separate briefly for air.

Noah doesn't say he missed me too. He just kisses me again, which is also nice. In the ten years since we broke up, I've never met a guy who could kiss like Noah. Not even Theo could compare.

"Hang on," Noah says as we separate again. "Let me get on the couch."

He puts his fist on the couch, and transfers his body over in one quick movement. He smooths out his shorts over his stumps then we go back to kissing again. My fingers slide under his T-shirt, feeling the smooth skin on his back, and I can feel him fumbling with the hook on my bra. This is getting steamy really fast.

As Noah shifts, I feel the stump of his leg poke me in my own leg. It startles me, and I pull away from him. I look down at his leg that just poked me.

"What's wrong?" he says.

"Nothing," I say quickly.

But he figures out what just happened. He looks down at the remains of his legs, then back up at my face. "You don't have to do this, Bailey. I know you're grateful but…"

"I *want* to do this," I say. I try to take his hand in mine, but he pulls away.

"We both know how you really feel," he reminds me. "You made it really clear ten years ago, didn't you? So… let's just… pretend this didn't happen."

I grit my teeth. "Noah, please stop it. I wouldn't be kissing you if I didn't want to."

"You can see why I find that hard to believe."

"I don't, actually." I frown at him. "Everything that happened… that was… well, you know… that was a long time ago. I was still in shock. You said yourself that most women are… okay with it."

"Are you kidding me?" His voice raises several notches and I'm starting to worry that Gwen and my

263

father might hear him. "You think most women are okay with me *not having legs*? I was *exaggerating*. Most women flip their shit when they find out."

"Well, what about that woman you went out with last night?" I say.

He shakes his head at me. "Yeah, that was great. An awkward dinner, then she wouldn't even kiss me good night. I drove around for two hours after, feeling like shit—that's why I got home so late."

"Noah…" I reach out to touch his shoulder but he swats me away.

"Please," he says. "The last thing I want is your pity." He rakes a hand through his short, dark blond hair. "Look, it's not your fault. I'm not mad at you anymore. This is just… the situation."

He leans over to transfer back into his wheelchair. I watch the muscles in his chest and arms tighten as he lifts his entire body, and *my* whole body tingles. God, he's freaking sexy. How could he accuse me of not wanting him?

Well, aside from the fact that I snuck out of his apartment ten years ago, leaving behind my engagement ring. But that's not fair. I was still in shock about the whole thing then, and I was dealing with my mother's illness. And I was a *kid*. It was a lot for me to deal with. If it happened now, I never would have behaved that way.

"I swear to you, Noah," I say. "I'm not faking anything."

He shakes his head at me. "Stop. Please. I mean it."

He pushes his palms against the wheels of his chair until he's left the room. I want to burst into tears with frustration. As much as I want him, there's nothing I can say to convince him of that.

Chapter 28
PRESENT DAY

Even though I'm on vacation this week, it's hard to take a break from my work. I've got a lot of clients, and the truth is, I think of a lot of them as friends. Or even family. Just because I'm in Maryland this week, it doesn't mean my clients' problems have taken a week off.

So while Lily is getting breakfast, I start making calls. First I call Keisha Robinson, who recently aged out of foster care and then found herself knocked up two months ago by an irresponsible jerk (I can relate). Next I call Linda Green, who isn't technically my client—her elderly mother is. Linda tells me how she went to visit her mother with food and found her cleaning her house—completely naked.

"Do you think that means she needs to go to a nursing home?" Linda asks me.

I can't tell Linda the answer to that one. I assure her that as soon as I return home, we can look into a few independent living facilities. In the meantime, as long as Mrs. Green keeps the nakedness confined to her home, it's okay.

My final call is to my current favorite client, Luke Collins. Luke was at a college graduation party when he dived into a swimming pool headfirst and broke his neck. As a result, he is paralyzed from the neck down, left only with a little movement in his upper arms. He spent a big chunk of time in rehab, where he learned to do basic things like feed himself and operate a power wheelchair, but nine months later, he's still dependent for bathing, dressing, and getting in and out of bed, and he always will be.

Luke's father died when he was young, so he's been staying with his mother since his injury. They've been struggling to get services for Luke, so his mother is helping him with absolutely everything. The situation is a disaster. The last time I visited their house, his mother was disheveled with huge bags under her eyes—I insisted she go relax while I cleaned the kitchen and made lunch for Luke. I'm worried that if they don't get help soon, it's only a matter of time before she cracks.

After four rings, I hear Luke's voice on the other line: "Hey, Bailey."

"Hi!" I say brightly. "How's it going?"

There's a long silence on the other line. "Been better."

"Is it your mother?" I ask.

"No, Mom's fine." He lets out a long sigh. "Hannah came by yesterday…"

I cringe. Hannah is Luke's girlfriend of three years—they dated nearly all through college. Before his accident, they had been discussing marriage. The parallels to my own situation have not escaped me, especially when Luke expressed frustration at how infrequently Hannah had been visiting him lately.

"How is she doing?" I ask.

"She dumped me."

I saw it coming as much as Luke probably did. I'd met Hannah on one occasion, and it was clear how uncomfortable she was with everything. She cringed visibly when Luke asked for her help with even the most simple things, like when he was struggling to get a splint on his hand so he could feed himself. I could see Hannah wasn't adjusting well to her boyfriend's situation.

Believe me, the parallels to my own situation didn't escape me.

"Oh, Luke," I murmur. "I'm really sorry. That sucks."

"Yeah," he sighs. He's a good kid. Before this happened, he had planned to go to grad school to become an archeologist. *I wanted to be Indiana Jones.* Now he's rethinking all his life plans. "It was inevitable though. She couldn't deal with it."

"Yes," I say, "although she's been there for you for nine months. That's worth something."

"Is it?" he snorts. "You met her, Bailey. Whenever she visited, it was like she couldn't wait to leave."

I wince. I'm sure ten years ago, Noah could have said the exact same thing about me. And just like Hannah, I bailed on him when he needed me.

"She probably just needs time," I tell him. "In another few years... who knows?"

"No." I can hear the hurt he's feeling. "You didn't see her face. It's over. For good." And then his voice breaks. "I can't even blame her. I can't imagine a girl being attracted to me like this."

I grip the phone tighter. It was just what Noah said when I asked for a break all those years ago. "Don't say that, Luke."

"What are you talking about?" His hurt is quickly morphing into anger. "I need my *mom* to help me take a fucking *shower*. What chance do I have of any kind of serious relationship?"

"It's not always going to be that way," I remind him. "We're setting up services for you—"

"I'll always need help though."

I can't argue with him there. Maybe it won't always be his mother bathing him, but he'll never be able to do it by himself.

"Can I talk to your mother, Luke?"

"She's busy."

"I can call her on her cell phone..."

He lets out a long breath. "I don't want you to worry her more than she already is, Bailey. Please. I'll be okay. Promise."

Of course, the person I really want to talk to isn't Luke's mother—it's Hannah. I want to shake her by the shoulders and tell her she's making a huge mistake. She might be giving up because it's hard right now, but if she loves him, she needs to stick around. Because if she doesn't, she'll regret it forever.

Things are quiet today, like we were all drinking too much and now we've got a collective hangover. I stay in the bedroom as long as possible, and when I come out, Lily is playing on the floor of the living room. I glance out the window and see Noah is sitting on the patio in his wheelchair, reading a book.

"Did Noah say anything to you before he went out?" I ask Lily.

She shrugs. "I told him I wanted to go explore, but he said that I should ask you. He said he was too tired."

Too tired. Noah has had boundless energy during this trip, but suddenly he's tired.

"Okay," I say. "Go put on your sneakers and we'll go explore together."

We both put on unintentionally matching outfits of blue jean shorts and light purple shirts. Now I've become one of those women who dresses her kid just like herself. I hate women like that.

When Noah sees how the two of us are dressed, a flicker of amusement flitters across his face, but it quickly fades. He goes back to the book he's reading, which isn't even a real book. It's something medical.

"We're going for a walk," I tell him.

He puts the book down on his lap and hesitates, his hands on the wheels of his chair, like he's thinking about going with us. "Don't go too far down the right bank of the river. There's poison ivy down there."

Poison ivy? What the hell? I didn't know that was a possibility around here.

"Um, okay, we'll just go to the left," I say, scratching subconsciously at my calf.

His brow furrows. "You know what poison ivy looks like, right?"

I stare at him blankly. What in our history would lead him to believe I know what poison ivy looks like?

Noah sighs. "They're usually green this time of year and they look a lot like oak leaves." Whatever those look like. "They usually have three broad leaves."

"Leaves of three, let it be!" Lily bursts out.

I laugh. "Where did you learn that?"

"Noah taught me the other day," she says in a way that makes me feel silly for having asked, as if there was any other way she could obtain information. "Noah, are you coming with us?"

It looks like she's over the trauma of seeing him without his prosthetics on. She doesn't seem at all bothered by the sight of his abbreviated thighs underneath his shorts.

"Uh, I think I'm going to pass," Noah says.

"But if you come, then if I get tired, you can give me a ride on your chair," she points out.

That comment makes Noah smile. "I think your mom is going to have to carry you."

Yeah, right. Lily weighs over fifty pounds—I can barely lift her, much less carry her any meaningful distance. He must think I'm somebody who swims five miles three times a week. And God knows what else he does the rest of the week.

I head off with Lily in the direction of the lake. I figure if we follow the bank, then we're less likely to be lost forever. I head to the left (he said *left*, right?) so that we avoid the poison ivy. I'm hoping Lily doesn't ask me to identify any insects or plants or anything natural. If she does, I'll have to make it up. Most bugs are beetles anyway, right?

When we get to the lake, I pick up a flat stone. "You know, you can skim stones along the water."

"What's skimming stones?" Lily asks.

During my junior year of college, Noah drove us out to a lake for a picnic and that's where he showed me how to skim a stone. "I can't believe you're twenty years old and you've never done this before," he said.

"So teach me," I said.

"The trick is to pick the perfect stone. It should be as flat, smooth, and circular as possible."

We searched on the shore to find the perfect stone. He rejected three of my choices as "ridiculous" before approving the fourth stone.

"Now you want your throw to be low—as close to parallel with the water as you can get without actually being parallel," he said. He demonstrated as he tossed his stone at the water and it bounced five times before sinking. "And you've got to have spin on it."

Getting a stone to skip along the water ended up being even harder than picking the perfect stone. I tried stone after stone, but each of them hit the water and sank. When I finally got one to skim the water, I was jumping around and yelling like an idiot. Noah laughed and kissed me until I forgot all about those stupid stones. Until today.

"So you've got to pick a stone that's flat and round," I tell Lily, as Noah told me.

"Like this?" She holds up a giant rock.

"No," I say patiently. I sift along the stones by the water until I find one that looks appropriate. "Flat and round and not too big. Like this."

I bend down to be level with the water and toss the stone. It sinks immediately. Damn it.

"What's it supposed to do?" Lily asks.

"It's supposed to bounce."

"It didn't do that."

"Yes, I *know*."

274

I try again with another half dozen stones until Lily gets bored. "You're really bad at this, Mommy," she says. Thanks, sweetie.

We walk along the water and point out the boats going by. Lily is skipping along the water, swinging her arms next to her. "I hope we get to go out on the boat again," she comments.

"Me too," I say, "but I'm not sure we will."

"How come?"

I think of the look on Noah's face last night when I jerked away from him. Why did I do that? I was just startled—it was an automatic reaction. "I don't know. We have to go back home soon."

Lily frowns in disappointment, but goes back to skipping. I wish I could live in the moment the way she does. That's the best thing about kids. They can be devastated about something in one minute, then forget all about it the next. Adults can't do that. I can't stop thinking about how Noah feels about me. I can't just enjoy this beautiful day with my daughter, even though I'm trying.

Lily is skipping along when I see her foot catch on a rock. She quickly goes sprawling across the sand. Of course, she's still small enough that she can fall without significant injury. But she's on the floor wailing like somebody just stabbed her.

"It huuuuuurrrrrrts, Mommy!" she sobs as she clutches her leg.

"It's okay." I give her a hug, but then I notice that my hand comes away dark red. That's when I noticed the dark red rivulets dripping down my daughter's shin. Oh my God, Lily is bleeding. A lot. "You scraped yourself?"

"That rock cut me!" Lily glares at the offending rock.

Lily is clutching her injured knee protectively. I know that I should take a look at it, but she won't let me, and the truth is, it's probably for the best. I'm just as squeamish as I ever was. I need to keep my wits about me to get the two of us home.

Thankfully, we haven't gone far. I can still see the cabin from where we're crouched on the ground. But I have a bad feeling Lily can't walk. I'm going to have to carry her.

"All right." I brace myself. "Lily, grab onto my neck."

She holds onto my neck and I heave her butt into the air. She's clinging to me, so that's making it easier to carry her. I just need to try not to think about all the blood dripping down her leg and likely staining my jean shorts.

The first two minutes of carrying Lily aren't so bad. The next two minutes are uncomfortable. The rest of the way is complete agony. I am so out of shape. By the time I get to the cabin, Lily might as well weigh a thousand pounds. My arms are rubber.

I see Noah has put his prosthetics on and he's climbing into his car. If he drives away, I'm toast. "Noah!" I yell.

He hears me, thank God. I let Lily slip out of my arms just as he's walking over. I see his eyes widen at the sight of her bleeding right leg.

"That was quite a nature walk," he comments.

Lily bursts into tears all over again. "It hurts so much!" she wails.

Noah looks like he's contemplating picking her up but decides against it. He reaches out his hand to hers and she takes it. "Let's get in the house," he says. "I've got my first aid kit and I'll get you patched up."

Noah and his first aid kits. They do come in handy an awful lot, though.

Lily limps into the house and sits down on the sofa. She's still got her hand covering her right knee protectively. Noah sits down on the couch beside her with his box of supplies.

"Lily," he says gently. "I know it's hurting a lot, but I've got to see it. I promise I'll get the whole thing bandaged up and it won't hurt anymore."

Her lower lip trembles, but she very, very slowly removes her hand from her right knee. And oh my God, it looks bad. I knew it was bleeding a lot, but I didn't expect a gash like that. It's so big and bloody and...

"Oh shit!" I hear Noah yell. I feel his arms catching me seconds before I hit the floor. I don't entirely pass out, but my legs feel as rubbery as my arms and I can't see because of all the spots in front of my eyes. He lowers me carefully onto the couch beside him and I lean my head against the pillows. After a second, my vision seems to clear but I still feel dizzy.

Noah looks between the two of us. "I don't know who to treat first."

"I'm fine," I say, feeling extremely foolish. "Help Lily."

I listen to him talking to her gently as he patches up her knee. They must love him in the ER—he's so kind and patient with her. I hear him telling her that she doesn't need stitches (thank God) and assuring her that the bleeding is already stopping. He applies some antiseptic ointment and then puts on a bandage.

"All better!" Noah declares.

I manage to sit up enough to see Lily beaming at him. She hops off the couch and skips off to her room, apparently entirely healed. That's what I'm talking about—living in the moment.

Noah turns to look at me. "And how's Mommy doing?"

"I'll be fine."

He raises his eyebrows at me. "I thought you'd have outgrown that by now."

I glare at him. "Well, I haven't."

"Well," he says, "it sure brought back memories."

We look at each other. I start to lean forward as if to kiss him, but he shakes his head and pulls away.

I bite my lip. "Thank you for your help with Lily."

He nods. "It's fine." He glances at the door. "I'm going out for a while."

"Noah…"

"I'll see you later." He rises to his feet, no longer looking at me. "I'll get more ice cream, okay?"

"Okay," I say in a small voice.

And then he's gone.

Chapter 30
PRESENT DAY

At around three in the afternoon, my ears perk up when I hear a key turning in the lock to the front door, but it turns out it's only Gwen and my father. They come in looking flushed and happy. Don't get me wrong—I'm thrilled my father is in love, even if it sometimes makes me feel that the memory of my mother is being pushed into the background. It also makes me long for what he has. I can't remember the last time I've been that hopelessly in love.

Well, that's not true. I can remember.

"How's my girl enjoying her week in the country?" Dad asks Lily, who is drawing at the kitchen table with my extra sketch pad. I offered her the coloring book, but she insisted that she wanted to be creative again like Noah told her to be. He's making quite the impression on both of us.

"Okay, Grandpa," Lily says.

"Do you want to go for a walk?" he asks.

Lily's eyes widen and she puts down her green crayon. "Mommy and I went for a walk earlier and guess what happened? I got a huge cut on my knee." She shows him her bandaged knee. "And Noah gave me aids."

"*What*?" Dad coughs.

"First aid, Dad." I roll my eyes. "He gave her first aid."

"Oh." He smiles awkwardly. "Well, how about we go out again? You can't get tired of all this fresh air, can you?"

Lily looks like she might refuse. I'm hoping she does, because if Lily and Dad leave, then I'll be alone here with Gwen. Gwen, whose son I dumped right after he'd lost his legs. Gwen, who has been taking jabs at me all week. She certainly hasn't made it a secret I'm not her favorite person.

But of course, Lily agrees to go out with my father on the condition that they're "very, very careful," whatever that means. I don't even have a minute to prepare a graceful exit before the two of them are gone.

And now Gwen and I are alone.

Gwen is sitting on the sofa, peering at me over the edge of her paperback novel, her blue eyes unreadable. She's got to hate me—she'd have every right. I can't believe this woman is going to be my stepmother. That's not going to be awkward *at all*. Best possible scenario: I run out of the room screaming, "You'll never be my real mother!"

"What are you reading, Bailey?" Gwen asks me as she sets her own book down on her lap.

"Nothing special," I mumble, dog-earing a page in my book. It's a one of those beach reads about the problems of people with so much more money than I'll ever have. I'd rather be sketching. Or really, be anywhere but here. Why didn't I go with Lily and my father on their walk? So what if they didn't invite me?

Gwen eyes me across the room, her brow creased. My stomach flip-flops. Now that we're alone together, she can say whatever she wants to me without any witnesses. She can tell me what a horrible person I am. She can say all the things she's been thinking to herself for the last decade.

"So," Gwen finally says. I take a deep breath, bracing myself. "Did you and Noah end up kissing last night?"

I nearly choke. That was *not* what I expected her to say. "Ex… excuse me?"

The stern expression is gone. A smile plays on her lips that actually reminds me a lot of Noah. "You think I haven't seen how the two of you have been looking at each other the last few days?"

Based on how hot my cheeks feel, they must be crimson. "I don't know what you mean," I mumble.

"Come on, Bailey," she says. "I'm not blind."

I toy with one of the pages of my book. "You… you know what happened between us all those years ago. I mean, you of all people…"

The lines deepen on Gwen's face. "Yes, I know. That was… hard for him." She sits down next to me on the couch. "He cried that day. He's not a crier…

he didn't cry when the doctor first broke the news to him over what happened to his legs. In fact, the day you left was the only time I've seen him cry in the last twenty years."

Wow. Way to make me feel horrible all over again.

"But he didn't see what had been going on all along," Gwen says. "You were there for him during those first few difficult months, and I know how hard that was for you. You turned green every time you walked into the hospital. And you were just a kid back then. Of course you were panicked and scared."

I lower my eyes. "I broke up with him right after the surgery though."

"Well, I won't lie and say that didn't do a number on his head. He was convinced he'd be alone forever. Honestly, we both really hated you for a while." She shakes her head. "But that was silly because... well, you know Noah. Women love him. Legs or no legs."

"That's not what he told me last night."

Gwen sighs. "Oh, what sob story was he feeding you? It isn't true. At all. Let me tell you, Bailey, a few months ago, he broke up with a woman he'd been seeing for two years. The only bad thing he could say about her was, 'I didn't like her as much as I liked Bailey.' He's got this idea in his head of the perfect relationship and it all comes from what he had with you. I got so frustrated with him because he still thought about you so much, even though…"

I don't know what to say, partially because I feel the same way. I married Theo because he was the complete opposite of Noah, but I never felt half as strongly for him. Noah was my great love. And I blew it.

Gwen pats my leg. "Anyway, hopefully you and I can put the past behind us. Whatever else happens, your father and I would love for Lily to be the flower girl at our wedding."

I smile at Gwen. "She would love that. Thank you."

Gwen smiles back and goes off to her bedroom, leaving me alone with my thoughts.

———

I wake up in the middle of the night in agony.

Lily's feet are in my face, so there's that. But also, a muscle in my neck has gone into horrible spasm. I literally cannot turn my head to the right without pain so bad that I see stars. It's knife-through-the-skin kind of pain.

I look at my watch. Three in the morning. Great.

I don't know what to do. I don't know if I've ever experienced pain this horrible before. Yes, I've experienced childbirth, but to be honest, that wasn't that bad. I had a C-section and couldn't feel my lower body the whole time.

I sit up in bed, hoping if I reposition, I might feel better. I don't. My neck is still extremely painful. It's so bad, I want to throw up.

I get out of bed and walk around the cabin. I can't see any way I'll be able to sleep with this going on. Maybe I need to go to the hospital.

When I'm by the door to Noah's bedroom, I pause. It's three in the morning and it would be really rude to wake him up. He was friendly to me today, but subdued. There was no flirting or teasing like there had been before our kiss. But every time I've ever been hurting or in pain, Noah has helped me. And he *is* a doctor.

Before I can stop myself, I'm knocking on his door.

After a few seconds, I hear him call, "Yeah?"

"It's Bailey. Can I come in?"

When he answers in the affirmative, I enter his room. I see him fumbling with the lamp next to his bed, and when it turns on and I can see him more clearly, it's a rush of déjà vu. I've seen Noah hundreds of times in the middle of the night looking just like this—eyes bleary with sleep, hair tousled, wearing an old, wrinkled T-shirt. But just like in the hospital, I can see that the blankets now end abruptly where his legs were cut off.

"What's wrong?" Noah asks, pushing himself up into a sitting position. "Everything okay with Lily?"

"No, it's…" I wince with pain. "My neck. It's killing me."

"Well, you did carry a fifty-pound kid all the way from the lake," he points out. "And you're not really in shape."

I glare at him. "Gee, thanks."

"Just saying…"

I rub at my sore neck. "It really hurts, Noah. Like, a lot. I can't even move my head."

"Okay." He pulls the covers off and I can see that he's wearing just his boxers below the belt. He scoots to the edge of the bed. "Let Dr. Walsh have a look."

I sit down next to him on the bed, partially turned to face him. He places his fingers gently on the place where my neck meets my shoulder and I practically scream with pain. He raises his eyebrows. "I guess I don't have to ask if that's tender."

My eyes are tearing up. "God, it hurts *so much*."

"Can you rotate your head?" he asks.

He demonstrates the normal way a person should be able to move their head forward, backward and to the sides. All the directions hurt a little, but when I try to turn my head to the right, it literally feels like I'm being stabbed with a thousand knives.

"What's *wrong* with me?" I wipe my eyes, which are now actively watering from pain.

286

"Your upper trapezius is in spasm," he explains. "Muscle spasms can be extremely painful and debilitating."

"So what do I do?"

He hesitates. "I've got a muscle relaxant you can take. It's… mine. And I've got some ibuprofen in the bathroom."

Noah digs around in the dresser next to his bed and pulls out a small bottle of pills. He shakes one out and hands it to me.

"Just one?" I ask.

He shakes the bottle. "You've never had this before. One is going to knock you out, okay? We don't need to put you in a coma." He jerks his head in the direction of the bathroom. "There's ibuprofen in the medicine cabinet. They're regular strength, so take four of them."

"Four?" I say. "Isn't that a lot?"

Noah gives me a look. "Are you intentionally trying to question everything I tell you to do? Who's the doctor here who sees twenty-thousand people with neck and back pain every year?"

Fair enough. I go to the bathroom, where I swallow the muscle relaxant, along with four tablets from his bottle of ibuprofen, even though the instructions say *very clearly* not to take more than two at a time. While in the bathroom, I notice that my hair is sticking up everywhere in an excellent

287

impression of the Bride of Frankenstein. Oh well. I don't even care anymore—I just want the pain to go away.

I come back to Noah's room. He's sitting up in bed, waiting for me. I sit down beside him. "It still hurts," I report.

"Well, what do you expect? You swallowed those pills one minute ago. It's not like I injected them directly into your vein."

"This sucks," I mumble. "It just hurts so much."

Noah looks at me for a minute. Finally, he says, "Turn around."

I turn to the side so that my back is facing him. After a moment, I feel his fingers on my shoulders. He's not applying any real pressure, but gently rubbing the area. At first it's uncomfortable, but as he slowly and patiently works his way deeper, my muscles start to melt.

"Wow, this really helps," I comment. "Is this what you do for patients?"

"Patients?" He laughs. "No, not patients. Not if I want to keep my medical license."

I don't know if it's the medications or the massage, but the pain has eased up considerably. Enough that I can pull away and turn back to face him again. "Thank you for that," I say. I reach over and put my hand on top of his.

288

Noah gives me a wary look. I smile at him, but suddenly, I feel incredibly sleepy. I mean, *really* sleepy. So tired that I lie down on Noah's bed, resting my head on his pillow, without even asking if it's okay.

"Um," Noah says. "What do you think you're doing?"

"I'm sleepy."

God, I'm tired. I don't think I've ever felt this tired before.

"Well," he says, "maybe you should go back to your bedroom."

I should. I definitely should. But damn, am I tired.

"Bailey?"

I shut my eyes for just a second, enjoying the softness of Noah's bed. His bed is so soft and comfy. It's like five times more comfy than my bed. Maybe ten times more.

"Bailey." I feel him shaking my shoulder. "I think the muscle relaxant I gave you is knocking you out. I probably shouldn't have given you the whole pill."

"I love the whole pill."

He rolls his eyes. "I'm sure you do. Listen, you've got to go back to your room."

Back to my room! He's crazy! How can I go back to my room when I can't even lift my head? And I'm not kidding. I literally cannot lift my head. It must weigh a thousand pounds. How do people walk around all day with their heads on their shoulders when heads are so heavy? The head should be on the feet. That would make so much more sense.

"Too tired," I mumble into the pillow.

"I know you're tired, but you can't spend the night in my bed."

"Why not?"

Noah looks frustrated. He's got that pouty look on his face that he always gets when he's frustrated. He's so freaking cute right now. How did I ever let go of someone this cute?

"Our parents wake up really early," he reminds me. "If you spend the night here, they're going to know it. And Lily will probably wake up and be freaked out that you're gone."

"Don't care," I tell the pillow.

Do I care? My father finding out I just slept with his fiancée's son seems like something I would care about. Except I really don't. All I care about is never moving from this glorious bed. I want to live here. Lily will have to have her wedding in this room because I will never leave this bed. This is the best bed there ever was. And I am sooooo tired.

"Bailey…" Noah drops his head down to the pillow so he can look me in the eyes. He has such gosh-darn nice blue eyes. So nice. God, I miss him. "Please get up. Come on."

How could I have walked out on him? What was I thinking? There's nobody out there like Noah. Nobody. I could look a million years and he'd be the only one.

How could he have though I didn't find him sexy? He's just as sexy now as he ever was. And I'm going to prove to him I think so.

My right arm feels like it weighs close to as much as my head, although maybe only five-hundred pounds. It feels like I'm moving through molasses but I manage to get my right hand on the bare end of one of Noah's stumps. I place my palm firmly on top of it, and then I knead my fingers into the loose skin.

"Whoa!" Now it's Noah who jerks away from me. Ha, what a hypocrite! He struggles to sit up in bed, then does his best to cover the ends of his stumps with his boxers, even though they're not quite long enough. "What are you *doing*?"

I giggle sleepily. "What? I'm proving to you that I think you're sexy."

He shakes his head at me. "You really don't have to do that."

"But I do," I murmur. "I do. I do think you're sexy. So sexy. I really, really, really do. Really, really…."

What was I saying again?

"You need to go back to your room," he announces. He grabs his wheelchair by the side of the bed and transfers into it. He smooths out his boxers again, then picks up a pillow from the bed. He lies the pillow down across his legs. "Come on, I'll give you a ride."

"No," I say. "Stay here."

Noah frowns. "This is not cute anymore, Bailey."

God, he's hot when he's pissed off.

He leans over me and I grab him around the neck. He holds onto his wheelchair with one hand and uses the other arm to lift me onto his lap. Wow, he's strong. He's so, so strong.

I keep my arms around his neck even when I'm on his lap. I stare into his blue eyes and he stares back. I can see him swallow hard.

"I still want to stay here with you," I say.

"It… it's not a good idea."

"I want you, Noah. I want you so, so bad. Please…"

Our lips are already only six inches apart. We're so close. I can feel his hot breath. God, I want him. I want him even more than I want sleep. I want him and sleep. Those are the two things that I want more than anything, in that order.

And now he's kissing me. I can feel his soft lips on mine, his tongue making my body tingle, the stubble of his five o'clock shadow grazing my chin. My hands slide into his hair, to the back of his neck, pulling his face as close to mine as it can get. I don't just want to kiss him. I want to devour him.

Want. Want. Want.

"I can't say no to you, I guess," he says when our lips separate. But he's smiling this time.

I cling to his neck, my body pressed against his chest. "I…" I feel my head swimming, but there's something I need to tell him. Something important. "I think I still love you, Noah."

Noah stiffens. He doesn't say anything for long enough that I forget exactly what I said to him and why I'm waiting so eagerly for a response. Finally, he says, "Let's get you back to your room."

I'm too tired to fight with him anymore.

I lean my head against his shoulder and he wheels the two of us out of his bedroom, and into mine. He wheels us right up to the bed, where Lily is still passed out cold. I feel the chair bounce slightly off the side of the bed, then Noah locks the wheels of the chair.

"Okay, this is your stop," he says.

My body still feels like it weighs two tons, but it's considerably less painful to make it from Noah's chair to my bed than it would have been to travel all the way from his bed to mine. His bed to mine? That was really far. No way was I making it. Why not make me run a marathon while you're at it?

It's nice to be back in my own bed. This one is really comfy too. Even better because Noah isn't nagging me to get up. I can stay here forever if I like. That would be nice.

"Good night, Bailey," he says softly.

"Good night, Noah." I take one last look up at his blue eyes. I wish he were climbing into bed with me. I wish I could feel his body pressed against mine, his strong arms encircling my body. I really wish that.

Except Noah doesn't move. He remains there, sitting with me as I drift off. And the last thing I hear him say, which I may very well have imagined is, "I think I still love you too, Bailey."

Chapter 31
PRESENT DAY

When I wake up, my neck still feels sore, but much improved from the night before. But I can't stop thinking about what happened in Noah's room.

Did he really give me a massage? Did I really kiss him and beg to spend the night in his bed? Did I really grope his leg?

Oh my God, did I tell him that I loved him?

And more importantly, did he say it back?

I take my time in the shower, hoping that Noah might have left by the time I get out. No such luck. When I get out, everyone is in the living room—Gwen and Dad are reading together on the loveseat, Lily is coloring, and Noah is on the sofa, fiddling with something in his tackle box. He's wearing his prosthetics now with shorts so that I can see the metal that forms his shins and the robotic hinges that make up his knee joints. When I walk into the room, he immediately drops his eyes and looks very busy.

"Good morning, sleepyhead!" Gwen says.

"Good morning, Sleepy Mommy," Lily giggles.

"Hi," I mumble. I grab a loaf of bread from the counter, intending to make myself some toast for breakfast.

Gwen rises from the couch and walks over to me. "I was thinking we might take Lily to town to look at some dresses she could wear when she's flower girl."

I yank out a piece of toast but nearly drop it in surprise. "How soon is the wedding?"

Gwen shrugs. "We were thinking this summer. There's no point in waiting, is there?"

Wow, that's a lot sooner than I expected. It's still hard to wrap my head around this whole thing. Another woman being married to my father—it seems impossible. "Uh, let me just get breakfast and then we can go."

She waves her hand. "Oh, please don't hurry. We were thinking we'd take Lily, and you could stay here." She looks back at her son. "Noah mentioned he was going to go fishing again this morning. Maybe you'd like to go with him?"

Noah looks up sharply at the sound of his name.

"Um, maybe," I say.

Or not.

Twenty minutes later, Gwen and my father are hustling Lily out the door, leaving Noah and me all alone. Part of me wants to yell after them, "Wait for me!" Instead, I turn to Noah, who is rising from the sofa with his tackle box, and say, "You can go by yourself if you want."

He shrugs. "Do you… want to come?"

Being alone on a boat with Noah in the middle of the lake? I'm not sure how to feel about that. "Do you want me to come?"

He looks at me a long time. Finally, he says, "Yes."

That's settled then.

Noah holds his fishing pole and tackle box in one hand, and his cane in his other hand. We walk down to the dock together without talking much. I desperately want to bring up what happened last night, but I don't know how to begin. Maybe when we're in the middle of the lake, the inspiration will come to me.

At the dock, there's an attractive brunette climbing into the boat next to Noah's. She's wearing short shorts and a bikini top with the most perfectly even tan I've ever seen. I can't help but notice the way her eyes light up when she sees Noah, even with his prosthetic legs readily visible.

"Noah!" She waves at him. "I haven't seen you all season. Where have you been?"

He grins at her. "Putting in extra shifts in the ER to pay for all this crap."

"We should go fishing together again sometime," she suggests in a way that makes me think "fishing" is a euphemism for something else.

"Sure, Jenny," he says. "I'm going back to New York soon but I'll give you a call next time I'm here."

Well, girls are still hitting on Noah right in front of me. It looks like nothing has changed in ten years.

After Jenny takes off in her boat, I can't help but notice that the interaction has put a smile on Noah's face. We climb into his boat and he whistles as he unties it from the pier.

"Did you sleep with her?" I blurt out.

He looks up in surprise. "What?"

Why did I say that? What's *wrong* with me? "Never mind."

He smiles crookedly. "There wasn't a lot of *sleeping* involved."

"Ugh." I roll my eyes at him. "Good to know you're enjoying yourself out here."

Noah doesn't say anything, just turns over the engine and steers the boat out of the harbor.

He drives us to a secluded area in the lake. I watch him attach the weights and bobbers to the fishing line, then tie the hook to the end. He pulls out a plastic container of worms from his tackle box. He holds them in my direction. "Want to do the honors, Bailey?"

I shake my head. "I'll pass, thanks."

Noah picks up one of the worms and laces it through the hook. He picks up the end of the fishing line and throws it into the water with the same underhand motion that he uses to skim stones in the water. I look out in the distance and see the red bobber.

"Now we wait," he says.

I don't know how Noah does it. When he fishes, he just sits there, staring out at the water. He doesn't read, just listens to the radio playing (but not too loud so it doesn't scare the fish). I asked him about it once and he said he likes to be able to hear his own thoughts.

I like the quiet too. It inspires me. But unlike Noah, I have my sketchpad. I'd never come out on a boat without it.

The fish aren't biting today. We've been out here for half an hour and Noah has repositioned the hook once. He doesn't seem all that bothered though. I watch him staring off into the distance, his blue eyes cloudy, the wind tousling his dark blond hair. I have the urge to draw him again, but he might take it the wrong way.

"I should have called you when your mother died," he suddenly says.

I look at him in surprise. "What?"

He clears his throat, looking embarrassed. "I should have… I mean, I *wanted* to. When I heard what happened, I knew you were probably devastated and I wanted to call you. I thought about it. I picked up my phone to do it, and I even had your number up on the screen at one point."

The truth is, I had been desperately hoping Noah would call me when my mother died. When I was at the deepest depths of my grief, the only thing I longed for was his arms around me. My father was lost in his own depression and couldn't offer the comfort I needed. All I could think about was Noah. I never wanted him back so badly as I did then. I *needed* him.

When I was at her funeral, I prayed he would show up. I kept looking around for signs of him. I didn't care if he was in a wheelchair or on a new set of prosthetic legs—I wanted to see him so much.

But he never showed. And that's how I knew there was no chance he'd ever forgive me.

"Why didn't you?" I ask.

He picks at a piece of lint on his shorts. "I was finally getting back to a good place in my life. I was starting medical school again, and… I knew if the conversation didn't go well, it would end up being a huge setback for me. I know that sounds selfish, but… well, I was young and stupid."

"I wish you had called." I grip my pencil tighter in my hand. "I would have really liked hearing from you."

"I'm sorry," he murmurs. He blinks a few times, staring down at his legs. "Was she sick when you… when we…?"

"Yes," I say. "I found out the cancer was back a week after your surgery."

"Jesus, Bailey," he breathes. "Why didn't you tell me?"

"I didn't want to use her as an excuse for the way I treated you."

He's quiet, taking that in. "I wish you had told me."

"Maybe I should have." I look out over Noah's shoulder, at the vast lake beyond our boat. It seems like the water is endless. "My mother really liked you. She was so angry with me for... what I did. She knew I'd never find anyone else like you ever again." I take a deep breath. "She was right. The truth is, I've regretted that day for the last ten years. I meant what I said last night. I'm still in love with you."

Noah is silent.

"I never loved Theo half as much as I loved you," I say. "I've thought about calling you a hundred times, but I was afraid you hated me."

"I didn't hate you," he says. "I was angry at you, but... I didn't hate you. I couldn't." He heaves a sigh. "The truth is that I never stopped loving you."

We stare at each other, letting the impact of his words sink in. My heart is pounding in my chest. Noah loves me. He's never stopped loving me.

I lean forward and he bridges the gap to kiss me. A minute later, we're making out like the boat is going down. The last two times we kissed, he pushed me away, but I know he won't do it this time. I feel his hands touching my hair, my back, my chest, desperate to touch every inch of me.

"Do you have a condom?" I whisper in his ear.

The last time I asked him that on a boat, he said no. But this time, he fumbles around under the seat and triumphantly pulls out a string of five condom packages.

"Should I be worried that you have such a well-stocked condom supply on this boat?" I ask him.

"Well, it's not a rowboat," he points out. "It's not going to capsize if we roll around on it. It's pretty safe."

I raise my eyebrows at him. "And I suppose you know that from experience?"

"Hell yeah," he says. He grins at the expression on my face. "What do you think I am—a priest? I'm a thirty-three-year-old single guy."

Fair enough.

I run my hand over the metal of his prosthetic socket. He watches me, his brow furrowed.

"Do you usually take them off when you…?"

Noah shrugs. "Depends."

"What do you prefer?"

"Honestly? I prefer them off. When they're on, it's like two weights dragging me down. But most women prefer I keep them on."

302

"Take them off."

He frowns. "Are you sure?"

"Very sure."

Noah presses on that white button on the inside of his thigh which seems to release the suction holding them in place. He yanks his left one off, then his right. He lays them on the floor, in front of the seats. Last, he pulls off the gel socks that cover both of his stumps. When he's done, only his bare skin is left. He shifts in his seat and the stumps flail in the air for a moment before he gets resettled.

He squints at me. "You're not freaked out?"

"Noah, stop it."

He sighs. "Look, after all this time, I get that they're not the most attractive things in the world." He rubs his left lower limb self-consciously. "My last girlfriend… I was with her for a while, and she wanted to get married, but… I knew she still wasn't entirely cool with the whole thing. When I got home from work, I just wanted to take my prosthetics off and get in my wheelchair, but I didn't feel comfortable doing that around her. She'd make a comment about how isn't it easier to be on my feet, and even when she didn't, I'd know she was thinking it."

I feel my cheeks grow warm. I suspect at least some of his self-consciousness must stem from the way I left him all those years ago. But what he needs to understand is I didn't leave because I wasn't in love with him anymore. I left him because I was deeply depressed and couldn't cope. But I find him as sexy now as I ever did.

"I heard…" I put my hand on his thigh, under his shorts. "I heard that after an amputation, the residual limb can get very sensitive. Like, *extremely* sensitive in certain situations."

Noah's eyes widen as he gets my meaning. "Well… yeah. That's… um, true."

I run my hand up, then down his thigh. His eyes widen further and I can hear him swallow. "Bailey…"

"Let me show you how sexy I think you are," I whisper.

"Okay," he manages.

Noah gets down onto the floor of the boat. I get on top of him and we're making out once again. Every time I touch that scar tissue at the end of his legs, he lets out a groan. By the time he gets the condom on and dives inside me, I can tell that he's desperately struggling to hold out for the sake of my own pleasure. But as it turns out, he doesn't have to wait very long. I'm just as turned on as he is and I climax almost immediately. It's lucky we're on a lonely boat in the middle of a lake because I'm not quiet when I do.

When it's over, we lie together on the floor of the boat, sweaty and sticky in each other's arms. I rest my head against Noah's muscular shoulder and he pulls me close.

"I never stopped loving you either," I say.

He smiles at me and squeezes me tighter. He's staring off into the distance, his blue eyes clear this time.

"What are you thinking?" I say.

"I think…" He kisses my forehead. "That we've got a bite on the line."

The fishing pole Noah set up is bobbing slightly. Looks like he's right.

Chapter 32
PRESENT DAY

I can't stop smiling.

Noah had to make a run to the store after we get back, but before he left, he kissed me so deeply that my knees almost gave out from under me. I missed kissing Noah all those years. Nothing has ever been able to match it.

And now I'm lying in bed, thinking about him. I can still feel his large, warm hands over my body. I can still taste his lips on mine. Like I said, I can't stop smiling.

My post-coital bliss is interrupted by the sound of my phone buzzing next to me. I roll my head to see who's calling. It's Theo.

The last person I want to talk to right now.

I consider letting it go to voicemail. After what he did last night, I never want to speak to that asshole ever again. But unfortunately, Theo isn't some creep I met in a bar last night. Theo is the father of my daughter. Like it or not, he's a part of my life. For Lily's sake, I need to remain on decent terms with him.

That means if he's calling from jail because he got pulled over for a DUI, I probably need to go bail him out.

I pick up the phone, bracing myself for an angry outburst. I'm relieved when Theo's voice on the other line is subdued. Almost contrite. "Hey, Bailey."

"Hello," I say.

He's silent for a moment on the other line. "I'm sorry about last night," he finally says. "I was drunk."

"Yeah, no kidding."

"You know that's not me," he says. It's true to some extent—Theo's never manhandled me before. But he's certainly gotten drunk and done stupid things in the past. It's his kind of his *thing*. "You know I wouldn't have… I mean, I'm sorry I grabbed you like that."

I take a deep breath. I'm not sure what Theo would have done if Noah wasn't there to protect me. I'd like to think it would have been fine. But I don't know for sure. "It's all right. Just don't ever do it again."

"And I'm sorry I tried to beat up that guy in the wheelchair," he says. "That was… I mean, I'm really embarrassed about that."

I almost laugh. *Tried to beat up that guy in the wheelchair.* Ha. If he's embarrassed, it's because Noah kicked his ass. "I'll tell him."

There's a long silence on the other end. I'm hoping that means our conversation is over, and I can go back to thinking about when Noah was touching me. And fantasizing about what he might do to me tonight.

"But, listen…" Theo breaks the silence. "I might have been drunk, but I meant a lot of what I said last night. I know I screwed things up with you, Bailey. I regret that every day of my life."

I snort. "You're only saying that because you thought I was with another guy last night."

"Maybe you're right," he admits. "But maybe it took thinking you were with someone else to open my eyes. You're the greatest thing that ever happened to me, and I just threw it away."

I don't know what to say to that. *Yeah, you did.* But the time for bitterness is over. It was never going to work out with me and Theo. He wasn't ready to be faithful, and I realize now that I had never gotten over Noah.

"Bailey," he says softly. "I've had a chance to do a lot of thinking lately and… I really think we should give it another try. You and me. You know?"

I suck in a breath. Theo has said things like this many times before, but he's never sounded quite so serious. Something has changed. Maybe it's the fact that Theo is getting close to forty or maybe it was seeing me with Noah last night, but he sounds like he really means it this time.

"Theo, I just don't think—"

"Hear me out first."

I bite my lip to keep from telling him there's no point. "Fine."

"I know I was a crappy husband and a crappy father," he says. "I know I cheated on you and I haven't been there for Lily. But when I saw you last night, I just… I realized how much I love you. That's why I went so crazy. I love you, Bailey. And I want us to be a family again. You, me, and Lily."

I'm shaking my head, even though he can't see it.

"I know what you're thinking," he says. "You're thinking I haven't changed. But I swear to you, I have. I won't mess around on you this time. I swear it."

Theo, me, and Lily. A family. That's what we were once. I was never confident things would work out with Theo—he was always my rebound guy from Noah—but I wanted to give it the best possible try for Lily's sake. But from the start, Theo never took our marriage vows seriously. He never took fatherhood seriously.

But maybe he's finally grown up. Do I owe it to Lily to give her biological father another chance?

I hear the door to the cabin opening. It's Noah. He's back. I can hear him whistling in the kitchen. I forgot how he always used to whistle when he was in a really good mood.

Theo's voice comes to me on the other line: "Bailey?"

309

"No, Theo," I hear myself saying. "I'm sorry. It's too late."

"Bailey." His voice breaks on my name and I feel a twinge of guilt. "You can't even give us one last try? For Lily's sake? Doesn't she deserve that?"

For Lily's sake.

I don't say what I'm thinking, which is that Noah has been a better father figure to Lily in the last week than Theo has managed in six years. Above all, Lily deserves a mother who's happy. And there's only one man I know who can make me truly happy.

"I'm sorry," I say again.

Theo is quiet for several moments. "It's that guy from last night, isn't it?"

I swallow hard. I didn't want to mention Noah, because I didn't want to set off Theo's temper. But he's right. If Noah hadn't come back into my life, there's a chance I might have been persuaded to give our relationship another shot. Just another reason I'm grateful to Noah.

"I could see the way you were looking at him," he says. "It was really obvious."

"Oh," is all I can say. There's no point in denying it.

I brace myself for Theo to start another jealous rant, but he doesn't. Maybe he really has matured. But even if that's the case, it's far too late.

"I blew it," he concedes. "And I'll always have to live with that. But... I'm going to try to do better for you and Lily from now on, okay?"

I do my best to keep from snorting again. "What does that mean?"

"It means," he says, "I'm going to go out and get a real job. The band isn't happening. Me and the guys... we had a talk the other day and decided to go our separate ways."

I actually gasp. "You broke up? Seriously?"

"Yep." He lets out a little chuckle. "It's been long enough, right? I'm going to hit the job ads on Monday. Figure out a way to get back on track with the child support payments again."

I grip the phone in my hand. He's trying. He's really trying this time.

"Hey, Bailey!" It's Noah's voice coming down the hall to my room. "I bought some snorkels for us if you want to try it out tomorrow. I got one for Lily too. We don't have to go deep or anything, but I thought it would be fun if—"

Noah's face appears at my bedroom door, but he stops talking abruptly when he realizes I'm already on the phone, a smile frozen on his lips. I wonder if he realizes who I'm talking to. I have a feeling from the look on his face that he's got some idea.

"That would be great," I say into the phone. "Really great. It would help us a lot."

"I know," Theo sighs. "I'm just… I'm sorry I screwed up on… us. I'll never forgive myself for that."

Noah blinks a few times, giving me a questioning look like he's not sure if he should leave or not. I gesture at him, indicating he should stay. He sits on the edge of my bed, an uneasy look on his face.

"Listen, Theo," I say quietly. "I have to go, but… we'll talk more later, okay?"

At the sound of Theo's name, Noah's eyes widen.

"Okay, Bailey," he says. "Have a good time on your trip."

I hang up the phone, feeling a rush of relief. That was the best phone conversation I've had with Theo in ages. He didn't get pissed off at me. There was no yelling or accusations. And he promised to start giving us child support. I hope this is the start of a better life for me and Lily, although I'm not holding my breath.

Noah raises an eyebrow. "So… that was Theo?"

I nod.

"What did *he* want?" He laughs, but it comes out strangled. "To get back together?"

I nod again. "He wanted a fresh start."

"Jesus." He rakes a hand through his short, dark blond hair. "He's persistent, isn't he? So, um, what did you say?"

I slug Noah gently in the arm. "What do you *think* I said?"

"I think," Noah says quietly, "that the guy is an asshole. But he's also Lily's father, and I wouldn't entirely blame you if…" His blue eyes meet mine. "I mean, it's not like we've been back together for *months*. It's only been a day. We don't know if you and I…"

Except I know. I've known Noah Walsh since I was eighteen years old, and he's the most decent man I know.

And he's also the sexiest.

"I don't want to be with Theo," I say as I run my hand up his shoulder. "I want *you*. I want to go snorkeling with you. And fishing, even though it's super boring."

Noah laughs. "Stop it. You know you love fishing."

"Um, fishing is objectively boring," I say. Noah clutches his chest in mock hurt. "But I have to say, I love fishing with *you*."

"I'm glad." He leans in closer to me, his lips nearly touching mine. "Because I love fishing with you too, Bailey."

And then he kisses me.

God, I can't wait to go fishing with him again.

Chapter 33

PRESENT DAY

This is really not good. Not good at all.

I'm sleeping too well in this cabin—it must be the country air. Or maybe it's not the country air. Maybe it's the fact that Noah has been keeping us busy every minute of the day. Yesterday morning, he took Lily and me snorkeling, which she absolutely loved. I was a little frightened, but he was so calm and reassuring, it was hard not to love it too.

Then after snorkeling, he packed a basket and drove us to a spot where we could have a picnic. He brought chairs for himself and me, since he explained it's hard for him to sit on the ground, which I appreciated, considering my back hurts when I sit too long on the ground anyway. Lily ran around in the grass, trying to find ladybugs and caterpillars, then we walked to the lake, where he showed her how to skim stones properly. She mastered it in about five minutes.

"Wow," Lily said to him, "you're a *lot* better at this than Mommy."

I couldn't argue with that one.

After I put Lily to bed, and Gwen and my father retired to their own room, Noah and I wasted no time sneaking off into his bedroom. Last night was our final night in the cabin, and I wasn't about to miss out on some incredible sex. Noah was always pretty good in bed, but I have to say, the boy has gotten new skills in the last decade. Maybe it was good to have some time apart. In any case, we couldn't get enough of each other.

The night before, I snuck back into my own bedroom to spend the night, so nobody would be the wiser. But after Noah left me completely breathless, somehow I just… fell asleep.

And now, inexplicably, it's morning.

Noah is sound asleep beside me, despite the fact that the clock next to his bed reads a quarter past eight, and he always wakes at the crack of dawn. His dark blond hair is mussed, and he's got a day's growth of golden stubble on his chin. He looks so sexy, blowing air softly between his lips, that for a moment, the panic abates.

Then I hear the noises from outside the bedroom door and realize everyone is awake but us.

Not good. *So* not good.

"Noah!" I shake him. He groans softly but doesn't open his eyes, so I shake him again. "Wake up!"

One of his blue eyes cracks open. For a moment, he looks confused, but then a smile stretches across his lips. "Hey," he says, "I thought I might have dreamed you."

I raise my eyebrows at him. "Dreamed me?"

"Yeah." He rubs his eyes with the back of his hand and smiles sheepishly. "Sometimes I used to have dreams about meeting up with you again and then… well…"

I bite my tongue to keep from telling him I've had similar dreams. I'd always wake up and feel deeply disappointed upon seeing the unused pillow beside me. But this time it's real. I've woken up and he's still here.

But there are more practical matters at hand.

"Noah," I say, more firmly this time. "We overslept. It's after eight!"

He yawns loudly. "You wore me out, woman."

I smack him in the arm. He grabs his arm and pretends to be hurt—as if I'm capable of injuring him. "Everyone is awake, you know. They're going to know we spent the night together."

He shifts in bed, the covers bunching around the stumps of his legs. I've woken up next to Noah hundreds of times before, but this part is different. He used to always wrap one leg around mine when we slept, but he can't do that anymore. He also doesn't kick me in his sleep anymore though, so overall it's a win.

"I don't know what the big deal is." He yawns again and kisses me on the shoulder. "Our parents already know anyway."

"No, they don't."

"They definitely do."

I shake my head. "Maybe they suspect. But they don't *know*."

He grins at me. "What—you think the walls of this cabin are soundproof?"

"Noah!" I bury my face in my hands. "Don't say that!"

"It's okay. I think it's adorable that you're so loud."

I groan. I really don't want to think about my father overhearing the incredible orgasm Noah gave me last night. If I'd really thought about it, I would have put a pillow over my face. Because not screaming wasn't a possibility.

"Look," I say, staring into Noah's blue eyes. "I just don't want Lily to know yet. It's hard on kids when their parents are in a relationship with someone new."

"But Lily loves me," he points out.

"Exactly. She thinks you're the greatest. So if it doesn't work out, she'll be extra disappointed."

His light brown eyebrows bunch together. "Why wouldn't it work out?"

I let out an exasperated sigh. "I don't know. I mean, relationships sometimes don't work out. Look at me and Theo. And… well, you just broke up with that girl a few months ago."

"Yeah…" He reaches out and brushes hair from my face. "But you're the love of my life, Bailey."

Then he presses his lips against mine, and I get that weak, fluttery feeling I always do when Noah kisses me. The truth is, I feel the exact same way. Even though it's only been a few days since we reconnected, I can't fathom any reason why Noah and I wouldn't work out—the thought of it is almost physically painful. But I've had so many bad experiences in the last decade, I need to protect myself. And my daughter.

He pulls away and frowns at the expression on my face. "Fine," he sighs. "Let's think of an excuse why you'd be in my bedroom all morning."

I nod gratefully. Unfortunately, coming up with an excuse isn't as easy as it sounds. Everything we think of sounds horribly phony. Helping him put up blinds? Giving him an art lesson? Our options are limited.

It also doesn't help that I'm wearing the exact same shorts and tank top I'd had on yesterday.

Noah decides to get dressed because we're getting nowhere fast. He throws on a wrinkled T-shirt from NYU School of Medicine, and puts his baggy blue jeans on over his limbs. His prosthetics are at the head of the bed, waiting for him. He fits the left one on, supporting his weight by holding onto the bed as he slides into it. He told me he always starts

318

with the left, because that's his stronger limb, thanks to the multiple surgeries he had on the right. He's relatively fast at putting the prosthetics on, but it's definitely an ordeal. I can see why he'd prefer to use a wheelchair first thing in the morning.

While Noah is trying to get his right prosthetic to sink into place, we hear a knock on the door. I'd recognize that tapping anywhere. It's Lily.

"Noah?" her little voice calls out.

He freezes, looking over at me with raised eyebrows. Like *I* know what to do. "What's up, Lily?" he calls back.

"Do you know where my mom went?" she asks. "I can't find her anywhere! She's missing!"

Noah and I exchange looks. I let out a sigh and go over to the bedroom door. When I open it up, Lily's eyes go wide.

"Mommy!" she exclaims. "What are you doing in here?"

"I…" I glance over in Noah's direction. He shrugs. "I, um, had a problem with my phone and he was trying to fix it for me."

That sounds believable, right?

Gwen sidles down the hallway, just in time to catch an eyeful of me standing in Noah's room as he adjusts his pants legs. Her lips curl into a knowing smile. "I see you found your mother, Lily."

"Uh huh." Lily spins in place for no particular reason. Sometimes she does that. Like she just gets it in her head she wants to spin and she does. "Noah was helping her fix her phone."

"Was he?" Gwen glances behind her. "But didn't I see your phone charging in the living room, Bailey?"

Oh great.

"My other phone," I correct myself. Even though I do not, in fact, own another phone. I'm lucky I can afford one. I'm not made of phones. "He was helping me with a different phone."

Lily is still spinning, and has spun herself all the way back to the living room. Out of earshot. It's fortunate, because Lily definitely knows I don't have two phones because that would be "too 'spensive." Still, Gwen leans forward as she says, "It's okay, Bailey. You're welcome to be in my son's room whenever you want."

All the blood rushes to my face. The fact that Noah is snickering into his hand doesn't make matters any better. Well, at least Lily doesn't know. Lucky thing six-year-olds are really gullible.

"Anyway," Gwen says, a twinkle in her eye, "I just wanted to let the two of you know that we'd like to head out soon. Lenny wants to get a jump on traffic."

"Oh." My heart sinks. Gwen is my ride back to the city, so when she leaves, I've got to leave. I'd hoped to get to spend more time with Noah today. At least a few more hours. "I guess we'll get ready then…"

Noah clears his throat. "I could drive you back."

I turn to look at him. "I thought you didn't have a shift for another two days. We have to get back today."

"Yeah, well…" He smiles at me. "I've already got the booster seat, so… might as well drive you."

"And I'm sure you'll be using it plenty," she comments. And she winks at us.

Oh Lord. This is so embarrassing.

But on the bright side, I get to be in a car with Noah for hours. And I'll see his apartment in the city. Maybe this week is over, but Noah and I aren't. We're just beginning.

Again.

———

"It's been so lovely having you here this week!" Gwen envelopes me in a giant hug as I stand by her car, which is all packed and ready to go back to the city. It's the first Gwen hug I've received in ten years.

"Thank you for inviting me," I say. And I mean it this time.

When Gwen pulls away from the hug, she takes both my hands in hers. "You'll have to come over for dinner soon. Okay?"

"Sure," I agree.

Noah comes out of the cabin to see his mother and my father off. He made Lily chocolate chip pancakes for breakfast, which cemented his role as the greatest person she'd ever met in her entire life. I really want to tell Lily about the two of us, but it's too soon. I can't risk breaking her heart if it doesn't work out. It will be bad enough that my heart would be broken.

But I'm cautiously optimistic.

"Noah!" Gwen calls out. She holds out her arms to him, and he hugs her dutifully. "Thank you so much for being such a wonderful host. And also, of course, for offering to drive Bailey and Lily home."

Dad honks the horn from within the car. "Come on! Let's get on the road, Gwen! We're going to hit traffic if we wait."

Gwen nods and hurries to the driver's seat of the car. She blows us a kiss, then they rev up the engine and are gone. We watch their car disappear into the distance.

Noah turns to me and grins. "They're gone. *Finally*."

I run my hand down his chest. "You know, we need to get on the road too in just a few hours."

"I could do a lot in a few hours…"

Noah leans forward and presses his lips against mine. God, he's a really good kisser. In ten years, I've never been kissed by anyone the way Noah Walsh kisses me. I could do this all day.

"I knew it!"

Noah and I jerk away from each other. I look up and see Lily standing on the steps of the cabin, her little heart-shaped face beaming. She's pointing at us gleefully.

"I knew you liked each other!" she cries.

I look over at Noah, who just grins and shrugs. He's apparently decided not to be upset over this.

"Lily," I say carefully. "Noah and I were just…"

"Kissing!" Now she's dancing around the grass. "You were kissing! With your lips!"

How else would we kiss other than with our lips? Is there something they're teaching them in school that I'm not aware of?

Finally, Noah puts his arm around my shoulder and looks down at Lily. "You're right, Lily," he says. "I do like your mom. A lot."

I look over at him and grin. "I like you a lot too."

"Noah likes Mommy!" Lily cries in a singsong voice. She seems so happy about the whole thing—it's adorable. "Mommy and Noah, sitting in a tree, K-I-S-S-S-I-G-G…"

Noah laughs and takes the opportunity to kiss me one more time. Okay, fine, Lily knows about Noah and me. It's not the end of the world. No, I don't want to disappoint her, but I've got this feeling that where Noah is involved, everything will work out.

Epilogue
SEVERAL MONTHS LATER

"Answer yes or no, Mommy," Lily says to me.

I'm attempting to work Lily's reddish-brown hair into a French braid, but she won't stop moving. She's been talking the whole time I've been brushing her hair and then just as I was doing the braid, she somehow got *hungry*. What have I done wrong as a mother that my child can't sit through me brushing her hair without a snack? Thank God Noah was around to rush out and see if he could grab her some crackers.

"Can you just sit still?" I mumble.

Why did I think I could put Lily's hair in a French braid? I don't know how to make a French braid. I am completely unqualified for this task.

"Yes or no, Mommy!" Lily demands.

This is a new game of hers. She asks me to answer a question, yes or no. But I don't get to know the question until I answer. So if I answer "yes," the question would be something like, "Would you eat boogers?" And if I answer "no," the question would be, "Would you *not* eat boogers?" Or something like that.

Can you tell I'm sick of this game?

"Hold still for just a second," I say.

"I've been holding still for five *hours*!" (A slight exaggeration.)

"I'm almost done," I lie.

At that moment, Noah bursts into the tiny room in the back of the church that I've been given to fix up Lily's hair. He holds up a little yellow package in triumph. "Lorna Doones!"

Lily's eyes light up and she rushes over to him, officially undoing any meager progress I'd made on her hair. "I love Lorna Doones."

Noah winks at me. "I know it."

I look at Noah in the dark suit he's wearing and I swoon for the tenth time today. He's so unbelievably hot dressed up in a suit, especially with a tie. But he also looks hot in the blue scrubs he wears to the hospital—they bring out the blue in his eyes. Or in a T-shirt and jeans.

Or wearing nothing at all.

Especially that last one.

"Noah?" Lily says around bites of her Lorna Doone.

He looks at me, taking in my harried expression, and smiles. "What's up, Lil?"

"Answer yes or no."

"Um…" He looks like he's really thinking about it. He's so good with her. When we were dating all those years ago, I never really thought about what

326

kind of father Noah would be. I never knew he'd kick ass at it. "No."

Lily's eyes widen. "No? You *don't* want Grandpa and Gwen to get married today?"

"No," Noah says patiently, "I wanted them to get married *yesterday*."

Lily cackles with laughter. She doesn't hero worship Noah any less since we've been dating for three months. I hope he's still around when she's a teenager, because he'll probably be the only one she'll listen to.

I hope he's around by then for a lot of reasons.

"I give up," I say, looking at Lily's loose hair. "I can't do a French braid. I'm going to have to do an American braid. Unless…" I look up at Noah. "Can you do a French braid?"

Noah makes a face at me. "I'm a straight male, so… no. I can't."

"Yeah, but aren't you always, like, sewing things up in the ER, *Dr. Walsh*?"

He rolls his eyes. "Yeah, and if anyone has a laceration under their hair, I'm glad to take care of that. But sorry, I don't do French braids."

Fine. Nobody's perfect.

I quickly arrange Lily's hair into a normal braid while Noah grabs the cane he's got leaning against the wall. He's worn his prosthetic legs for the wedding ceremony, but the church had a bunch of stairs to get in without any railing, so he took the cane. Even though he doesn't need the extra support when he's on an even surface like inside the church, he likes to have it around when he's somewhere he's never been before.

"How do I look?" Lily asks Noah when I finish her hair.

She does a little twirl so the skirt of her pink bridesmaid dress (that I didn't have to pay for, thank God) flies into the air. Lily helped design the dress herself, and it has a scary number of ruffles. But she loves it, which is more important than my daughter not looking like a doily.

"You look beautiful," he tells her. His eyes lift to me in my own dress—it's a rich green color and gives my boobs the perfect amount of lift for a woman who breastfed a baby for a year and a half without realizing it would cause them to sag *forever*. "Just like your mom."

I blush, even though he says things like that all the time. And my body tingles when he gets close to me and pulls me in for a kiss that's only just barely appropriate given we're right in front of my daughter. The truth is, for the last three months, Noah and I have been having difficulty keeping our hands off each other. He jokes that we're making up for lost time, although it was like that before too.

The only problem is finding time to be alone together. Lily and I share a bedroom, which means Noah and I have to hook up on the sofa in my apartment after she's fallen asleep, with an excuse ready in case she walks in on us. We're going to tell her he's giving me CPR. In any case, him spending the night is out of the question.

"Noah," Lily says in a sing-songy voice. "Answer yes or no."

He's gazing into my eyes. I don't think he even heard the question.

"Noah!" Lily barks.

He tears his eyes away from me to smile at her. "Yes, Lily?"

"Answer yes or no."

I give him a lot of credit for not rolling his eyes. "Yes."

A grin spreads across Lily's small face. "Yes? So yes, you're going to marry Mommy?"

Noah's blue eyes widen. He glances at me then back at my daughter. Thanks for making things really awkward, sweetie.

"Lily," I sigh. "You know that Noah and I haven't been going out for very long."

"Grandpa and Gwen weren't going out very long," Lily irritatingly points out.

I flash Noah an apologetic look. I can't help but remember that day when he got down on one knee in his graduation gown. That was one of the most amazing moments of my life. And then I remember the day when I put the ring he gave me on his bookcase just before I left his life forever. Or at least, I thought it would be forever.

Noah bends down to look Lily in the eyes, leaning on his cane to help him keep his balance while he gets down to her level. "Lily," he says. "The truth is that I do want to marry your mom."

He…

What?

"You do?" Lily looks even more excited than she did when *Dogcat* came out on DVD last week, and Noah bought her a copy. I'll never forgive him for that.

He nods. "Yeah. I've known your mother for a long time, and I'm starting to realize I don't think I could marry anyone else but her."

"Good thing she's single," Lily comments.

Noah laughs. "Yeah, good thing."

"She probably wouldn't marry anyone else too," she adds. "Because she never went out on dates with anybody. Or had any boyfriends before you."

"Lily!" I hiss. Not that we didn't all know I used to have a pathetic social life, but I don't know why Lily needs to keep reminding everyone about it.

"Listen," Noah says to Lily, "I was thinking maybe I could try living with you and Mom for a while and see how we all get along before we make any other plans. What do you think?"

She frowns. "Would you sleep in the bedroom with me and Mommy?"

"Actually," he says, "I thought maybe we could get a two-bedroom apartment so you could have your own room."

"My own room!" Lily is almost levitating with excitement. "Can I have a bed with a slide on it?"

"Uh…" Noah glances at me. Lily been obsessed with slide beds ever since she saw one in one of her friends' rooms. "Sure. I guess."

That's all he had to say. Lily is bouncing up and down, happier than I've ever seen her.

Noah straightens up so he can look me in the eyes. "What do you say, Bailey? I know it's soon, but… it's not like we don't know each other."

I take his hand in mine. It's always been my greatest regret that I let the love of my life slip away from me. And here he is, giving me a do-over.

"Answer yes or no, Mommy!" Lily says.

"Yes," I whisper.

And just like that, the worst mistake of my life is undone.

THE END

Dear readers,

Years ago, I read an article online about how if you write a letter to your readers at the end of your book, it will encourage them to review the book online. I excitedly wrote a letter at the end of my next book. And I waited.

And waited…

And waited…

Then I took a pee break.

Then I took a short nap.

And waited…

My point is, it didn't work. No amount of begging worked. Writing a threatening letter from Santa Claus didn't work. Providing a rough template of what should be included in a brief review didn't work. That letter where I offered $500 to each Amazon reviewer didn't work. (Oh? Did you miss that one?) *Nothing works.*

So instead of trying to be amusing, I'm going to get real for a moment here. That's right, Annabelle Costa is going to Get Serious. Here we go:

These reviews mean a lot to me. It's nice to get paid for my work, but the truth is, I treasure the emails I receive and positive reviews even more than any money I make. In a way, that's why I'm doing this. I've been writing long before publishing on

Amazon was a possibility, hoping only for positive comments online. Even the negative comments help me to grow as an author (well, sometimes).

It is so cool to me that real people read and buy my books. That's all any author wants. And hearing from you guys, either in reviews or emails is an incredible gift. I mean that from the bottom of my heart. And you have to know how much it pains me to be this cheesy, but I really mean it.

So I hope to hear from you. You can either email me at razberripie@gmail.com. Or please leave a review on Amazon here. Other authors say I'm supposed to tell you to like me on Facebook or follow me on Twitter, but honestly, I'd be happier with the email or review.

Thank you once again to all my readers,

Annabelle Costa

Acknowledgments

One thing I really struggle with when writing the acknowledgments in my books is how to spell the word "acknowledgments." Like, is there an extra E in it or not? Is it "acknowledgments" or "acknowledgements"? Spell check thinks both of those are right!

So I finally looked it up. Apparently, the non-E version is preferred in the US and Canada, whereas the E version is preferred in the rest of the English-speaking world. But both are technically correct. Huh. I hope you've learned something today. I sure have.

The end.

OH WAIT, I TOTALLY FORGOT TO THANK PEOPLE!!!!

This part is easy. Thank you to the lovely Molly Mirren, J. Saman, and Avery Kingston. And thank you to everyone at PD for your continued support for so many years.

Also, thanks to the real Lily. Without you, I'd never know how many cats could be squeezed onto one dress.

61420224R00201

Made in the USA
Middletown, DE
19 August 2019